Joy Complete

Voice of Joy series Book 3

By Sarah Floyd

DEDICATION

To my encouragers

I Thessalonians 5:11

ACKNOWLEDGMENTS

I would like to thank Maggie Carter, my beta reader for *Joy Complete*, for jumping in at the last minute to catch my errors. You're awesome!

I would also like to thank Wendy and Mary Pilot for their time and effort in improving my cover design. Mary, I owe you a lifetime supply of feta cheese, okay?

And, of course, I will always thank my husband, Jason, for supporting me in this writing journey, especially this spring, when working on my book was a constant for me as so many other aspects of life were changing.

CHAPTER 1

Joy hummed as she swept the first-floor porch of her rental property. She barely needed to clean this unit to prepare it for the new tenants, because the Goldman family had left it so tidy. What a shame to lose such wonderful tenants after five and a half years, but they had a good reason to leave – they were finally purchasing their first home. Joy paused her work to permit herself a rare moment of pride in her work as a landlady. Through her charity, Looking Up, the Goldmans had rented this apartment – part of a Victorian house – for a low price in return for their agreement to maintain respectable lives as faithful members of a religious group. Thanks to the money they had saved in Joy's affordable property, they'd managed a down payment on an old farmhouse near Barre. They were ecstatic, and Joy felt that her efforts had not been in vain.

Joy was still standing on the porch, savoring the brisk May breeze, when a blood-curdling shriek from inside the apartment jolted her back to her own life in a hurry. Annie. Her children were supposed to be inside playing while their great-aunt cleaned the kitchen. Annie's shrieks continued and were soon mingled with thunder across the hardwood floors. Joy flung down her broom and dashed inside.

Joy followed the pandemonium to the bathroom, where an astonishing sight met her eyes. Her Aunt Joann knelt beside the toilet with her arms around Joy's kicking, screaming daughter Annie. Annie's hands were submerged in the commode, which was overflowing with dirty water. Joy's sons, Micah, and Gideon, were kneeling nearby as well, staring at their sister. Both were soaked below the waist, presumably also with toilet water.

Joy stood in the doorway for a few seconds, her hand over her mouth, unsure whether to shout, laugh, or cry. In that space of time, Joann managed to lift Annie away from the toilet, but the little girl's weight threw her off balance, and Joann landed on the floor with a thud, sitting down hard in the growing puddle, with Annie writhing on her lap.

"Um," Joy said at last, alerting the rest of them to her presence.

"My kitty! Mama, my kitty!" Annie howled. She jumped up from Joann's lap to run to her mother, but she slipped on the wet floor and fell instead.

It was several minutes before Joy understood what had happened. First, she had to turn off the water to the toilet, strip Annie of her filthy clothes, and put her into the bathtub. Joann, who had hurt only her pride, marched the boys outside to the water spigot, attached the garden hose, and sprayed them down, clothes and all. To their delight, she also allowed them to rinse her.

Finally, all five of them gathered in a dripping group on the kitchen floor. Annie was wearing Joann's sweater and a pair of Micah's shorts that Joy had unearthed from the car – the shorts were left over from potty training days but still fit her skinny girl in the waist.

"Okay, kids," Joy said, flopping down beside them. "I know that Kitty is in the toilet, but I need to know how she got there."

"Mommy," Annie said, eyes filling with tears again. "I *told* you! Kitty is a *boy*!"

Joy hid her amusement with difficulty. Four-year-olds. They were amazing – hers in particular.

"Oh, I'm sorry. How did he end up in the toilet?"

All three children began talking at once, but Joy soon had the story. Annie had taken Kitty, her favorite stuffed animal, with her to keep her company in the bathroom. Once she'd finished, she'd thought Kitty might also need to use the potty, so she'd set the toy on the toilet seat. As she flushed, Kitty had fallen into the bowl and had jammed the toilet. The boys had heard her cries and had plunged into the overflowing water to watch her try to save Kitty. And poor Joann, who had been halfway inside the oven, scrubbing, had not been able to intervene until it was too late to keep the children from drenching themselves.

After a stern warning to let an adult know before trying to handle such a situation themselves, Joy hugged them all. She reassured Annie that she would do her best to rescue Kitty as soon as everyone else was clean and dry, and that no, Kitty wouldn't drown. She sank back down to the kitchen floor and put her head in her hands. She'd planned to make so much progress on the house today, but instead she'd have to waste two hours driving everyone back to Woodfield for baths and changes of clothes. Why, oh, why had she underestimated the power of three four-year-olds to create mayhem?

Her aunt's quiet voice broke into her thoughts. "Which of these things would you rather that I do? Drive the children back to your house for baths and return for you later, or stay here and plunge the toilet and continue working?"

Joy raised her head and stared at Joann. "Oh," she said. "Either one would be wonderful – but what about you? You're soaked too...and I never even asked you...did Annie hurt you?"

"I'll dry," Joann said, tossing her dripping braid over her shoulder. "And no, I'm not hurt. It takes more than a four-year-old to break me."

"I guess, if you're sure you don't mind, I'll stay here. You can borrow some of my clothes or drive on to your house long enough to change. Thank you so much..."

"Of course," Joann said, standing up stiffly. "And now you can have some time to yourself to think about what you need to do."

"That did cross my mind when I chose this option," Joy admitted. She hugged Joann and then kissed the children, handed off the car keys, and watched as Joann supervised them as they buckled their car seat harnesses. She waved as Joann drove away in the minivan, and then she collapsed on the porch stairs for a few minutes' peace before she had to return to the scene of the slime.

Joy closed her eyes and took a deep breath, hoping to soothe her nerves. She was so tired. Gideon had awakened her with his night terrors again last night, and she had not been able to go back to sleep until nearly sunrise. It was exhausting as well to maintain this rental property in addition to be a wife and mommy. She couldn't imagine what she'd do when the place began to need major repairs, or if she had bad tenants to handle.

Joy was also exhausted from the wild twists and turns her entire life had taken since her marriage to Paul five years before. It was obvious that the theme of her whole life was "did not go as planned." After an incredible honeymoon in Venice, Italy, she and Paul had settled into married life in the farmhouse in Woodfield. It was still a month until Paul had to begin his next year of teaching, so they used that time to adjust to living together as husband and wife. Joy was barely accustomed to waking up with someone beside her when she began to feel ill every morning. By mid-August, less than three months after her wedding, the woman who had been terrified to marry found herself expecting a baby to be born around her first anniversary. And when Joy had her first ultrasound, the technician squealed and informed the dazed couple that she could hear three separate heartbeats!

Instead of spending her first year of marriage focusing on learning how to be a wife, Joy was on the couch, moaning with nausea for six months straight. Instead of flourishing as a new landlady and hunting for more rental properties, she read dozens of parenting books and blogs, hoping to discover the secret to be a better mother than hers had been. And instead of having a beautiful, idyllic birth in a quiet hospital room on the babies' due date, she'd had a medical induction at 36 weeks and had come close to bleeding to death. And Micah had a tongue tie, and Annie had colic, and Gideon was intolerant to everything she ate.

Even now, four years later, Joy shuddered when she remembered her sleep deprivation and anxiety during her first few months as a mother. She could recall one night in particular, before she used any bottles, when she was feeding one baby or another 9.5 hours out of 10. She'd also never changed a diaper until her triplets were born, and suddenly, she was responsible for changing 30 or more every day.

Paul had been the epitome of an ideal husband and father. As the oldest of five, he'd had ample experience with babies, so nothing scared him. He bottle-fed, diapered, sang, and cuddled like a pro. Unfortunately, when the babies were born, he still had two months of teaching left in the school year, and he could only take one week off, so he wasn't home as much as he would have preferred.

Joann, as well as Paul's mother, Katie, had taken up the slack when Joy's energy failed. Both had cooked, cleaned, and watched babies at all hours of the day and night. Katie had stayed with Paul and Joy for the first two weeks after Joy and the babies came home, and Joann even moved in with them for a few weeks later when Joy developed mastitis and was bedridden for several days. That sacrifice meant the most to Joy – that her aunt was willing to take over the care of Joy's babies when she'd never been able to have her own.

Joy squirmed in her wet clothes and decided to go tackle the bathroom problem. She'd dig that stuffed animal out of the commode or die trying. The rental property budget had no funds for a new toilet, a visit from a plumber, or a strait jacket for Annie if she lost her most prized possession!

By early afternoon, the bathroom was spotless, and Joy had managed to snake Kitty from her underwater cave. She'd deposited the filthy toy in a Ziploc bag to wash once she got home. She'd also finished cleaning the kitchen, changed a burnt-out light bulb, and treated a few small stains on the carpet in the bedrooms. At the moment she realized she was finished with her day's work – after only two hours – Joann and the children pulled into the driveway. She hurried out to the porch again.

Annie was the first person to leave the van. "Mommy! Mommy! Did you rescue Kitty?" she shouted, running up to Joy.

"Yes, sweetie, but he's really dirty and gross, and he may look a little – um – different after we wash him."

"That's okay, Mommy. Thank you for saving him," Annie said, throwing her arms around Joy's waist.

Micah came running over next with a grocery sack. "Here's some clothes for you. Aunt Joann says you should take a shower right away."

"I thought you'd like to be clean as soon as possible after your battle with the toilet," Joann said, climbing the porch stairs. "I also brought sandwiches for our lunch. The kids and I can eat on the porch while you shower if you don't want to make a mess in the apartment again."

"Oh, yes," Joy said. "That's perfect." She finally noticed what Joann was wearing and snickered.

"What – oh, my wardrobe choice," said Joann, grinning. "I grabbed the first things I saw that were large enough."

Joy couldn't stop giggling. Joann was wearing one of Joy's long pajama t-shirts. It was hot pink and covered in screen-printed conversation hearts – a Valentines joke gift from Jennifer years before. With the shirt, she'd put on a pair of Joy's exercise capris – bright purple ones – and red socks. "You – you look like the Valentines section of Walmart," Joy said, still laughing.

"Hush, child," Joann said. "Someone will hear the commotion and see me!"

Joy snorted and hurried to the pristine bathroom to enjoy the rare privilege of a private daytime shower. This day had begun with such chaos, but it was improving, she reflected. Alone time *and* a relaxed shower!

Afterward, Joy headed to the porch to rejoin the others. She paused in the doorway to stare at her children and her aunt for the second time today, but this sight took her breath away for a different reason. The triplets had finished their food and were all in Joann's lap...she was sitting cross-legged on the porch floor so there would be room for all of them. They were listening to her talking with rapt attention, and then, as Joy stood watching, shielded from their view, Joann began to sing to them – in French. Joy strained to catch the words – her own French was mediocre after years of haphazard efforts to learn – but she was fairly sure it was a nursery rhyme.

Joy studied all of them as Joann's soft, tuneful voice continued. Micah Alexander, her oldest by three minutes, looked as much like her as a preschool boy could resemble his mother – tall, lanky, and brown-eyed, with fine, straight, medium-brown hair. He was an outgoing chatterbox who kept his parents on their toes with his constant questions. Gideon Jean, his identical twin, had similar features, but his build was heavier, so it wasn't too difficult to tell them apart. He was also much quieter and more reserved than Micah. Joanna Katherine, known as Annie, their little drama queen, looked nothing like her brothers. She was tiny – petite and small-boned like her grandmother Katie – and had the wild dark curls, blue eyes, and freckles like Paul. She was a bundle of emotions almost all the time, and she followed her great-aunt around like a puppy.

Joy felt a sense of relief when she turned her gaze to her aunt. Joann was looking so well these days. A bit older, of course, and her long braid was much greyer than it was dark now, but her eyes were bright, and she'd finally regained some weight after years of struggling with her health. She'd always have to be careful – to watch her diet and keep up with her medications – but the only issues that plagued her now were allergies and a mild case of asthma, side effects from the times she'd nearly died of pneumonia complications in the past. She worked and moved and spoke with the energy and grace of someone much younger than fifty-six.

Joann's song ended, and Annie begged her to sing another. "Next time," Joann promised as Joy joined them at last. Joann handed her a sandwich. "Do you feel better now?" she asked Joy.

"Are you kidding? I feel like I've had a mini vacation!" Joy took a bite of her sandwich, expecting ham or peanut butter. Instead, it was chicken salad, some of the best she'd ever tasted. "Where did you find this? Tomorrow is grocery shopping day, and the cupboards are bare."

7

"I raided your freezer for ingredients for our sandwiches, and I found a little bag of shredded chicken from a few months ago – it was marked January. I hope you don't mind. I wasn't in a PBJ mood, so I mixed up some chicken salad."

"You know you can raid anything in my house anytime, especially with this result. This is delicious."

Joann smiled at her and began to pick up the remains of the children's lunches. The triplets had migrated to the far end of the long porch and were occupying themselves with some tiny cars.

Joy leaned back against the side of the house and sighed. "You're so good to me," she said. "You make everything more fun, or interesting, or – or feasible somehow. And you help me far more than I could ever hope to help you – or anyone else."

"No, Joy. I'm not 'good to you.' I love you. There's a difference."

"And you know I love you. But saying so is about all I do…"

"Remember your seasons. This isn't your time to help everyone; it's your time to love your husband and raise your babies. Not to mention, you helped me enough to last a lifetime when I was so sick. And when you're done raising those babies, I'll probably be decrepit, and you'll help me again."

They laughed together until the triplets ran to them, clamoring to be told the joke.

CHAPTER 2

Joy's cell phone was ringing as she arrived home that afternoon after dropping off Joann at her house down the road. All was silent in the back seat – the children had fallen asleep on the fifteen-minute trip back to Woodfield – so she sprang from her seat and answered the call standing in the front yard near the van. It was Paul.

"Hi, honey," he said. "I'm almost ready to leave work, but I needed to ask you if you'd mind if I brought someone for supper tonight. I know you had a lot of plans for the day, so if not, that's okay…"

"Well…" Joy said. "It would be fine except for the fact that we have very little food in the house. I put off grocery shopping until tomorrow, so I don't have much to serve anyone…"

"How about if I bring home frozen pizzas?"

"That's fine – I do think I can manage a salad. Who's coming over?"

"An old student," he said. "Do you remember Jack?"

"Oh, yeah, he was the guy who decided to drop out to support his – his grandma, right?"

"Yes. He paid me a visit after school today. I'll tell you more when I get home."

Joy had carried her drowsy children into the house and deposited them onto the couch when her phone rang again. "Yes," she gasped, winded from 110 pounds of toddler transport and expecting Paul to be on the line again. Instead, it was Joann.

"I forgot to mention this earlier with all the unexpected ah, water works, but Alex wanted me to ask you if you'd like us to come over tonight to make homemade ice cream," she said. "Micah has been begging him to make some since the snow melted."

"Oh," Joy said. "That would be fun, but there's no hurry – Micah can wait a little longer…"

"I know." Joy could hear the indulgent smile in her aunt's voice. "But you know your son. He has his uncle wrapped around his little finger."

Joy explained that they'd have a guest as well, and Joann promised to prepare an extra-large batch of the ingredients. Joy ended their conversation with a warm feeling in her heart because of Alex's kindness.

Alex Martin was her aunt's second husband – Joy's uncle John had died several years ago while trying to save his friend from drowning. Joann had remarried over six years ago, to the quiet, gentle man Joy's children now called uncle. John would always hold an important place in Joy's heart – her father's younger brother had been one of the primary reasons she'd survived her bleak adolescence, but Joy now knew Alex better than she'd ever known Uncle John, and she gladly claimed him as family. Generous and kind, Alex had won Joy over with his immediate acceptance of her and his love for her aunt. His relationship with Micah, Gideon, and Annie was like that of a grandfather, a blessing since both of their blood grandfathers had died five years before.

By the time Paul arrived at the farmhouse with Jack and two large frozen pizzas, Joy had taken out the trash, removed the tiny Superman underpants from the dining table, and put away the clean dishes from the dish drainer...somehow, Joann had also found time to wash two days' worth of dishes!

Jack had grown a few inches since his sophomore year, when he'd last come to the Graham house. He wore black jeans and an old t-shirt sporting the name of a heavy metal band; he had never had a traditional appearance, but Joy noticed he had removed the multiple piercings he used to have, most likely at the request of his anxious grandma.

As they all ate the pizza and salad, Jack filled them in on the past three years of his life in between chatter from Micah and Annie. At first, Jack seemed shy, but once he started talking, the words tumbled from him. He'd grown up in a dysfunctional home – he'd never known his real father, and the parade of men who'd lived briefly with his mother had introduced many negative influences into his home. The only stable person in his family was his mother's mother, who lived across town. When she developed cancer, Jack was fifteen, and he'd confided to Paul one day after class that his grandma was refusing treatment. He'd also shared with Paul that he planned to quit school on his 16th birthday and move in with her to care for her. Paul and Joy had done their best to encourage him during the four months until that time, and Paul had helped him find a job at a local factory.

Now, Jack told them, his grandma had died and had left him her tiny, old house so he'd never feel compelled to go back to live in his mother's apartment. He was nineteen, still working in the factory, and would be eligible for a major promotion if he got his GED. But Jack was nervous, because he'd never been good at academics, and he hadn't paid much attention during his last year of school. He'd gone back to the high school today to find Paul, his favorite former teacher, to ask him for advice.

"What do you have to lose by going for your GED?" Paul asked him, refilling his water cup.

"Well, my free time, for one thing..." Jack began, grinning. "I already work all the time. I've been getting, like, ten hours a week in overtime lately."

Paul looked up at him. "I get the feeling that's not the main thing you're worried about," he said. "You've never shied away from hard work..."

"Nah, you're right, Mr. Graham. I don't care about the time that much. I mostly play video games and watch T.V. at night anyway. The big issue is – I'm not really – I mean, it's gonna be kinda – humiliating – going back to school after all these years. I never thought I would..." Jack's voice trailed off as he heard Alex and Joann drive up.

"Sorry, that's the people with the ice cream...Joy's aunt and uncle. Hold that thought – we'll finish our conversation later," Paul promised.

11

"No problem." Jack looked relieved to be able to shift the attention away from himself.

Alex came inside first, carrying the old-fashioned ice cream maker and a huge bag of ice. Paul introduced him to Jack, who he'd heard about but never met. Joann was a bit behind him – she'd lost the car keys under her seat and had to retrieve them. When Paul began introducing her, Jack dropped his fork on the floor.

"Miss Joann!" he croaked. "You – you used to work at the library!"

"I remember you!" Joann said, hurrying over to him. "Wait – don't tell me – your name is...Jack – is that right? You were the little boy who always came on a bicycle and used the computers to research – ah, to do research!"

"That was me! I can't believe you even remember my name!"

"I've always wondered how you were doing," she answered, smiling at him. "I haven't seen you in, oh, seven years or so! And now, look at you! You're all grown up and taller than I am." She paused. "Are you okay, Jack?"

"Yes, Miss Joann. I am. Things are a lot better now."

Paul, Joy, and Alex were staring at them, puzzled by their cryptic conversation. Jack noticed their confusion. "I – I'd like to explain," he said. "Is that okay? Do we have time for me to tell a story?"

They assured him that they'd listen. Alex threw the ice into Joy's freezer, and they all moved into the living room to talk.

"This lady was pretty important to me when I was in middle school," Jack began. "She was in charge of the children's room, you know, and I rode my bike to the library all the time to go in there to get online. I liked to look up stuff about sports and action movies and dogs and fast cars – you know, guy stuff. Miss Joann recognized me after a while and learned my name and would say hi to me when I came in. Sometimes, she'd ask me how I was doing or if I'd gotten to play in the snow that day or little things like that. I never told her, but sometimes, I'd sit and watch

12

her while she wasn't looking – not in a creepy stalker way, but because I liked to see her smiling at all the kids. I didn't see much smiling at home, and I wished I could have a mom like Miss Joann, who smiled a lot and talked to me like I mattered – you know – kinda sappy things like that." Jack paused to push his unruly hair from his flushed face.

"One day, I came to the library because I was scared. My mom's new boyfriend had started acting mean, and I'd found some pills in the bathroom that he said were for a cold. They weren't. The computer wouldn't allow me to research the drugs – there was a program on it since it was a computer for kids that blocked us from looking up drugs or porn or violent sites, but I didn't know that. I didn't know much about computers – I'd never had one at home – so I asked Miss Joann why it wasn't working.

"When she found out what I was trying to search, she sat down with me and asked me if I was taking those drugs, or if anyone was trying to convince me to take them. I started crying right there in the library – my mom's other boyfriends had smoked and drank and done weed, but this was the first time I'd found hard drugs in our house. I told her the whole situation, and she hugged me and told me I was right to be scared and to tell someone about it. After I stopped crying, she asked me about myself – nothing nosy –what I liked to do and what I wanted to be when I grew up and my favorite sports teams.

"The next chance I had, I went back to the library to see her. I wanted to tell her that my mom had broken up with the guy because he was getting so rough, and that he and his pills were gone now. But when I went to the children's room, Miss Joann wasn't there. I worked up the guts to ask about her at the main desk, and the man said she was really sick and in the hospital. And the next day, my mom ran over my bicycle in the driveway, and I never got another one. It was too far to walk to the library, and I never had money for the bus, so I never got to go back to see if she got better. But when things at home were extra hard, I remembered her, and later I told my grandma about her." Jack finally stopped talking and glanced up at Joann.

13

"So you were a huge help," he added. "And – and I'm glad you're okay."

"I remember that day too," Joann said, blushing at his praise. "I was afraid I should have called someone – children's services or the police – to make sure you stayed safe, but I didn't know your last name or address, and I was afraid you'd never trust me with anything else if I started asking you questions like that. I hoped you'd come back and talk again so I could learn those things gradually and help you somehow. I was concerned that I never saw you again, but I had missed over three weeks of work, and then I resigned a few months later."

"That's an amazing story," Joy said. "It's so incredible that you met up again here, under these circumstances!"

"I know. It's awesome," Jack said.

Alex slipped into the kitchen to start the ice cream, because the triplets' eyes were beginning to droop after their busy day, but Paul encouraged Jack to share about his current life successes again so that Joann could hear. She listened intently as he self-consciously summarized again the past few years. By the time he finished telling her about losing his grandma, there were tears in Joann's eyes. He concluded by repeating to her his nervousness about returning to school.

Joann didn't respond at first, but then she rose from the couch and crossed over to the recliner where Jack sat. "I'd like to give you a hug," she said. "Even though you are a six-foot tall man now, I think you could use a hug." Jack stood up and hugged her right back.

"You should be so proud of yourself," she said. "You have accomplished so much, and you've made good decisions despite being surrounded by negativity for a long time. And I'm certain your grandma would be proud of you too for even considering continued education." Jack grinned and stared at the floor.

"Do you have any friends who would be interested in taking the GED courses with you? Or co-workers?" asked Paul.

"I don't think so. Most of my friends are into different stuff now. I don't see them much anymore."

"Those classes are open to anyone, right?" Joann said. Joy saw her aunt's blue eyes snapping and smiled, anticipating Joann's next words.

"Yeah, for a fee. They're not real expensive."

"Would you feel better if I took them too, and we studied together sometimes for the test? I wouldn't embarrass you by sitting near you in class, but you'd know you could talk with me about all of it if you were struggling..." Joann said.

Jack's jaw dropped. "Why would you do that? There wouldn't be any point in you doing all that for me!"

"Actually, it would benefit me too. I quit school during my junior year, and I've always wished I had finished. I don't need a GED now because I'm no longer working outside the home, but it would be fun to go ahead and finally finish high school."

"You'd do that? Seriously?"

"Why not? I don't want my mind to deteriorate," she laughed. "This will be a good way to avoid it."

"Oh, cool! That would help so much," Jack said. He sat back in his chair, his entire body sagging in relief.

"Let's exchange phone numbers so you can give me all the information," Joann said. Jack called her cell phone, which was at her house – she still left it there frequently, to her family's chagrin – and she promised to save his number.

Jack stayed long enough to eat a huge bowl of ice cream, and to tell the kids good night, but he left soon after Joy guided their staggering selves upstairs to bed. His alarm would go off before six the next morning, and he lived half an hour away. Before he and Paul went outside to Paul's truck, though, Jack stopped to speak to Joann again.

"I wanna thank you again," he said, shy once more. "For helping me when I was a grubby little punk, and now with these classes. I don't know why you're such a – a nice person, and I'm not so good with words, but I hope you

15

know how much I – I appreciated it. Do appreciate it. And you." His final words were so husky that only Joann heard them.

"I…" Joann began, but she could think of nothing to say; Jack's sincere gratitude had caught her by surprise. "Keep me posted about the class schedule, Jack," she said at last, hugging him again. He nodded, and he and Paul disappeared into the darkness of the front yard.

CHAPTER 3

A few days later, during naptime, Joy sat on the floor in the big, old kitchen, sorting the mounds of laundry she'd neglected that week. She should probably be relaxing, she reflected, not working; after all, naptime was usually rest time these days since the triplets didn't always nap anymore, and it wouldn't last forever, but the temptation to accomplish tasks without twelve accompanying little hands and feet involved was often too appealing. Joy didn't mind doing laundry, or cleaning, or even cooking nowadays – she'd come such a long way from the self-centered socialite she'd been when she'd met Paul – but sometimes the sheer volume of housework and deep, philosophical preschooler questions to answer seemed relentless and overwhelming. And then there was that matter of the children's education – Joy winced as she rolled Annie's socks into matching pairs – she and Paul were discussing the possibility of homeschooling them next school year, a task that promised even more work for Joy.

Joy was still lost in thought when she heard a light tap at the door. She jumped and craned her neck to see through the half-open curtain on the kitchen door – it was only her aunt. Joy crawled to her feet and waved Joann inside.

Joann closed the door noiselessly behind herself and waited until Joy was beside her before she said anything…she was always sensitive to the kids' naptime.

"How did you know I need a hug this afternoon?" Joy spoke first, embracing the older woman.

"Oh, telepathy, of course," laughed Joann. "But do you have a few minutes? I have an idea to run by you…"

"Sure, but I need to keep sorting laundry, or my children will be naked tomorrow," said Joy. "Look at all this!"

Joann smiled. "Go right ahead – and I'll help you. I think I can tell Annie's clothes apart from the boys' at least."

"Oh, thanks. I didn't mean that…"

"Shhh. I can occasionally manage to do two things at once, but it's a strain," Joann teased her.

Joy returned to her seat on the tile, and Joann sank down beside her. "Joy, how long has it been since you and I did something fun together – just the two of us – something more exciting than folding laundry or maybe washing up the dishes after we've shared a meal?"

"Um...over four years?" Joy asked.

"That's right – really almost five since you felt so ill during your pregnancy."

"Wow," Joy said. "Five years. That's incredible, but I'm sure it's true. We see each other all the time, but you're mostly helping me or we're spending time with all of us together."

"What would you think about taking a little trip together this weekend, just you and me? I already asked Paul if he would mind if I kidnapped you."

Joy stared at her. "*This* weekend? Like, in three days?"

"Mmmhmm."

"I – I don't know what to say!"

"Say yes! We'd leave Friday as soon as Paul gets home and be back Monday afternoon..."

"Monday?"

"Memorial Day."

"Oh...right. But – I wonder how the kids would do – I've never left them more than one night, and only once even overnight at all, that time you and Alex watched them so Paul and I could celebrate our anniversary alone..."

"They were fine that time, and they were only two years old," Joann said. "And they'll be with their daddy the entire time."

"It does sound wonderful to have a long break like that...but I also don't think I should spend the money..."

"Dear heart, I know. I'm not asking you to."

"Oh," Joy said again. "I – I don't know, Aunt Joann. I don't think you should spend so much money on me either..."

18

"Joy, I've told you before. Money isn't something I have to worry much about these days. Please, say you'll go. It would be so good for you, and I'd enjoy spending some time with you one-on-one again."

Joy closed her eyes and smiled. A vacation. Uninterrupted sleep. For free. With one of her favorite people on earth.

"Okay, you've talked me into it," she said. "Where will we go?"

"Now, that is entirely up to you. I've planned most of our past adventures, and I've also gotten us into some tough situations. This time, you can have that privilege – and responsibility!"

"Surely you must have some plan – or at least a preference…"

"No plans. And you know me as well as anyone, dear heart – of course I have preferences, but I'm up for almost anything. You don't have to decide this very moment either, although we should make reservations tonight if possible, because of the holiday weekend."

"Reservations? So we don't have to camp in a tent on this trip?" Joy teased her.

Joann rolled her eyes. "Not unless you're dying to go on another camping trip."

Joy grinned. "Maybe not this time – since this is supposed to be a restful experience and all…"

They laughed together, reminiscing about their two nights' hiking trip on the Appalachian Trail that had ended in a significant injury and an emergency room visit for Joy. The six years that had passed did nothing to dim those memories, and they re-lived several of the highlights as they finished the laundry.

"I know where I'd like to go," Joy said, tossing the last of Micah's t-shirts into his pile of clothes.

"Oh, really? Where?"

"The White Mountains. Wasn't that where you went to hike when Alex proposed? I've always thought it sounded so interesting."

19

"Yes, I stayed in Bethlehem, New Hampshire that weekend. I'm surprised you remember."

"I had more brain cells back then...but what do you think? Could we go there?"

"I don't see why not, although some of the attractions may still be closed for the winter."

"Yay! Oh, Aunt Joann, this is starting to sound like so much fun!" Joy scrambled to her feet and bent down to hug her aunt's shoulders.

"I'm so glad," Joann said. "I'm looking forward to another adventure with my girl, and – oh, oh..." she moaned as she tried to stand. "My foot is asleep!"

Joy laughed, offered her hands to Joann, and pulled her to her feet. Joann leaned on her as she continued to wave her foot in the air.

"Have you been hiding a talent for modern dance?" Joy teased her.

"Didn't you know that Alex and I practice all the latest dance moves together daily?" Joann said, sinking into a kitchen chair at last. Only her sparkling eyes gave her away.

The thought of her calm, dignified step-uncle engaging in such an activity cracked Joy up again.

Joy sat across from her aunt at the table, and for the rest of the triplets' two-hour rest time, she and Joann chatted and enjoyed each other's company. During a pause in their conversation, Joy pushed a catalog from a corner of the cluttered table to the empty space in front of her aunt. "What do you think about this?" she said.

Joann leafed through it. "A curriculum catalog?" she said. "Are you thinking about homeschooling them?"

"Yeah, we are. Have I completely lost my mind?"

Joann didn't reply for several seconds. "No, of course you haven't," she said at last. "I'd wondered if you were considering that route since Paul's family homeschooled for so many years."

"You didn't answer my first question, though. What do you think about it?"

"I don't know much about modern homeschooling. I know there are dozens of methods and programs and approaches now, and groups that meet for lessons – what do they call them? Co-ops?"

"That's right."

"Anyway, you'll have to teach me more about it if you choose that route – the terminology and everything, because when I was young, only the children who lived in the far northern part of Canada, the areas too remote for schools, did homeschooling, and it was via correspondence courses."

"I guess it has changed quite a bit," Joy said. "I don't know if I can handle all the extra work, to be honest. Teaching three little ones who are very different from each other would be challenging enough without also cooking and cleaning for them and keeping up with the rental property."

Joann nodded. Joy watched her in silence, and then said, "I somehow get the feeling that you don't approve – or that you think I'm making a mistake. Are you – are you against homeschooling? I know many people are…"

"First of all, Joy, it's not my place to approve or disapprove of the decisions you and Paul make for your family, so you need to do what you feel is best regardless of my opinion. And no, I'm certainly not against the concept of learning at home – don't forget that I finished all my high school textbooks on my own at home after John and I married. But I can't help but wonder a bit if you'd find yourself too overwhelmed if you take on one of these – these complex, official curriculums, and try to recreate school at home. Do you understand what I'm saying?"

"Not exactly…"

"Well, once again, this is merely my uneducated opinion – I've never raised or schooled a child, obviously – but isn't one of the benefits of homeschooling the ability to have some flexibility? To – to allow the children to pursue their interests, and to learn more naturally? Could you perhaps – forgo the curriculum for a few years? You wouldn't have all the paperwork, and they could learn how to help you around the house as well as their 3 Rs."

"Wow, Aunt Joann, you're describing the unschooling movement! Are you sure you aren't a radical homeschooler who's secretly reading all the latest blogs?"

"Ha! Hardly – I told you – I know little about it, but the children I've spent time with seem to learn best when they follow their interests, and you're already so busy. On the other hand, dear heart, I will support you in whatever you choose; I hope you'll always remember that. And I will be happy to help if there's anything an old lady without even a diploma to her name can accomplish."

"Thank you – I appreciate your support so much. I'll talk to Paul – he's not sure we need curriculum yet either. But I want to do this right – to make the best choice possible for the kids, so that they can be and do whatever they dream – and most importantly, so they can grow up in the atmosphere of faith that I only experienced for three months of my childhood. It's so stressful sometimes to know what's best."

Joann took Joy's hand in her own big, bony ones. "Joy," she said. "You're doing beautifully. You have three bright, happy, loving children who are being raised in the Lord – in the 'way they should go.' I have confidence that you will do what's best for your family – and you should be confident in yourself too. You're an incredible mother. Don't second-guess yourself."

Joy sniffed, and a small shower of tears dropped on the table. "Thank you," she croaked. She reached for the tissue box on the table, but the triplets had used all the tissues for an art project that morning. She scrubbed her eyes with her fists and sniffed again – the tears kept coming despite her efforts to hold them in. "I'm so thankful for you," she said to her aunt.

"Here," Joann said, handing her a clean tissue from her pocket.

Joy blew her nose and grinned. "How are you always prepared for any situation? You always have a tissue when I need one, even when I can't find one in my own house!"

"Then I suppose you should also be thankful for my perpetual allergies!"

CHAPTER 4

Joann picked Joy up from the farmhouse in the early morning fog on Friday; Alex had offered to watch the triplets until Paul finished work that afternoon so the women could reach their destination earlier in the day. Joy had told the children goodbye the night before and had explained to them that their Uncle Alex would be there when they woke up the next morning. There were a few tears from Annie, who was snuggled into her toddler bed with a cleaner, sadder version of Kitty, but all three children cheered up when Joy told them that their uncle was making more ice cream after lunch and that their daddy was taking them to Shelburne Farms on Saturday.

Still, as Joann bumped down the gravel road toward the highway, Joy could hardly believe she was leaving her family behind for four entire days and three nights. She hoped the children wouldn't miss her too much, but a little bit was okay…

"They're going to have a wonderful time," Joann said into Joy's silence, taking one hand from the steering wheel long enough to rub Joy's shoulder. "And so are we," she added.

"I'm pretty obvious, aren't I?" Joy laughed. "And I know they will. They'll have Alex eating out of their hands five seconds after they wake up. And I'm looking forward to this trip with you − so much. But my mind won't calm down."

"I understand; it's perfectly natural. I brought a few things that might help. See if you can reach the grocery sack behind your seat…"

Joy stretched around and swung the bag forward to her lap − it was full of snacks. "Why, Aunt Joann! This is full of junk food!" She rummaged through Hershey's kisses, packages of trail mix, mini Pringles cans, and even a few full-sized candy bars. "You never eat this stuff!"

"I'm not usually on vacation either. Go ahead, have a piece of chocolate. It will put your mind into the appropriate vacation-ish mood. I'll have one too, to support you, of course."

Joy giggled. "It's 7:30 in the morning!"

"So? Our vacation has begun. Pass me some candy!"

By the time they'd reached the highway, they were munching on Hershey's kisses, breathing in a fresh, uplifting citrus scent from Joann's essential oil car diffuser, and singing along to the CD Joann had bought especially for the trip – Evolve by Imagine Dragons.

"I didn't know you listened to Imagine Dragons," Joy said as the second song ended.

"I don't – consciously, but I've heard you playing their music for years, and their songs come on the radio in the car, so I'm familiar with them. They remind me a little of U2 somehow. I think I like them."

Joy grinned. She'd lived near her aunt for years now – had seen her almost daily – and Joann still surprised her sometimes. She'd been paying attention to Joy's background music!

Joann didn't take the interstate, choosing to meander through the small New England towns and around the forested mountains as she drove east. If she and Joy saw something interesting, they stopped to visit it, so they had barely crossed into New Hampshire by noon. "How about a sandwich?" Joann asked as they entered a town with a few restaurants.

"Ugh, I'm not hungry after all that candy and those Pringles! Maybe I'll eat a small salad or something..."

Joann chuckled. "You know driving makes me hungry, so let's grab something from a café and have a picnic in the local park."

"Okay. You probably do need food – you didn't eat all the chips and trail mix that I did!" Joy said. She grimaced as she said it – junk food was not a common indulgence for her either; it made her gain weight almost instantly, especially since having children. She and Joann and Paul helped to keep each other accountable most of the time, because Paul and Joy wanted to stay healthy, and Joann avoided processed foods to help control the high blood pressure she'd had since her 30s.

The women took their lunches to a gazebo in the middle of the village green. "Mmmm..." Joy said, sniffing hers. She'd opted for a small container of broccoli cheese soup instead of a salad once she'd opened her car door and discovered how cold the temperature was at their higher elevation. She and Joann sat close on the floor against the side of the gazebo, shivering in the stiff breeze. "This is the coldest picnic I've ever had," Joy said, her teeth chattering.

"Do you need to move to the jeep?"

"No, I'll survive – if you eat fast!"

Joy finished first – she'd gulped her soup at top speed to warm herself, and despite her discomfort, she was able to appreciate the coziness of their location. The village green was surrounded by tidy, historic homes and buildings and by trees with tiny new leaves. She couldn't feel her fingertips any longer, but she felt a sense of excitement she'd been missing for a long time. "Besides," Joy thought. "Would it really be an adventure with Aunt Joann if the weather were predictable?"

Joann had tried to reserve a hotel room for them in Bethlehem, on the western side of the White Mountains, but all the nice hotels were booked for the holiday weekend. She'd managed to snag them a room at a chain hotel in North Conway, on the opposite side of the mountains. "It's a crowded place," she explained to Joy as they set out again. "But it's near a few short, easy hikes, and..."

"*Actually* easy?" Joy interrupted, her tone dripping with sarcasm.

Joann laughed. "Ah, yes, actually easy. I promise. There are also outlet stores in Conway, and an indoor pool at the hotel, if you'd rather not go hiking."

"Are you kidding? I'd love to go hiking with you again. I've missed it – okay, maybe not the outdoor toilet and blisters and bugs parts, but I've missed spending that time with you doing something you enjoy so much. And this time, I'll try not to roll down the side of a mountain and break myself."

"If you do, I'll kill you," her aunt replied. "You scared me out of my mind when you did that, and I couldn't have gotten you out safely if we'd been any farther from the road. On second thought, we'll stay our entire visit inside the L.L. Bean outlet, and you're not to touch the display kayaks."

"Yes, ma'am!"

The final leg of their road trip led them over the mountains on the famous Kancamaugus Highway. Panoramic views of the highest peaks in New England greeted them around almost every sharp curve, and a few times, Joy begged Joann to pull over long enough for her to snap a photo. The tops of some of the mountains, including Mt. Washington, were hidden in the clouds, and Joann speculated that snow might even be falling at those elevations. At one of their photo stops, Joann slid another CD into the player, and Joy leaned back in contentment as beautiful acapella hymns filled the vehicle. She hadn't realized until that moment that the mountains made her feel like praising God.

Joann checked them into their hotel by late afternoon, and after they'd unloaded the car, they agreed that it was too late to hike but too early to eat supper. "Do you want to shop?" Joann asked. Joy raised her eyebrows in disbelief. "No, really, I don't mind. Shopping isn't too painful unless I'm attempting to buy clothes for myself."

"How about swimming in the pool? It didn't sound too busy when we walked past a few minutes ago..."

"Oh, that would be lovely right now, a swim in a warm pool. That wind outside cuts right to my bones. Good idea, Joy."'

"You may be embarrassed to be seen with me in my swimming – uh – outfit, though," Joy said, holding up the ratty t-shirt and exercise capris she'd pulled from her suitcase. "I bought a rash guard shirt and board shorts for my honeymoon, you know, so I'd be covered, stylish, and comfortable in the water at the same time, but that was one very large pregnancy ago."

27

"Wait until you see my ensemble. It's even worse."

Joy had to laugh when Joann stepped from the bathroom in her outfit. Her aunt wore a sleeveless t-shirt of an unknown original color – it was so faded and paint-spattered – and long athletic shorts.

"Are those Alex's shorts?" Joy giggled.

"Yes…you know I don't wear shorts, and I could hardly swim in blue jeans. I am wearing a swimsuit too, but it shall not see the light of day. It's from when I was in high school and wore swimsuits in public."

"Seriously? Your swimsuit is – what – forty years old? It's still holding together?"

"Oh, hush!"

"Oh, well, what can I say – it still fits you…that's impressive."

"I didn't say it fit well!"

Joy snorted and hurried to change her own clothes.

Although the hotel was almost booked, they had the pool to themselves for half an hour. Joy eased into the water and swam a few strokes, not accustomed to swimming anymore, or to swimming fully clothed. She grimaced at the sensation of the heavy, wet t-shirt – maybe new modest swimwear would be on her Christmas list this year!

Joann climbed into the shallow end of the pool, but she began swimming right away and was soon underwater in the deep end. She swam to the far edge of the pool and then back to Joy and stood up, breathing hard. "Whew," she said. "I'd forgotten how long – it's – been – since I swam – underwater."

"Exhausting, isn't it, if you aren't used to it?"

"Not that – I suppose I haven't tried to swim since having asthma. I should go more often – to build up my lung capacity; this is ridiculous," Joann said, trying to breathe more deeply now.

Joy bit her lip and murmured a response as Joann ducked underwater again. It had been about 5.5 years since the night that Joy had half-carried her aunt to her jeep and driven like a possessed woman to the hospital, where the grace of God and modern medical knowledge had allowed Joann to recover from drug-resistant pneumonia, lung abscesses, and resulting heart complications. Even though Joann was much healthier now, Joy couldn't help but feel a pang of alarm whenever her aunt even hinted at an issue with her health. She watched Joann a few seconds longer as she swam a lap and then stopped to catch her breath again. Then, forcing the difficult memories from her mind, she swam up behind her and splashed her in the face. Joann whirled, sputtering and in shock, and retaliated, laughing like a child.

After a few more minutes of swimming, and then showers in their room, they left for supper. They decided to eat at a Chilis since the nearest one to their homes was over an hour's drive, and they were too ravenous to try anything exotic that night.

The restaurant was bustling with holiday tourists, so although Joann and Joy were seated immediately, their orders were not taken for a long time, and they had to wait almost an hour for their food.

"Ohhh," Joy said, leaning back against the booth seat and yawning. "I'm starving! My bowl of soup disappeared hours ago. I was afraid the waitress would hear my poor tummy growling like a lion."

"I'm starving too," said Joann. "Driving and exercising make me hungry every time." She took a long drink from her ice water. "Are you relaxing yet?"

"Oh, yes," Joy said, laughing. She had called Paul and the kids while Joann was taking her turn in the shower. "They all sounded so happy that I finished relaxing the minute I heard their voices. I may not even have trouble at bedtime."

"I'm so glad, but I'm not surprised. They have such a good relationship with their daddy; I knew they'd enjoy themselves and be just fine."

"Paul is so good with them. I suppose being the oldest of five prepared him for how to be an amazing daddy. I'm thankful one of us knows what we're doing."

29

"Dear heart, I'm hearing so much discouragement in your voice right now, and other times recently too. Has something happened to make you doubt your abilities?"

"Aunt Joann, you're going to make me cry again right here in public," hissed Joy, her eyes already welling.

"Do you think anyone will notice? Look around." Joann's gaze traveled to the boisterous family beside them and the loud group of women in front of them. "You don't have to share with me, of course, if you're uncomfortable. I hope you know that by now. But it concerns me to hear you criticizing yourself like this…"

"I've been more anxious lately, yes. I – I guess what triggered it was a conversation that Paul and I were having a few weeks ago about music – we were discussing that we needed to be more careful about what we listen to because the triplets are really starting to pick up on song lyrics and ask questions about them. We were also discussing that we remembered several things from when we were four, and that it was weird to think that the kids are probably making memories now that they will have for the rest of their lives. And it struck me later that night that my time for parenting practice is over. It's crunch time now. I mean, if you feed and change and love a baby, and don't drop him on his head, he won't have bad memories of your parenting mistakes. But four-year-olds can remember when you mess up, so I need to do a better job of being the parent I need and want to be…"

"Oh, Joy," Joann said. "You're a wonderful parent now, and you always have been…"

"Then why can't I keep up? Everything is still so overwhelming, even though they don't need bottles or diapers anymore. If the house is clean, we eat TV dinners for supper. And if we have healthy, balanced, well-planned meals, the laundry is piled higher than my head or the floors crunch under my feet when I walk on them. And don't even get me started on what my house looks like if the rental property needs work that week."

"It's a process, Joy. Your children are still very young, and they need your attention almost constantly.

30

You can't do everything at this stage. You'll keep learning new rhythms as they grow older, and it will become easier to juggle the responsibilities."

"But I don't want to learn anything!" Joy wailed, forgetting her self-consciousness. "I'm too stinking tired all the time to learn!" She laid her face on her arms on top of the table.

"You're not getting much sleep because of Gideon's night terrors, are you?"

"No. And because I stay up late so I can have some down time, and some time with Paul, and once Gideon wakes me up screaming, it takes me hours to fall asleep again. Then Paul's alarm goes off at 6:00."

"No wonder you're discouraged! You must be sleep-deprived. How can I help, kiddo?"

"Oh, I don't know. You help me out so much already. And, as talented as you are, even you can't make my child sleep."

"No, but I do have essential oils that might help both of you sleep better...oh, I know, you're a skeptic, but what do you have to lose? You can use mine for as long as you like...I have plenty. If they don't work, you're no worse than you were before."

"Uhhh..." Joy said. "I just hate the thought of being a part of such an annoying fad."

"People have been using plants to help heal themselves since Bible times," Joann said. "It isn't a fad to use natural remedies in most parts of the world. I've used lavender or products made with lavender to help me relax for many years, long before I could afford to buy essential oils. And you know I avoid all the marketing hype with them; I use them because they work for me, and because I've been able to avoid taking as many medications because of them."

"Okay, we'll try some when we get back," Joy said. "I guess it's dumb to continue to avoid the oils on principle alone, but I'm never going to be one of those moms who goes around with, like, diffuser jewelry hanging from seven body parts and an aromatherapy force field following her like a cloud."

Joann laughed until tears ran down her tanned cheeks. "That's not necessary. I think you can realize some benefits from oils without doing all that," she said. "But let's think about other ways I can help. I rarely babysit for you even though I live half a mile down the road. I know you trust me with the kids, so why don't I do that more often?"

"I suppose because I want to spend time with you myself, so when you're around, I usually am too…"

"Well, you know I love to spend time with you. That's why we're here, after all. If I watch the triplets more often during the day, though, you can have that alone time you need. You can study your Bible in peace, or read, or write…"

"Ha! I haven't had time to write since they were born!"

"I know. You're a creative person, and you need time to have that outlet. I can also watch them sometimes in the evenings instead so that you and Paul can have a chance for some privacy without needing to stay up so late. I can even pick them up at, say, five pm, after they've had some time with their daddy, feed them supper, and bring them home for their bedtime."

"Oh," Joy said. "Oh. Oh, wow."

"It's a relief to think about it, isn't it? Having more breaks? I suppose I would have thought of it sooner if I'd been a parent myself. I'm sorry it's taken me so long to come up with these strategies. Will you let me try them? Will you let me try to lighten your load a bit?"

Joy only had time to nod before the server arrived with their food, but she could feel her shoulders beginning to sag with utter relief at the thought of Joann's suggestions.

CHAPTER 5

Joy was awakened the next morning by the sound of their room door banging closed. She opened her eyes slowly, letting them adjust to the semi-darkness and wondering how long she'd slept. Wait – she could see the sunlight pouring through a crack in the heavy drapes. It had to be at least 7:00, and she'd been asleep by 11:00 at the latest...she'd slept all night long! Joy couldn't remember the last time she'd slept for eight hours; Gideon woke her with screaming at least five nights a week, and her body awakened her in anticipation on the other nights. She stretched, luxuriating in the smooth sheets of the big bed.

"Good morning," Joann said then, carrying a well-laden tray to her bedside. "We have breakfast! I know you're still not a breakfast person, but I ordered you a little anyway, and I hope you don't mind if I go ahead and eat mine – I've been awake for two hours."

"Two hours! What time is it?"

"Almost 8:30."

"What? You've got to be kidding!"

"Nope. You were exhausted. I was hoping I wouldn't wake you until you'd had a chance to catch up on some sleep."

"Well, I'm awake now! The day's half over!"

Joann laughed. "I remember when you used to growl at me if I called you before 9:00."

"Yeah, yeah. Don't remind me that I didn't grow up until I was over 25! Is that – is that a chocolate chip muffin?"

Joann laughed again and passed her the muffin and continued to eat her own vegetable omelet.

"I think this is the second time I've had breakfast in bed since I moved to Vermont," Joy said. "The other time was my first morning in Venice. Paul went to the restaurant across the street that morning, ordered a bunch of food from a menu he couldn't read, and brought it to me when I woke up."

"What did he order?"

"Poached eggs, fresh fruit, some sort of dry bread, and calf's face jelly – we think."

"Tasty?"

"I wouldn't know. I only ate the fruit and the bread. Paul wasn't a fan, though." Joy grinned, remembering her new husband's face as he swallowed two poached eggs and several spoons full of jelly, determined not to waste the food.

"What should we do today, Aunt Joann?" she asked a moment later. "I can tell that the weather is at least a little better."

"That's entirely up to you, dear heart. I'm up for anything – except that jelly you mentioned."

"Let's go hiking. You said you knew of some short trails."

"Yes…hmmm…there are two waterfalls not far from here that are easily accessible…how does that sound?"

"Perfect!" Joy stuffed the last bit of her muffin into her mouth. "I'll be ready in fifteen minutes!"

The first waterfall Joann had chosen was Sabbaday Falls, several miles back up the Kancamaugus Highway. The trail to the falls was gently inclined and followed the stream through the forest. "This is beautiful," Joy said happily, staring at the canopies of miniature bright-green leaves overhead.

"Yes. I'm enjoying the difference between now and the last time I visited years ago – that time, I hiked up here in snowshoes!"

"This is much better to me. I always walk like an injured giraffe in those."

The waterfall was rushing with excess water from the melted spring snows. At the top overlook, Joy and Joann sat on a bench for a while to appreciate the view. Joy pulled the hood of her jacket up again to protect herself from the chilly breeze. Her aunt sighed. "Thank you, Joy," she said, closing her eyes.

"For what? You're taking me on this incredible vacation…"

"For hiking with me again, even though it's not your favorite activity."

"Of course! We need to go more often again. Maybe now that we don't have to carry the kids so much, they could come with us sometimes too. They'd love it."

"That would be wonderful. And other times, we could go alone as we did in the old days."

"Yes," Joy answered firmly. She'd only been away for a day, but she realized already the necessity of taking some time for herself – and of exercising more. This easy hike – and it truly was easy – in 50-degree weather – had exhausted her!

"Moving water has such a pull for me," said Joann, her eyes still closed. "Perhaps it's because I grew up spending so many days at the Coaticook Gorge, but it has always been important to me. I'm so glad I have the creek on my property now."

"Mmmm," Joy murmured.

"What about you? Does something in nature draw you as well? Or do I sound like a hippie?"

Joy laughed. "Not at all like a hippie. Hmmm, I don't know. I'm not as – as practiced – or – or skilled as you at setting aside my thoughts and focusing on the natural beauty around me. And since I was raised in the city, it isn't such an innate part of my identity. But I love moving water too. And mountains. And fall foliage. And I do notice them much more now than I did before I came to Vermont."

"Alex is the same way. He appreciates beautiful scenery, and he is almost always ready to oblige me if I want us to go somewhere outdoors, but he also was a city person before he moved to Vermont, so it's not something he usually seeks for himself. I'm so thankful he's satisfied to live way out in the country with his woodchuck wife."

Joy snorted. "You're hardly a woodchuck...but you do spend an awful lot of time eating the garden!"

Her aunt slugged her on the arm, and they headed back down the trail as soon as Joy had taken a selfie of them in front of the falls.

After a quick lunch in town, Joy and Joann drove in the opposite direction to Glen Ellis Falls. As they drove higher into the mountains, they could see patches of snow under the trees and a few inches still hanging from the rocks in some of the streams. The parking lot for the waterfalls was even mounded with snow in the shady areas.

"I think it's still wintertime up here," Joy said, zipping up her coat as they hurried toward the trail.

"Almost," her aunt said, pointing to a trillium blooming nearby.

"What is that?" Joy said, crouching to photograph a close-up of the delicate petals.

"A purple trillium. We have them at home too, although I usually see them in late April or early May because of our lower elevation."

"I've never seen one...or at least, never noticed one before."

"They're one of my favorite spring flowers."

"Could we go on some botany walks with the kids? I'd like them to know how to identify as many wildflowers as you do...and other useful plants too. I can recognize the basics now, but you could show them ones like trillium, and we could count it as homeschooling."

"I'm sure that can be arranged."

To access the waterfall, they had to walk through a metal pipe that ran under the highway. Joy reached the pipe first and stopped short. "Oh." The walkway through it was a solid sheet of ice.

Joann came up behind her and laughed. "I wasn't expecting that on Memorial Day weekend. They must have had an extremely cold spring up here."

"Will the entire trail be like this?"

"I doubt it, but this area hasn't been exposed to much sunlight." Joann peered through the pipe and then dropped to her knees. She turned around and noticed Joy staring at her. "I don't want to fall down."

Joy's mouth dropped open as Joann began crawling across the ice. She'd assumed Joann would have recommended they go somewhere less icy, but no, she should have known better than to expect her aunt to take the easy way out of anything. Joy took a deep breath and began crawling after her. It was another adventure to add to the list of unexpected activities she'd shared with her.

Joy caught up with Joann by the end of the tunnel, gratified that she could at least crawl faster than someone a quarter century older than she. They helped each other up and were relieved to discover that the trail was indeed almost clear. It followed a steep gorge on the left, in which the roaring mountain stream tumbled toward the falls. The hike was not long in distance – maybe a quarter of a mile, Joy estimated, but it was quite steep, and the drop-offs down to the waterfall were guarded only by a few primitive log handrails. Joy focused on her footing and avoiding the icy patches on the way down, so she barely registered the views until she had reached the base of the falls. She grasped the stone wall and looked up – and shouted in surprise.

Glen Ellis Falls was one of the most beautiful sights she'd even witnessed. It was brimming with dozens of inches of melted snow and spring rains, and some of the rocks were still lacy with icicles. It was so lovely that it gave Joy a strange ache in her chest. "Spectacular, isn't it?" said Joann, putting her arm around Joy's shoulders.

"I want to stay here and stare at it forever!" Joy sat on one of the nearby stone stairs and continued to watch the water plunging down the gorge – it was mesmerizing. Joann spent a few minutes taking photos from various artistic angles and then joined her niece on the step. They sat without speaking for a long time, drinking in God's creation.

Joy sighed, and then sighed again, and then realized she was crying. She turned her face toward the gorge, not wanting to draw attention to herself, but their seat was narrow, and her shoulders were shaking. Joann stayed silent, but she took Joy's hand in her firm fingers and squeezed it, waiting for the words that would come in their own time.

"I had forgotten," Joy murmured at last, wiping her eyes. "I had forgotten – me…myself. I've been so busy and preoccupied and – and stressed and – and I think I forgot to feel much else."

"Yes, dear heart. Cry it out."

"But – but being here – and looking at this – this incredible beauty – I'm feeling something again. Something – something creative and exciting. Like that I might not always feel like a sleep-deprived robot – at least not forever. I – I almost think I could write again after another day or two of this – and I've written only a few pages since I got pregnant with the triplets."

"Oh, Joy…"

"Will you – will you help me, Aunt Joann?" Joy asked, sniffing. "Will you help me remember to exercise, and to spend more time in settings like this? Will you remind me to use my time for creativity instead of just catching up on housework?"

"Yes, yes, I will do everything I can."

"I have so – many blessings – in my life," Joy wailed. "I have an amazing husband, and wonderful children, and you, and a house and a car, and places like this to visit, and other family nearby, and so many other things. I'm thankful to be able to stay at home with the kids without giving up on Looking Up entirely. I have almost everything I could ever need or want, so I don't know why life has overwhelmed me to the point that I'd forgotten how to access such – such vital parts of who I am."

"I don't know why exactly, kiddo, because I've never done anything even close to what you're doing. I've never had my own multitude of little humans depending on me for everything, day in and day out, while still running a house and loving a husband and working as a landlady. You're working more jobs simultaneously every minute of your days than I've worked in my entire life. I should think that you've every reason to have been overwhelmed, but you're rocking it, as your generation would say."

Joy began to giggle – Joann's occasional forays into popular slang never failed to crack her up. "Thank you," she said.

"I *will* help you," Joann reiterated, making solemn eye contact. "I promise. Even supermoms need a boost every now and then." Joy hugged her, and they started their climb back to the jeep.

CHAPTER 6

The rest of the long weekend in Conway passed rapidly and without much more emotional upheaval for Joy. They enjoyed another swim in the hotel pool, a little shopping, a day of worship and fellowship with the brethren of the church of Christ in Conway, and several good phone calls with Paul and the triplets. Joy even spent a few minutes writing on Sunday evening; it wasn't fiction, but she did manage to journal about how she'd felt at Glen Ellis Falls. By checkout time on Monday, Joy felt calm, well-rested, and ready for their trip home. They planned to drive home by a direct route to arrive by suppertime since Paul had to work the next morning.

Joy shut the back hatch of Joann's jeep; she'd loaded all their luggage while Joann was checking out in the lobby. Her phone rang with Paul's ring tone, and she answered in surprise; he'd usually called her in the evenings.

"Hi, sweetheart," Paul said, his voice stressed. Joy could hear the triplets in the background.

"What's the matter?" she said, her anxiety re-surfacing.

"We are all fine, but Wilson is in the emergency room. It sounds like he may have had a massive stroke."

"Oh, no!" Wilson Roberts had been the preacher for the East Montpelier congregation for many years – longer than Joy had lived in Vermont – and they all loved the funny little man and his wife.

"Is he going to be okay?" asked Joy, trying to remember how old Wilson was – 65? 70?

"It's too soon to know. They got him there pretty fast, but it's hard to tell with strokes – if that's even what happened. I'm about to get the kids ready for the day, and then we're going to Alex's, and they'll stay with him while I go to the hospital. At naptime, I'll come back, and Alex will go."

"That sounds good. We'll be back as soon as possible. Aunt Joann is checking out right now."

"Be safe, Joy. Love you!"

"You too. Love you." Joy ended the call and wiped her eyes. Poor Wilson. She prayed right then that he would not only live, but also keep or regain his ability to preach. She couldn't imagine him ever wanting to do anything else. And his poor wife, Francis. She was a quiet, nervous woman, and Joy suspected she was beside herself with worry for Wilson.

Joy reported the news to her aunt as soon as she returned to the car. "Oh, dear," Joann murmured. "How awful. I know Francis said a few weeks ago that he'd been having blood pressure problems again. I hope they were able to treat him in time." She took a deep breath. "He's not very old to be having a stroke either...only a decade older than I am. Let's go. I need to be with Francis."

Joy was thankful that Joann was driving back, because it was a rainy, gloomy day, and the highways were sometimes obscured by fog. Joann drove cautiously but fast, navigating the wet mountain roads with confidence. As usual, she needed no map, no GPS, no directions printed out. Her memory was as good now as it had been five years ago.

They had made a stop for fast food to go when Paul called Joy again to let her know he was heading back to the triplets. "How is Wilson?" said Joy, gripping the armrest. She had put on the speaker phone so her aunt could hear his update too.

"He's stable but still in the emergency room. They're still running tests, but it was a stroke, and his speech and his right side definitely seem to be affected."

"Oh, that's so tough. I was hoping his speech and memory would be okay."

"I know. I think his memory isn't too muddled at least, because he recognized both his wife and me."

"That's a relief. How is Francis?"

"A mess, as you can imagine. I spent most of my time trying to comfort her and praying with her."

"Aunt Joann is going straight to the hospital as soon as she drops me off," Joy told him.

"That's great. She is exactly the person Francis needs," he said, forgetting that Joann was listening too. "There's something about her that always keeps people calm."

Joann blushed and shook her head. "Oh, hush now, Paul Graham," she said, alerting him again of her presence.

"Oh, hi," Paul said, laughing a little. Joy laughed too. "Paul, she looks like a fire engine," she said.

"Oh, well. I'd say the same thing to your face, Aunt Joann."

It was late afternoon when Joann dropped off Joy and her luggage at the big farmhouse. They had run into some road work – the Northeast Kingdom had chosen Memorial Day weekend to repair some frost heaves, so they had been delayed. "I wish the end of our getaway hadn't been so stressful," Joann said as she turned onto their gravel road. "But otherwise, I had a wonderful time."

"It was so wonderful, Aunt Joann. It was exactly what I needed. Thank you so much for convincing me to go, and for treating me to such an amazing vacation. I will never forget it."

"You're welcome. I'm so thankful you went with me. We'll do it again in the future. And I'll remember our conversations about your hectic schedule, dear heart. Don't worry. Things are going to get easier for you now."

"Oh, Aunt Joann!" Joy hugged her tight.

Joann kissed her on the forehead. "I'll be at the hospital until visiting hours are over tonight. Now, go hug those babies. I know you're dying to see them."

"Yes, I am!"

Joy sprinted down the driveway with her bags, but before she reached the porch, the front door flew open, and small people came spilling through it toward her. Joy dropped her burdens and knelt on the grass beside the driveway as the triplets threw themselves at her, chattering like magpies.

Paul followed at a similar pace. He bent, poked his face among the children's heads, and gave Joy a long kiss on the lips. "I've missed you," he whispered afterward as the kids backed up a few inches, shouting, "Ewwwww!"

"I've missed you too – so much. Thank you for making it possible for me to go."

"So you're glad you went?"

"You have no idea how glad! But I'm even more glad to be home with you."

The kids had resumed talking as fast as possible then, so Paul and Joy couldn't say more to each other for a while. Joy smiled as Micah, Gideon, and Annie told her all about their visit to Shelburne Farms – Micah talked a lot about the covered bridge on the grounds; he had a huge fascination with all covered bridges. They also gave her all the details about Alex's ice cream from Friday – he'd outdone himself and crafted a special Twix candy bar flavor for them, and about playing Candy Land with him for two hours that afternoon. Annie said that Kitty had missed her.

When all three children happened to stop for breath at the same time, Paul spoke up. "I'd intended to have a nice supper ready for you tonight but spending most of the day at the hospital threw off that plan. We've also, ah, eaten most of the other food in the house…"

Joy grinned at him. "It's okay. I never expected you to have leftover food. As for supper tonight – could the budget handle some Chinese takeout? We could take some to Alex and Aunt Joann too, and to Francis if she wants it. I don't know about the others, but I know for a fact that Aunt Joann has eaten a bowl of oatmeal and a chicken sandwich today, and that's all. And I'd really like to see Francis for a minute."

"That's fine. I'll stay in the car with the kiddos while you visit her, so we don't have to drag them through all the germs."

"Yes! Good thinking."

It only took the five of them thirty minutes to get ready. Joy reflected that maybe in another or year or two, they could even manage to be on time consistently to appointments. On the way into town, Joy filled Paul in on some more aspects of her trip. She saved the emotional parts – her self-discoveries – to share with him when they did not have an audience.

After a quick stop at their favorite Chinese restaurant, a tiny place between Montpelier and Barre, Paul drove to the hospital. Joy jumped out, her arms full of fragrant containers of food, and left Paul and the kids to do damage to a huge mound of chicken lo mein.

None of them were in the emergency room anymore, so Joy asked at the information desk and found out that Wilson was in the process of being transferred to a room in ICU. She hurried to the fourth floor. Alex and Joann greeted her in the ICU waiting room.

"Welcome back, Joy," Alex said, giving her a hug. "It sounds like you and Jo-Jo had a nice trip."

"Oh, yes. Thank you so much for helping with the triplets."

"Anytime. Well, okay, I lied. I am too old to keep up with them full-time," he laughed. "Did you know that Micah asked me 53 questions before breakfast on Friday? I counted – and there were no repeats either."

Joy bit her lip to avoid howling with laughter. "I'm not at all surprised." She sobered quickly. "Is Wilson in a room yet?"

"Yes, they are settling him right now," said Joann. "He's very tired, so Francis is telling him good night so she can leave for a while. She's been here since 6:30 a.m."

"I can't stay long – Paul and the kids are in the car – but I brought all of you some Chinese takeout. I didn't think any of you were taking time to eat, and I want to give Francis a hug tonight."

"You're a mind reader, Joy," said Alex. "How did you know I've been craving Chinese food all day?"

Joy set out the food right there in the waiting room since there was no one else around. She'd brought Alex's favorite – sweet and sour pork as well as snow peas and rice with chicken for her aunt – the only semi low-sodium option on the menu, and some basic beef, broccoli, and rice for herself and Francis since she wasn't sure what Wilson's wife preferred.

Francis came back into the waiting room as they were arranging the food, and she was shocked to see Joy. "Why aren't you home with your babies?" she asked.

"They're in the car with Paul. I couldn't wait to give you a hug and speak with you in person," Joy said. 'I'm sorry you've had such a terrible day."

Francis hugged her close. "Thank you," she said. "It has been a terrible day, but at least he's alive. It could have been even worse."

"I'm so thankful it wasn't."

"Still," Francis said. "I don't know what we're going to do. He won't be able to walk or talk well – or preach – for a long time, if ever. And nothing about our house is handicap accessible. And I don't even drive except in town."

Joann took Francis's hand. "We'll all be here to help both of you through all of those challenges."

"In the meantime," Joy said. "How about some supper?"

Francis noticed the feast before her for the first time. She burst into tears. Joy was alarmed until she noticed that Francis was also smiling. "This is – this is perfect," she said. "I'm so hungry, but I didn't want cafeteria food. Thank you so much, Joy."

Joy scarfed her food and then said her goodbyes. Joann was going to take Francis home after their meal, since Wilson was stabilized and sleeping, and Francis desperately needed rest.

"Whew, what a day," said Paul as they drove home, greasy and full of noodles, a few minutes later.

"I know. It seems unreal that I woke up in a hotel in Conway this morning," Joy said.

"Oh, man," Paul said. "I almost forgot to tell you. Something else happened today. Mom called and told me that Marie and Luca are leaving Venice."

45

"Really? Where are they going? I thought they'd be there forever since all Luca's relatives live nearby."

"That's the shocking part...they want to move to Vermont."

"What?" Joy sat up ramrod straight in her seat. "You're kidding!"

"I'm serious. Luca plans to set up a CPA practice somewhere around here and is hoping to find a congregation in the state that will let him preach sometimes – he's not been using his Bible degree much where they live now."

"Paul, maybe he could preach for us, at least for the time being, until Wilson heals!"

"I thought of that too...it would be a blessing since none of the rest of us are used to preaching much."

"Oh, come on. I've heard you preach a couple of times when you filled in, and you did a wonderful job. But it would be the perfect opportunity for him to do some preaching."

"I'll email him tomorrow to tell him about our situation. It may be that Wilson will be able to preach again in a few weeks, and I pray that he can. Realistically, though, that isn't likely since his speech has been significantly affected. Since Luca isn't trying for Wilson's job, it would be a good way to give him some recovery time without making him feel like we were pushing him out."

"I still can't believe they're leaving Italy. When are they coming?"

"I think in August. He is a little nervous about Vermont winters and wants to move well before the first snowfall."

Joy clapped her hands like a child. She would be counting the days until August now.

Marie was Paul's oldest sister. She was Joy's age, and the two of them had become close friends before Marie had left to marry Luca four years previously. Joy also was fond of Luca, a 35-year-old native Venetian who spoke almost flawless English. Joy and Paul had spent time with him on their honeymoon to Venice when they had stayed on his family's property. Marie and Luca had two little girls, aged three and one, but Joy and Paul had never met them. Only Katie had met little Eva and Lucia – Marie had finally convinced her mother to fly to Italy for a month the previous year, when Lucia was a newborn.

The triplets were in bed, and Paul was in the shower, when Joy received a text message from her aunt. "I'm in your driveway. I have some oil for you," it said. Joy giggled, threw Paul's heavy robe over her thin pajamas, and stepped onto the porch. Joann met her at the porch stairs.

"Here's some lavender oil," she whispered. "I saw your lights still on downstairs when I drove by, so I hurried home to grab some for you in case Gideon needs it tonight. You could even put a few drops on his pillow if he's already asleep."

"Thank you," said Joy, hugging her aunt. "You didn't have to give it to me tonight, though...you've only been home...what...five minutes since we got back?"

"It only took me a few seconds to grab it. Don't worry about returning it...I have another bottle, and you can buy your own later if it works for him. Even if it doesn't keep him from waking, it may calm you afterward so you can go right back to sleep."

"You're the best, Aunt Joann. Now, please, go home and get some rest."

"I will. Good night, dear heart." Joann kissed Joy's cheek and disappeared into the darkness.

CHAPTER 7

By the end of the week, it was obvious that Wilson would not be preaching again anytime soon. His speech was so garbled that even Francis couldn't understand most of his words, and his right side was almost paralyzed. His frustration showed as he struggled to communicate, so Alex gave him an old iPad, and during the brief intervals the nurses allowed it, Wilson tapped out words with his left hand. Unfortunately, his ability to spell had also been affected, so most of his messages were incoherent.

The men of the East Montpelier congregation had a meeting to discuss some plans for the immediate future, because Wilson had filled so many other important roles other than preaching alone. Paul shared with the other men about Luca's upcoming arrival and vouched for his scriptural beliefs, and they all agreed that Luca would be a good temporary preacher if his plans were successful. They reached a consensus to contact Luca and explain the situation and ask if he would be willing to preach from his arrival until the next spring, if Wilson also comprehended and approved of the idea. Alex encouraged the men to discuss the plan with Wilson in his hospital room, for although the preacher couldn't speak, he seemed to have a good grasp of his mind, and Alex was hoping to preserve as much of Wilson's dignity as possible. When Alex and two others went to visit and explained, Wilson gave them an immediate left-handed thumbs up sign.

Paul and Joy called Luca and Marie via Skype one rainy Saturday in June and let all the cousins talk together for a few minutes. Although Eva was almost a year younger than the triplets, she had an advanced vocabulary, and she had an involved conversation with them about her favorite movies. All the children were ecstatic at the thought of living near each other so they could be friends "for real," as Annie said. After a few minutes, Marie put her girls to bed for the night, Joy took the triplets upstairs for their quiet time, and Paul and Luca continued to chat. Paul waited until Joy and Marie had returned before he mentioned Wilson's illness and their congregation's need for a temporary preacher.

"I am so sad to hear of your preacher's sickness," Luca said. "But, of course, I would be happy to help. It is the perfect opportunity for me, since I have learned so much about preaching, but I have never had the chance to practice. And I will not need a salary – your little church should save their money. I have researched the area well, and I will begin practice as a CPA in one of the small villages nearby...many villages have no CPAs."

"Oh, Luca, that sounds like an ideal situation for you," said Joy. "I'm so surprised – but so excited – that you are all moving over here."

"We are too," Marie said, smiling, but something about her tone and expression caught Paul's attention.

"Is something wrong?" Paul asked, grasping the edge of the table where the computer was resting.

"We've made the decision to move over there for two reasons," Marie said, glancing down. "The first reason is that Luca and the girls have all tested positive for celiac disease this month, and we think America with all its health food stores and gluten-free options would be an easier place to begin this journey than here in a place where life revolves around traditional pasta dishes."

"Oh, no," Joy said. "That's awful. I had no idea you weren't feeling well, Luca, or that the girls were having problems."

"We have not shared our health journey until now except with my family here, because their reaction was not good...at first, they believed our symptoms were insignificant – that the children must have stomach aches because they ate too much candy, or that I must be too stressed. But then, once we were diagnosed, my parents were terribly upset. My mother cried for a week, and she has been making gloomy predictions of our sad futures without lasagna since then. It was easiest not to speak of it until we had made plans for our health," said Luca.

"Celiac is no fun, I'm sure," Paul said. "One of my best friends from college has it, and it is very tough for him. You're right, though, that our culture is a good place to adapt to that lifestyle…especially here in Vermont. You'll have plenty of options for an interesting diet. But what was your second reason?"

"Our other reason is that I'm worried about Mom, Paul," said Marie.

Paul and Joy exchanged looks. Joy suddenly found it a little difficult to breathe. She and Paul had been talking about Katie the day before – how she had just sort of – slowed down. They had insisted she see her doctor as soon as possible, and she had obediently scheduled an appointment for the upcoming week, another indication that something was amiss.

"What has worried you specifically?" Paul said, unaware that he was gripping the table again.

"It's hard to put my finger on it," Marie admitted. "But when she visited us last year, I noticed that she had aged so much, Paul…like, far more than I would have expected in three years' time. And she got tired so easily, even after she'd had plenty of days to get past her jet lag. She'd play with Eva outside for ten minutes and then need to sit down to rest or catch her breath. I quizzed her about it, but she always made the excuse that she was getting old. But she's barely over 60, and you know as well as I do that Mom resists the idea of being old and feeble more than anyone."

"We've noticed similar things," Joy said quietly. "She loves spending time with the triplets, but she doesn't play outside with them anymore or even offer to babysit often. She seems content to be the sit-down grandma – she reads to them and colors with them, but she doesn't get down in the floor with them much anymore either."

"Do you think she's depressed again?" said Marie. "After all, she's living alone now since Jennifer's in grad school down south."

"Maybe, but it's more than that," Paul said.

"I think so too. I don't know if we'll stay in America forever...naturally, Luca hates the thought of leaving his entire family here. But I'm feeling such an urgency – such a pull to be back in Vermont for a while, and Luca agrees."

"I'm ashamed to say that I have a tendency to take Mom's presence for granted sometimes," Paul said. "After all, I've never lived more than an hour or two away from her. And I don't always focus on her health as much as I should these days either...I should have seen these changes in her sooner."

"Don't criticize yourself too much," Marie said. "It's more difficult to see gradual changes when you're with someone all the time."

Paul and Joy ended their online conversation soon afterward, Marie's words having worried Paul so much that he couldn't focus on anything else. "I can't believe that my sister, who lives on another stinkin' continent, is moving back because she's known for a whole year that something is off with Mom, while I, the oldest in the family, have only picked up on it in the past *month!*" he said, pulling at his hair, which was still a jumbled mess the majority of the time.

"Paul, sweetheart, you take very good care of your family," Joy said, putting her arms around him from behind. "You're not going to notice everything. And maybe we're all wrong. Maybe Katie is feeling down – or not sleeping well – or has a little arthritis that she's too self-conscious to mention. It might not be anything serious."

"I may be as dense as a post, but I know my mom when I wake up enough to pay attention. In fact, I – I'm going to call her right now to get to the bottom of this."

Joy sat down at the opposite end of the old couch from Paul and tried to make a grocery list for the next week, but it was impossible to concentrate on the list even though she could only hear one side of their conversation. Soon, Paul switched his phone to the speaker option so Joy could listen more easily.

"Mom, I've been worried about you lately," he began.

51

"You always worry," Katie said.

Paul pulled his hair again. "You've changed the past several months, though, Mom. You – you seem exhausted all the time. You – you used to be full of energy and ready for anything, even a couple of years ago."

"Paul, you mentioned these things a few days ago. I'm going to the doctor on Thursday at your insistence, remember?"

"But you always resist going to the doctor or anything…we've had to lecture you for years to keep your inhaler with you! And you gave in so quickly this time. Are you feeling sick? Is there something you're not telling me?"

Katie hesitated, and in her pause, Paul added, "Mom, I'm not the only one who's noticed. Joy is concerned too, and I just finished talking with Marie. Part of why she's moving back to Vermont is because she's worried about you."

"Oh," said Katie quietly. "Oh, I had no idea."

Paul winced. "Maybe I shouldn't have told you that," he said. "But Marie has been worrying about you since your visit. Mom, what's going on?"

"I don't know, sweetie. I haven't said anything because I didn't realize you'd noticed a difference. But yes, I am always tired, no matter how much I sleep. My joints ache almost every day. It's getting harder to breathe too, even when I'm sitting still, or I've just used my inhaler. I – I didn't fight you about the doctor's appointment because I was on the verge of calling him myself."

Joy covered her mouth with her hand. Paul's face grew even paler than usual. "You – you should have told me," he said at last.

Katie sighed. "We've had so much worry the past few years already. I didn't want to add to it, and for a long time, I did blame my symptoms on other things – a cold, jet lag, allergies, a bit of depression, turning 60, etc. It's only been recently that I stopped making excuses to myself and accepted the likelihood that something more serious is going on."

"But if you had told me an entire year ago, we could have potentially gotten relief for you sooner, and you wouldn't have had to spend so much time exhausted and in pain!"

"I know that, Paul," she said.

"But – oh, never mind. Here – Joy – I'm – I'm going outside for a bit…" Paul thrust the phone at her and bolted.

Joy's shoulders sagged…she had no idea what to say either. "Hi, Katie," she said. "I've heard your conversation already – Paul put you on speaker phone."

"Hi," said Katie. "Are you angry at me too?"

"Oh, I don't know…maybe a little. I wish so much that you'd told us."

"I suppose the desire to protect our kids from sadness and hard times never goes away, even when the kid is past 30 and a father himself. Paul has lived most of his life worrying about and taking care of one of his parents – first Jean, and then, me. I hate to continue to add to that burden."

Joy took a deep breath. She'd taken several communications classes at Brown University, and she had years of experience working as a realtor and then as a landlady, but none of that had adequately prepared her to mediate between her husband and her mother-in-law. "I think that, at this point, taking care of you comes naturally for Paul," Joy said, selecting her words precisely. "And I can't – I can't speak for him, of course, but I think he'd like the ability to continue to take care of you…the choice to do so. If he doesn't know that you've been feeling so badly for months, he can't have that choice anymore – he can't take care of you."

"How old are you, Joy?" asked Katie.

"Um…thirty-one…" Joy said, puzzled.

"That's what I thought, but you are wise beyond your years. You're completely right. I should have told him. I apologize, and I'll call him back later, after he's calmed down a bit, and I'll apologize to him."

"We – we just want to help," Joy stammered, reeling from Katie's rapid acceptance of her explanation.

Joy loved her mother-in-law and felt a much stronger connection with her than she ever had with her own mother, but Katie's stubbornness was legendary. She prayed that Paul could forgive his mother soon.

The days until Katie's appointment crept by for the entire family. Paul was irritable and jumpy and could not focus well on his end-of-the-year teaching responsibilities. Joy had to bite her tongue several times to keep from snapping at him that she was worried too, but she refrained, realizing that his stress about Katie was also exacerbated by the fact that he always struggled in May and June, around the anniversary of his dad's death.

Paul offered to drive his mother to the doctor, and even to go in with her to the appointment, but she refused, laughing, saying that he wouldn't want to hear all the questions she'd have to answer about menopause. Paul wrinkled up his nose and did not argue with her, but Joy, after laughing at both of them, suggested accompanying her instead, and Katie agreed.

Katie's doctor was kind but professional and thorough. He asked her dozens of questions, examined her from head to toe, and spent a long time listening to her heart and lungs. He also gave her a form to take to the lab for an extensive bloodwork panel.

"Katie, I'm most concerned about your breathing," he said at last. "Let's check your oxygen level." He helped her breathe into his oximeter, read the result, shook his head, and took a second reading. "Your oxygen level is not good…it's no wonder you've been short of breath. And you say this has been going on for over a year? Well, I don't think it's pneumonia, or you would have been dead by now, quite frankly, but we must figure out why your airways are so much more constricted and to see if your lungs are affected. This may take a while – and a lot of testing – but we'll figure it out."

The doctor lifted Katie's blouse once more to listen to her lungs again and noticed a small, raised, red area on her back. "What is this?"

"That? Oh, I think it's a scar from an old bite of some sort. It gets dry and itchy in the wintertime, but the rest of the year, I forget it's there."

"Katie, have you been bitten by a tick recently?"

Katie laughed. "Not this year, but plenty of times in the past. I owned a farm for many years, and we pulled them off daily in the spring and fall."

"Do you remember having a tick bite in the location of this spot?"

"Actually, I think I do…Joy, do you remember when we took pictures of Annie in that field of daffodils year before last? I had a tick on my back that night after I was back home and ready for bed. Jennifer was already asleep, sick, so I managed to pull it off myself. I think that was where it was."

"Did you have a rash afterward?"

"Oh, no, I've never had the Lyme rash, if that's what you mean. I always watch for it."

"The rash only appear in a small percentage of cases of Lyme," the doctor said. "What about a fever? Did you have a fever after it – within a month or two?"

Katie was silent as she tried to remember. Joy jumped into the discussion. "Yes, yes, you did," she said. "That was the year we all had the flu in May, every one of us, even Alex and Aunt Joann, remember?"

"Oh, yes. And I only had a fever and exhaustion – never any coughing like the rest of you – and it only lasted two or three days."

"Katie, I'm not going to give you a diagnosis until we run all the tests I'm planning, but I'd say there's a high chance that you have chronic Lyme disease, and based on your breathing, I'm concerned that the bacteria has been attacking your lungs."

"Oh," said Katie. "Oh, oh my."

"Yes, we need to do blood tests and x-rays as soon as possible. I'm sending you to the hospital lab after we're finished here, but it will take a while for the results to come in. In the meantime, I'm prescribing an antibiotic and breathing treatments for you, and you should also go to a health food store and buy a homeopathic remedy called Ledum. I don't know much about homeopathy, but I have many colleagues who insist that Ledum is effective in treating bites, even long after the fact."

Katie nodded, her face pale and her hands trembling.

"If it is Lyme, will – will she be able to make a full recovery?" Joy asked through a throat tight with fear.

"I hope so. It would have been better if I could have seen you when you first began having symptoms, Katie," said the doctor. "The Lyme bacteria is tricky and can be quite aggressive. I've treated dozens of cases of it from bites that were a few weeks or a month or two old, but more than two years have passed, so I'll be honest, I don't know what we will be facing. If your tests are positive, I would suggest consulting with a Lyme-literate doctor – they're the experts in chronic Lyme disease. I can provide you with some names and phone numbers of my colleagues if it comes down to that."

"I understand," Katie said, staring at her lap.

"I know you don't like coming to see me, Katie," he said. "I know you prefer to heal as naturally as possible, and I respect that and don't take it personally. But this time, Katie, your body has taken a beating. You are not well, whether it is from Lyme or for another reason. You're going to have to trust me, or another doctor, and to trust modern medicine, or I fear that you will not recover."

"I know. I'll take have the tests and take the medication and treatments," Katie promised.

"I'll help," Joy jumped in. "Paul – my husband – Katie's son – and I will help make sure she does all of it." Katie rolled her eyes at Joy. "You *do* have a reputation for canceling checkups and avoiding pills," Joy muttered. The doctor couldn't hide his smile.

Instead of driving home from work that afternoon, Paul drove to Katie's house, the spacious little home he'd built for his mother and sisters after his father's death. Katie's appointment had been at 1:30, so he'd assumed Joy would have already brought her home and gone to get the triplets from Joann, but the house was dark and closed when Paul pulled up at 3:30. He waited for several minutes and was contemplating calling Joy when she drove up at last.

"Paul's here," Katie whispered as she caught sight of his car. "He's going to be furious."

"He's going to be very worried about you," Joy said.

"He's going to be furious," Katie said again.

Katie told her news concisely, but with all the necessary details. She didn't even flinch when Paul shouted, "*What*?!" when he heard that she'd contracted Lyme over two years before. Joy watched them from nearby, remembering anew that she'd married into a family of fast, hot tempers, and feeling thankful that Paul controlled his expertly so much of the time. Today, however, was not one of Paul's shining moments of self-control.

"So you've had a deadly bacteria rampaging around in your bloodstream for two stinking years? Great. Just great," he bellowed, and then he whirled and strode to the back of Katie's house. A minute later, Katie and Joy heard the thwack of an ax meeting firewood. Joy knew that by the end of the afternoon, Paul would have tired muscles and an aching shoulder from his old arm injury, Katie would have enough wood to last her forever, and she herself would have a big laundry project to clean and mend the dress clothes he was still wearing.

"That went well," said Katie, sniffing.

"It's because he cares so much," Joy whispered.

"I know," Katie said. "I know."

CHAPTER 8

That Saturday, Paul left before breakfast to go to his mom's house to apologize for his temper and to take her out for breakfast and a long drive so they could work out their frustrations. Joy had planned to stay home with the kids to get caught up on housework, but when Joann called to suggest an outing to the big park in Montpelier, Joy jumped at the opportunity to enjoy the pleasant, sunny weather.

First, they went on the nature walk through the forest and meadows on one side of the park. The town had cleared a good trail, complete with benches along the way, and the triplets loved looking at the different types of wildflowers blooming nearby. Joann could name almost all the flowers, and Joy smiled as she noticed her eager learners soaking up the information like sponges.

After their little hike, they ate celery and peanut butter and string cheese, and then the kids raced over to the swings, begging to be pushed in the "big kid" swings. Joy and Joann pushed them as high as possible, but the boys soon grew bored and wanted to play catch instead.

"Noooo…" Annie whined. "I want to swing! You can play ball at home."

"I don't mind throwing the ball for them," said Joann in an undertone to Joy. "You could keep pushing Annie." Joy smiled gratefully.

"Okay, Annie, you can keep swinging if you ask nicely instead of complaining," Joy said.

"Please, can I swing?"

"That's better. Micah, Gideon, Aunt Joann says she'll play catch with you so Annie can swing some more."

"*You* can play catch?" Micah said, staring at Joann.

"I certainly can, but today, I'll have to pitch the ball to you and Gideon. Your gloves won't fit my big hands."

"Okay!" said Micah. "Come on, let's go over there! Let's race. Can you run a race too, Aunt Joann, or are you too old?"

"Micah!" Joy scolded, turning her head to hide her grin from him. "That's not a polite question to ask."

"Sorry. But are you?"

Joann winked at him. "I think I can manage a short race. Are you ready? How about you, Gideon? All right...on your mark, get set, go!"

Joy could watch their game from her post at the swing set, and she observed proudly that both boys were becoming skilled at catching their baseball from short distances – a skill they had definitely learned from Paul rather than from her! In a little while, Gideon stopped catching and was wanting to practice his pitches. Joann knelt beside him on the grass and helped correct his form on his overhand pitches. To Joy's surprise, Gideon threw several pitches so well that his brother caught them. He was so excited that he began jumping up and down, and then both boys ran to Joann, who was still kneeling, and threw their arms around her in bear hugs.

"Mommy!" Annie's voice on the breeze interrupted Joy's focus. "I'm done swinging now. I want to play on the playground now with Aunt Joann. See, they are coming back."

"Ask her if she wants to," Joy said, slowing her daughter's swing.

Annie was out of her swing and attached to Joann before she and the boys had even reached the playground again. "Can you play with me now? Please? I want to go on all the big slides with you."

Joann grinned self-consciously at Joy and allowed herself to be led to the huge climbing structure. For the next ten minutes, Annie and her patient aunt "chased" the boys up steps, ladders, and pseudo rock walls and down tall, steep slides. Joy snapped several photos with her phone and posted them to Facebook, being sure to tag Joann meticulously in each photo. She'd be dead meat when her aunt noticed them, but the moment was too hilarious to keep to herself.

Finally, when the kids decided to chase each other while hanging from the monkey bars, Joann bowed out.

"I'm sorry, kiddos," she said, breathless but laughing. "That's where I draw the line. No monkey bars for me!" She sank onto the grass beside Joy, moaning a little. "Oh, to be a foot shorter and a half-century younger," she said, brushing wisps of hair from her eyes.

"Oh, I don't know – your advanced age and extreme height didn't seem to be holding you back out there," Joy giggled.

"Yes, well, if I'm not at worship tomorrow, you can assume that I'm paralyzed," Joann said, her eyes twinkling. "I almost got trapped in that tallest tubular slide. I was already imagining the newspaper headline: 'Elderly lady rescued from playground equipment with the Jaws of Life.' But then Gideon came down the slide and dislodged me quite effectively."

"Ouch!" Joy said. "That sounds painful. He isn't lightweight."

"It wasn't my favorite form of exercise."

The two women watched the triplets in silence for a few minutes. "They are always going to remember that, I think," Joy spoke up after a bit. "That you played with them, I mean. It's so important to them. Paul still talks about his parents playing on playgrounds with him as a child...even his dad did before he got so sick. Paul and I try to play with them as often as they ask so they'll have those memories too. I know they think it was a special treat today for you to play with them on the playground too."

"Hey, it's a good excuse to try out all those interesting slides," Joann said. "I don't seem like a strange, creepy old woman when I'm playing with them, but some people might question my sanity if I played alone."

Joy laughed. "You should come here sometime alone – late at night or at daybreak or something – and climb and slide to your heart's content without an audience to judge you."

Joann bit her lip. "Yes...I should...again..."

"*Again*? You mean you've done that before?"

Joann nodded, blushing. "I did, once, at 6:30 in the morning, shortly after I moved to Montpelier. Of course, that was a few years and a few aches and pains ago, but I was still a spectacle, I'm sure. I couldn't sleep and was taking a walk and feeling lonely and sorry for myself, and as I passed the park, I studied the equipment and felt a sense of disappointment that I'd never had an opportunity to experience a huge, modern playground like that. And then I looked around me, realized I was alone, and climbed and slid until I gave myself such a friction burn on the slide – on my backside – that I could hardly sit for a week!"

Joy cracked up. "Oh, Aunt Joann!" she said, hugging the older woman beside her. "I love you! You're awesome!"

"I love you too, dear heart." Joann watched as Annie scrambled up a tricky chain wall. "And I love your wonderful children. Thank you so much for sharing them with me sometimes."

Joy couldn't speak from the rush of emotions that tightened her throat.

Joy and Paul waited to discuss his day with Katie until the kids were in bed that night. To Joy's relief, both Katie and Paul had apologized and forgiven each other – Katie for keeping her failing health a secret for so long, and Paul for losing his temper with her.

"I still don't understand why she didn't tell me," Paul said. "But I'm going to have to let that go and focus on the present and the future. She has a huge fight ahead of her, I'm afraid, and I need to do everything I can to help her." Paul took off his glasses, rubbed the bridge of his nose, and groaned.

"Do you have a headache?" Joy asked.

"Kinda. From stress, I'm sure."

"Hang on. I'll be right back." Joy jumped up from the couch, hurried into the kitchen, and returned with the bottle of lavender oil from Joann. "Now, sit on the floor with your back against the couch."

Paul grinned as Joy climbed behind him on the couch and began massaging a few drops of oil into his temples.

61

"Ahhh…" he said. "That feels amazing. Don't ever stop."

"I don't know if lavender helps headaches, but it will help you relax at least."

"Joann's really converted you to this oil thing, huh?"

"Oh, I've only tried lavender so far. But Gideon isn't having as many night terrors since I began using it on him at bedtime, and when he does have them, he calms down so much more easily. Also, I've used it on myself after he's awakened me, and it's helping me go back to sleep sometimes instead of lying awake, tense, for the rest of the night."

"Hey, if it's working – why not use it?"

Joy expanded her massage onto Paul's scalp. "You need a haircut, sweetheart," she said, her fingers tangling in his crazy waves.

"I know, I know. Once school is out next week, I'll get one."

Suddenly, Joy stopped rubbing his head. "Paul!" she exclaimed. "You have *grey* hair!" She brushed the hair above his ears. "I see – one, two, three – at least three silver hairs – and here's one on the other side too!"

"I know," Paul said, laughing at her. "They've been there for a while. It happens. And my hair is so dark that they show up well."

"I can't believe we've reached this stage," Joy said. "I feel so old all of a sudden."

"Hey, you aren't the one going grey. And besides, once I get grey enough, maybe people will stop thinking I'm in college and will give me more respect. Did I tell you that one of the grouchy subs at school – the man who must be 85 years old – mistook me recently for a senior – for a *high school student*? Yeah, maybe going grey isn't so bad…"

They laughed away the rest of Paul's tension headache.

CHAPTER 9

Paul finished his school semester on Thursday of the following week. He came home, kissed Joy and the kids, and shut himself into his study to finish scoring the exams and submitting the grades on his computer. He worked without stopping until after sundown, except to tell the triplets good night, so that he could celebrate the next day.

Joy was sorting socks on the couch when Paul came staggering from the study, yawning. "Done!" he announced, collapsing onto her piles of socks.

Joy kissed him. "Finally," she said. "You must feel so relieved."

"Yes...this month has dragged on forever!"

The Graham family slept until 9:30 the next morning because no one set an alarm, and Gideon slept through the night. When Joy woke up after 10 hours' sleep to the warmth of sunlight on her face, she could hardly remember who or where she was. She couldn't remember what had awakened her either – a noise – a dream? Then, she heard a muffled giggle, and she pried open her eyelids and saw three mischievous faces peeking around the doorway to the bedroom.

"Good morning, Mommy!" Annie sang out. "Are you awake?"

"Yes, but let's be quiet so we don't wake Daddy up..." Joy whispered.

"Too late," Paul moaned, putting his pillow over his head.

"Yay!" the triplets cheered, and they all catapulted themselves into their parents' bed.

"You don't have to go to work for lots of days, right, Daddy?" asked Micah, wedging his face under Paul's pillow to look at his father.

"Right."

"Woohoo!" Micah screeched into Paul's ear.

"Can we go to Stooo-urts? Please?" Gideon begged. All three children loved the breakfast sandwiches at Stewart's, the local gas station, and it was a family tradition to eat breakfast there on special occasions.

"Okay, okay, if it isn't too late," Paul said, rolling over and blinking in the bright sunlight. "What time is it?"

"After 9:30," Joy said.

"We'll have to hurry if we want breakfast at Stewart's," he told the children. "They stop making breakfast soon. We can go if you can all get yourselves dressed and at the door in ten minutes. Do you know how long ten minutes is?"

"How long it takes to walk to Aunt Joann's house!" Annie said. "Come on, let's go!" She ran down the hall at top speed, her brothers at her heels. Paul and Joy laughed at the triplets' excitement.

Everyone was downstairs in the prescribed amount of time, although Micah's t-shirt was on backward, and Gideon was wearing his sister's purple flip flops since his own blue ones had been swept downstream in the creek the day before. "Are we ready?" Paul asked. Joy glanced over at him, grinned, and smoothed down his wild bedhead hair.

"Let's go!" she said. "Happy summer!"

That evening, Paul, Joy, and the kids continued their celebration of summertime by going to Joann and Alex's for a cookout. Katie went as well, as did Jennifer, who had packed her suitcases and driven north as soon as she'd heard of her mother's health problems. After a delicious meal of grilled chicken, Paul and Alex settled into the Adirondack chairs on the side deck, where the triplets were drenching themselves at the water table Joann had set up for them. The women retreated to the back screened porch, away from the mosquitos.

"How are you feeling now that you're having breathing treatments and medication?" Joann asked Katie, who she hadn't seen since her doctor's visit.

"Better in some ways…my joints are becoming less sore. But I still feel exhausted and short of breath. I have an x-ray scheduled for Monday, so I'll know more after that.

It's hard to be patient; I'm taking all this medicine, so I expect quick, definitive results." Katie laughed ruefully.

"But your doctor is convinced that it's Lyme?" Joann continued.

"Oh, I didn't realize you hadn't heard. Yes, it's Lyme. My bloodwork came back positive yesterday."

"At least you have an answer now, although I know it is a tricky disease to fight."

"Yes, I'm thankful to be getting answers now. I also have an appointment with a Lyme-literate, naturopathic doctor next week, and I'm hoping for even more answers from her."

"How can I help?" Joann said.

"I don't need much right now," Katie said. "I've got my baby home for the entire summer – she insisted on switching all her summer courses to online – and she's barely letting me lift a finger around the house." She beamed at her youngest daughter beside her on the outdoor couch.

Jennifer grinned back but said nothing, and as Katie and Joann began speaking again, Joy studied her youngest sister-in-law. Jennifer didn't look much different than she had at 18 when Joy had met her – the pigtails were gone, but the freckles, mischievous sparkle in her eyes, and deep tan remained. She was still short, solid, and preferred to dress in old, comfortable clothes. But sometime in her year in South Carolina, pursuing her master's in counseling, Jennifer had grown up, Joy realized. She didn't dominate every conversation, she rarely asked personal questions, and Joy had even heard rumors that Jennifer had acquired a boyfriend.

Joy's thoughts were broken when her aunt rose from her chair and crossed the porch to Jennifer's side. "I haven't even had a proper hug from you yet," Joann said as Jennifer stood up.

Joann held the younger woman at arm's length for a minute. "I'm so proud of how you've grown up," she said. "You're doing such a good thing for your mother this summer. She will never forget your sacrifice." Then she pulled Jennifer into a tight hug. Joy watched, smiling. She remembered when Jennifer had been overcome with hero worship for Joann; having her approval was probably pretty nice for Jennifer even today.

Monday evening, Alex ate supper with Paul and Joy and the kids at their house while Joann went to her first GED prep class. She would take classes on Monday and Thursday evenings for three months and then take the GED on October 1st if she felt ready; otherwise, she could take three more months of classes. Joy had invited Alex to eat with them often on those nights and had promised to put aside a plate for Joann to eat when she finished class.

Joy was still washing the supper dishes when Joann drove up that evening. Surprised, since Joann's class was supposed to last until 8 pm, Joy rinsed and dried her hands and hurried to greet her at the kitchen door.

"You're early!" she said hugging her aunt.

"Yes, the instructor didn't want to overwhelm anyone on the first night, so she let us out 30 minutes early."

"How was it? How did it feel to be a student again after all these years?"

Joann hesitated. "It did feel strange," she said. "But I'm glad I'm going." She took a huge paperback book from her shoulder bag and held it out to Joy. "This is the book we're going to be using for our practice questions, and the teacher will explain some of the concepts in class too."

Joy flipped through the pages of sample questions. "Multiplying decimals...reading charts and graphs...parts of speech...basic algebra...Aunt Joann, you could do all this stuff in your sleep! You've taught me some of these concepts. You'll be bored out of your mind after three days, not to mention three months!"

Joann bit her lip. "Oh, I'm sure there are some things I never learned, or have forgotten. I didn't have the best education, as you know."

"Aunt Joann, you know you don't really need this class. You could pass that test any time you wanted. You're doing this for Jack, aren't you?"

66

"Mostly, dear heart. You should have seen him tonight – he was fidgeting all through class and systematically chewing off all his fingernails. But I also would like to finish high school at last…it's only taken me 38 years!" She yawned. "Where is everyone else?"

"In the boys' room, playing Uno. Paul is teaching the triplets how to play. I doubt they even heard you drive up – they're making such a racket!" As if on cue, Paul roared so loudly that the women in the kitchen could hear him well.

"I'll go tell Alex you're here. The kids only have 15 minutes until they have to stop playing and start getting ready for bed anyway," Joy said.

"No, don't disturb their game. Alex can see me in 15 minutes," Joann said.

"Okay, they'll be done soon – Paul's watching the time. Meanwhile, here's your supper – it's meatloaf, potatoes au gratin, and green beans. Would you like me to microwave it for you?"

"No, no, go ahead with whatever you were doing," Joann said, taking the plate from Joy. "I can reheat it myself. Thank you for saving it for me, but please don't feel obligated to do it regularly. I can make a sandwich or a salad when I get home."

"Are you kidding?" Joy said. "It takes almost zero effort for me to increase the portions I cook enough for you to have a warmish meal after class. Besides, how often do I have a chance these days to do a favor for you? Please let me do this."

"Thank you, kiddo," said Joann, kissing Joy's cheek. "I will be glad not to need to cook on these evenings if you insist."

"I insist!"

The following day, Alex and Joann watched the triplets while Paul and Joy went on an all-day date, something they hadn't done in far too long. They drove to Burlington, window-shopped, had a picnic on the shores of Lake Champlain, played a few leisurely games of tennis at a local park, and had long, uninterrupted conversations. "It feels like I'm playing hooky from life," Paul said, laughing. "I'm with you, in the middle of the day, doing unnecessary things, in a different city – a different *county* – than our children!"

"Isn't it wonderful?" said Joy, leaning against him as he drove through the city streets.

"So wonderful."

After dinner at a Mexican restaurant, they headed back to Woodfield. They sang along to the radio together – the local pop station was playing hits from their teen years, but once they reached Montpelier, Paul turned the volume down. "Joy," he said. "How many books did you sell last year?"

Joy snorted. "I didn't even count, but the royalty amount on our tax form this year was something like $37, so probably about ten. Why do you ask?"

"Oh, I was remembering what you told me when you came back from your trip with Aunt Joann – that you'd lost yourself and were trying to come back, and that you were wishing you could write again. And I thought that maybe if I spent some time marketing and advertising your book, so you started selling more copies again, it would give you a little boost of encouragement to write again."

Joy's eyes welled with happy tears. "Oh, oh, Paul," she said. "That is the nicest thing I've heard in a long time. What an amazing idea!"

"Well, my first project this summer has to be helping Mom, of course, but that won't take up all my time, so I'll plan to see what I can do in advertising. Your book is much too well-written and interesting to be so obscure, and I think we can change that."

"Thank you, oh, thank you!"

"No, thank *you* for all you do for me and our family. I know the last few years have been exhausting and not what you expected, but you have done such an incredible job taking care of us. If helping more people discover your book will make you feel more like yourself again, it's the least I can do."

"Pull over, sweetheart," Joy said.

"What?"

"Pull over. I'm going to kiss you until you can't breathe!"

The next day, Paul took the triplets fishing, and Joy invited her aunt to come to lunch while they were gone. First, though, Joy spent the entire morning in solitude on the front porch, attempting to write. It was difficult to keep her mind from wandering to the dirty dishes in the sink and the mound of clean but unfolded laundry on her bed, but she forced herself to put words on paper. By noon, when she saw Joann's jeep approaching, she had managed to write a fanciful children's story – not something she was expecting to write; she preferred adult fiction...but it was a start.

Joy rose from the porch swing, stretched, and descended the steps to meet Joann in the driveway. She hugged her aunt and began chattering about her writing success right away as they walked toward the house. It wasn't until she let Joann get a word in edgewise, and actually made eye contact with her, that she realized Joann's voice was hoarse and her eyes were red.

"Oh, are you getting a cold?" she said, her writing forgotten.

"No, it was a cat," Joann said.

"A cat? Oh, yeah, you're allergic. What were you doing around a cat?"

"Alex and I visited Wilson at the rehab center this morning, and while we were there, Francis remembered she'd left the oven on in her haste to go visit him. We promised to go turn it off." Joann had to stop speaking to sneeze several times. "We did a little – tidying – too – Francis hasn't had time to think about cleaning lately, but I'd forgotten that they've adopted a cat – a long-haired one that sheds at a dreadful rate. There was cat hair everywhere. Ah – achoo!"

"Oh, no! That's awful. Why did you stay?"

"I didn't stay long, believe me, because I knew if I even sat on the couch, I'd be covered in hair also, and then my head would explode before I got home."

"Can I do anything to help?"

"Yes, let me have some tissues!" Joann gasped. "I was not prepared for an allergy attack today."

They postponed lunch for a few minutes until Joann had stopped sneezing. She rinsed her face in cold water, splashing it across her eyes and cheeks without hesitation since she never wore makeup, and then she took out her contacts and put on her glasses since her eyes were still itchy and streaming. Finally, her symptoms began to subside.

"Sorry about that," she said, breathing a sigh of relief.

"I feel sorry for you. You look miserable."

"Not miserable now that I have taken out my contacts anyway. Just uncomfortable."

"Is your breathing affected? Will this give you problems with your asthma?"

"No, I can breathe easily. It's such a blessing, Joy, but I only need my inhaler around smoke or when I exercise hard or am sick these days. Sometimes, I almost forget I even have asthma." Joann leaned back in her seat on the couch and smiled at Joy.

"That's so amazing," said Joy, relieved.

"Isn't it? God is such a powerful Healer. Have I told you about my last checkups with my doctors?"

"No, I didn't know you'd had them."

"Well, I don't talk about them much, I suppose, but I did see my cardiologist, my pulmonologist, and my general practitioner last week, all on the same day to get it over with, and they ordered the usual annual tests. The results came in over the past two days, and the doctors were all pleased. I still don't have osteoporosis – my bone density hardly changed this year. And my lungs are normal and healthy. The doctor can't even see where those abscesses were years ago. He said it looks like those bouts of pneumonia never happened. I weigh 140 pounds, the most I've ever weighed, which seems a strange source of pride, but you know how hard I've worked to reach a healthy weight. And I'm only taking medications for my heart rhythm and my blood pressure – the same ones I've been on since before you first met me. Of course, I'm also taking about six thousand vitamins and supplements, because I'm an old lady, but I only have the two drugs, other than my inhaler as needed."

"Aunt Joann, that's the best news I've heard in forever! Thank you so much for telling me. I often wonder how you're doing – I know you're basically well or you would have told me – but I try not to pester you about it anymore."

"I know, dear heart, and I appreciate your perception. So, now, I've given you a full update...I expect you to refrain from asking me any health questions for at least six more months," Joann teased her. "And I think it's time you fed me some lunch, eh?"

Joy snickered, and they both moved to the kitchen. They shared a simple meal of sandwiches and salads and then remained at the table for a while, chatting about Joy's writing. As they finished, Joy saw the mail truck pause at her mailbox. "Oh, yes, Paul's been waiting on a package – his new glasses prescription has gone through our insurance at last. I need to grab the mail right away to see if they came." As she stood up from the table, her phone rang.

"I'll get the mail," Joann whispered as Joy took her call.

When Joann came back inside a minute later, a stack of envelopes in her hand – but no package – Joy was already off the phone. "It was an auto-reminder about the kids' dentist appointments," Joy said. "Hm, no glasses yet. Rats. Paul is tired of waiting...you can pile the mail on the counter somewhere..."

"Joy," Joann said, setting down all the mail except the top envelope. "You might want to see this now.'"

"What is it?" Joy said, confused by her aunt's grave expression. She took the thick envelope and read the return address. "It's from my mother – that is odd. She doesn't write letters. And if she does, she doesn't address the envelopes herself..."

"Would you like me to go on home so you can read it? It was rather heavy…it might take a while…"

"No, please stay," Joy said. "It's probably another attempt to convince me to bring the kids down to Hilton Head to meet her. We do plan on it someday, but only at a time when Paul can come too – and beaches are not our favorite places in the summertime…" She tore into the envelope.

A folded sheet of paper and four plane tickets fluttered onto the table. "What?" Joy exclaimed. "Plane tickets? Seriously?" She picked up on of the tickets. "Gideon Graham. Of all the nerve. And I'll bet they're non-refundable too!" She pushed the tickets away from her and rubbed her forehead in frustration.

Joann read one of the tickets that Joy had pushed aside. "Joy, these tickets are for this month – in less than two weeks," she said. "And they aren't to Hilton Head. They're to Harrisburg, Pennsylvania."

"Oh, good grief," Joy said. "I guess I've got to read the letter now. It had better have a good explanation…starting with why there doesn't seem to be a ticket for Paul!"

Joy unfolded the letter, written on plain, unlined stationery, with shaking fingers. "Dear Joy," she began, reading aloud. "Wait? She called me Joy, even in a letter?" Joy shook her head and continued reading.

"I am certain this letter will come as a surprise to you, but there are some news items about myself that I must tell you without further delay.

"First of all, I've sold my beach condo and relocated to rural southern Pennsylvania. I will explain my reasons for this to you when I see you. I wish my grandchildren could have seen the ocean from the condo complex's private beach, but it is too late for that now.

"Secondly, I have enclosed plane tickets for you and the children to visit me in my new home. I did not include one for Paul because I assumed that he could not leave work for a week on such short notice. You are most likely angry at me for arranging your time in this way, but

72

we must have some important conversations in person as soon as possible. And no, I am not terminally ill.

"I will not be meeting you at the airport. My neighbor's relative, Jacob Fischer, will be waiting for you by baggage claim, holding a sign with my name on it.

"Bring simple clothes for the children. I am renting a cottage on a farm, and they will want to play outside while we have our conversations.

"Your mother, Amelia
P.S. I am no longer using my previous cell phone number."

Joy threw down the letter and buried her head in her arms. "What is going on?" she moaned. "*Why* can't I have a normal parent who says, 'Hey, come visit me?' But nooo, Amelia Carnegie has to send me cryptic letters and try to re-arrange my entire life!"

"What a strange letter," Joann said, patting her arm.

"I know, right?" Joy lifted her head and looked at her aunt. "She's left the beach, gone back to Pennsylvania, which she hates, and is living on a farm of all places!"

"Maybe she's decided to become Amish," said Joann, chuckling. "The envelope is postmarked Carlisle, Pennsylvania – I believe that's in Lancaster County."

Joy burst out laughing. "Oh, yeah. My mother, Amish! That's a good one. Can you imagine?" She glanced back at the letter and scowled. "But did you catch that she doesn't even remember – or care – that Paul's off work in the summers?"

Joann nodded. "I noticed, dear heart. What do you plan to do?"

"Ha! I can't do anything," Joy said, jumping up to pace the kitchen. "There's no way I'm spending a week down there with her by myself with the kids, and there's no way the budget would allow Paul to buy himself a ticket, especially at summer rates mere days in advance."

"Joy, you know that Alex and I could help out with that…" Joann began.

"No, no, we wouldn't want to do that unless it were an emergency," said Joy. "Besides, Paul doesn't need to leave his mom right now. There's no way."

Joann sat in silence for a moment, staring into space. "What if I came with you? Alex will be away most of that week, presenting at a medical conference in Newark, a place I have no desire to visit…"

"Well…that would be a huge help. I am dying to understand what's going on – but also terrified at the thought of going down there after all these years away from her. But it would be expensive for you to get a ticket."

"I'm not concerned about that. Talk to Paul and see what he says, and I'll talk to Alex, but I think it's the most reasonable answer to this – ah – unreasonable situation…"

"Unreasonable is an understatement. It's infuriating. I don't even have a way to contact her quickly because she refuses to use email." Joy was embarrassed to feel her eyes filling with tears.

"You could tell her you can't come, you know," Joann said gently. "Or you could invite her to come up here. You have to conserve your own energy and protect your own emotions too."

"I know. But I don't believe she would come, and I have to know what she's talking about! And I'm not going to listen to any garbage from her this time."

"I'm certain you can handle it…I just wanted to remind you that setting boundaries for her is still okay."

"Yeah…I'll talk to Paul as soon as he gets home. I expect them in about an hour."

"Keep me posted, kiddo. I'm heading home now if you're all right."

"Oh, I am. I'm annoyed and confused, but I won't let it take over my life. Don't worry."

CHAPTER 10

Paul was even more frustrated than Joy at the contents of Amelia's letter. "Who does she think she is, the queen of England? Ordering you around and planning your schedule from hundreds of miles away and baiting you with bits of information?" Paul pulled at his hair, wild again only two weeks after his haircut.

"Do you think I should stay home, then?"

"I didn't say that. You're going to have to make that decision, although I do believe you should take Joann with you if you go. I'd go in a flash, cost notwithstanding, if it weren't for the situation with Mom."

Joy bit her lip and nodded, her stomach knotting. Katie's condition had stopped improving, although she was undergoing heavy treatments in both conventional and homeopathic medicine. Her fatigue had increased to the extent that she hadn't left her house in days except for Sunday worship. Her doctors' theory was that the bacteria were responding to the treatments by putting up an even stronger fight, but everyone was worried about her.

"I guess I'll go, unless your mom gets a lot worse, as long as Aunt Joann can find a plane ticket," Joy said, sighing as she leaned against Paul. "The thought of leaving you for a week makes me sick, but this feels important, and I think I need to go. And I suppose it's time for the kids to meet their grandmother."

"I'll miss you like crazy, but it's probably a good decision, sweetheart. It sounds like you and Amelia might even be able to resolve some issues with nothing to do for a week except sit on a farm and talk to each other."

"Maybe...if it is possible for opposites to resolve anything. I think it might be easier to reunite North and South Korea than for my mom and me to work through our past," Joy said.

"Hey, even North and South Korea are beginning to negotiate," Paul laughed.

Joy rolled her eyes. "I'd better call my aunt," she said, pulling herself up from the couch. "She'll need to buy her ticket immediately."

Joann answered on the first ring, so quickly that Joy was startled.

"Oh!" she said. "Hi – already!"

Joann laughed. "We must have read each other's minds," she told Joy. "I had my phone in my hand, ready to call you. There's a special deal on plane tickets online for the airline you'll be flying to Pennsylvania. It opens at midnight tonight and continues until 9 a.m. tomorrow, but there's a limited number of seats available on your flight. I wanted to ask if you'd made up your mind."

"Yes, I guess I have, unless there's an emergency with Katie. I'm going to go, as long as you are absolutely sure you don't mind going with us."

"I don't mind at all...that's why I offered. As I said, Alex will be away five of the seven days anyway, and I had no other concrete plans except GED class."

"Oh, I forgot about your class. Are you allowed to miss two classes in a row? Won't Jack be upset?"

"They don't track absences, just charge you again if you can't pass after three months. And I already called Jack to ask him if he would feel comfortable enough to go twice without me. He promised that he would be fine, and he said he'd take extra notes for me so I wouldn't fall behind."

Joy grinned. Several classes into the course, Joann was still keeping up with minimal effort. She'd even admitted to Joy that her pride was sometimes the only thing that kept her awake in the classes.

"So, if you've decided, I'll buy my ticket as close to midnight as possible tonight," said Joann.

"I hate that you have to stay up so late," Joy said. "Would you like for me to buy it for you instead?"

"No, you've three little ones to wake you early in the morning. I can sleep when I'm dead." Joy agreed and ended the call, wincing at Joann's joke.

All too soon for Joy, it was the weekend before she and the others would leave on Tuesday. She stared at her children's clothing piled on her bed, ready to go in the suitcase they would share. They had plenty of "simple" clothing, all right – so simple that most of it was covered in grass and berry stains and holes, and the boys' pants and shorts were all too short or tight. They'd hit a growth spurt this summer, and the September budget was scheduled to include new wardrobes for all the kids. However, this was July, and Joy didn't want two of her three kids to appear before Amelia as ragamuffins. She considered a quick trip to the dollar store, but she couldn't bring herself to buy any of the flimsy outfits covered in cartoons her children never watched.

Suddenly, Joy remembered the gift card Alex and Joann had given her for the children that past Christmas – it had been for an online clothing company, hadn't it? But the children had recently received an enormous mound of winter hand-me-downs, so she'd stashed the gift card in a drawer for another time. Joy dashed to her room to ransack the drawers of her bureau.

"Bingo!" she yelled aloud after a quick search. She took the card to her desk and opened the company's website. To her delight, Just the Basics proved to be a children's clothing line full of practical play clothes in bright colors and simple patterns – no lace or other trim or superheroes. And, for a small fee, they offered next-day shipping! With a few taps of her computer's touchpad, Joy had filled in the worst of the gaps in her boys' wardrobes – and with adorable clothes that she could endorse. Now if only Just the Basics carried clothes in her size...Joy couldn't think of how she'd find a week's worth of casual but presentable clothing in her own closet either!

Tuesday morning's sunrise saw Paul, Alex, Joann, Joy, and three half-asleep kids driving in Joy's van toward the Burlington airport. Joy tried to calm her jangled nerves as she reviewed her mental packing list once again. She smoothed the legs of her new grey capris. At least she had enough clothing now. Joann had made a last-minute

Walmart run the night before to refill her prescriptions, and she'd called Joy to ask her if she was interested in any cheap capris. Joy had taken a leap of faith and told her to buy her two pairs, and they'd fit perfectly, to her surprise. And then, when Joann had found out that Joy was struggling to pack a week's worth of clothes, she'd dug up an old pair of jeans that had never fit her well, cut them off at the knee, and hemmed them into an additional pair of capris for Joy.

Typically, when all seven of them rode together, Joy drove, Joann rode shotgun, and the men chivalrously crawled into the tight backseat, but this morning, Alex and Joann claimed the back, saying that Paul and Joy needed to sit together since they'd have to spend a week apart.

Joy glanced over her shoulder. The children had all fallen back asleep, and Alex and Joann were murmuring to each other in the back. "I'm so nervous about this trip," she told Paul quietly.

"I know, sweetheart."

"What if it's awful?"

"Well, worst case scenario, you can leave. It's not hard to rent a car and come home – you'll only be about seven or eight hours away."

"That's true. I – I hadn't even considered that option. Sometimes, my anxiety makes me dumb."

"No, Joy. Never dumb. A little forgetful, maybe, but never dumb." Paul lifted her hand to his lips and kissed it.

By mid-morning, Joy, Joann, and the children were spread across an entire row of airplane seats, with a triplet at each window and a strict rotation schedule in place so the third child would have an equal amount of window time. Joy, who had flown dozens of times before, tried to sit back and relax while her aunt shared the kids' enthusiasm – Joann had only flown twice.

"Oh, look, Annie, there's a big river!" Joann was saying, leaning around her great-niece to point it out. Joy smiled. Perhaps this journey would have its good moments as well.

They landed long before Micah, Gideon, and Annie grew bored. Their descent was rapid and bumpy due to storm clouds surrounding the Harrisburg airport. Joy was hardly concerned about the excessive turbulence, and she pushed any pangs aside so she could enjoy the children's reactions – they were convinced that landings were like riding a giant rollercoaster. Joann did not enjoy the unexpected excitement – it was the first time she'd experienced air turbulence – and once the wheels bounced three times and landed safely on the runway, she sat back in relief, ghostly pale under her tan.

"Are you okay?" Joy asked her as the plane taxied toward the gate.

"Yes – or rather, I will be once I stop shaking. Was that – that wild ride *normal*?"

"It happens occasionally. I should have warned you."

Joann nodded and took several deep breaths. "I suppose I'm not quite as adventurous as I used to be."

Joy laughed at her. Her aunt was always up for adventure.

They were the last ones to struggle off the plane, and they were delayed further in going to baggage claim by the necessity of a bathroom stop for everyone. "I hope Jacob Fischer hasn't given up on us," Joy said as they rushed to their appointed meeting place.

"If you want to take Annie and watch for him, the boys and I can grab our bags," Joann suggested.

Joy's worried were unfounded, because the first thing she saw when they stepped off the escalator at baggage claim was a slender, middle-aged man holding a poster with her mother's name handwritten on it. "Jacob Fischer?' she said, approaching him.

"That's me. You must be Joy," he said, shaking her hand in a friendly manner. His voice held a trace of an accent that Joy couldn't place, and he was dressed in simple work clothes.

"Thank you for taking us to my mom's house," Joy said.

"Oh, I will only be taking you about halfway. She rents her cottage from my cousin, Titus Yoder, and he will meet us in Bird in Hand and drive you the rest of the way to the farm. It's not possible for him to travel to the airport today."

"Well, thank you, regardless," Joy said.

"You're welcome. Do you have suitcases?"

"Yes, four of the, plus three car seats."

"Show them to me as they pass, and I will get them for you."

Once their luggage had been located, Jacob led them outside and into a parking garage to a brown 15-passenger van. He loaded their suitcases and backpacks into the back and then even installed one of the car seats while Joy and Joann secured the others. "You're very good at this!" Joy said when Jacob managed to finish his car seat installation long before she finished hers.

"I should be. I have ten children, and two of them still use car seats."

"You have ten kids?" Micah said. "That's a lot!"

"My cousin Titus has even more. He has 13. You'll meet them while you're staying on his farm."

"Whoa!" Gideon said. Micah was speechless.

Joy didn't make any comments about Jacob's family size, but her mind was churning. Was her mom actually living on an Amish farm? Or maybe Mennonite? Because she was pretty sure the Amish didn't drive vans, but she was fuzzy on the differences between the two religions.

"Is anyone hungry?" Jacob asked as they traveled through the edge of the city.

"Yes!" shrieked all three children at once.

"You're in luck. My wife packed some lunch for all of you in case you were hungry. Joann, if you will look in that basket at your feet, there is plenty of cold fried chicken and biscuits for everybody."

"Oh, how kind of her!" Joann said, investigating the basket.

"Yes, please tell her thank you for all of us," said Joy. "It has been a long time since breakfast, and now we won't be starving the minute we hit my mother's door."

"She's good about feeding people," said Jacob. "So is Hannah – that's Titus's wife. I suspect she'll invite you for supper at least once or twice while you're down there."

"This is yummy!" said Annie, attacking her chicken.

"Lily makes the best chicken in the county. But don't tell Hannah I said that!"

After several more minutes had passed, they rode through an old-fashioned village, slowly, because the roads were busy with children and animals. Most girls wore long dresses and white bonnets. They also passed a few buggies drawn by horses, much to the triplets' delight. Jacob made a turn into the parking lot of a small restaurant that advertised chicken and dumplings and hand-churned ice cream.

"Here's where we'll meet Titus," he said. "He's not here yet," Jacob added, glancing around the parking lot, which was full of vehicles as well as three buggies.

"What color of car does he have?" asked Micah, craning his neck in every direction.

Jacob coughed slightly and turned around to face Joy, who was in the seat behind her aunt. "Joy, your mother hasn't told you anything about her life here, has she?"

"Nooo…" Joy said.

Jacob smiled at her gently and then said, "Micah, my cousin Titus doesn't drive a car. He's Amish, which means that he drives horses and buggies instead, like the ones over there."

The children all began chattering together in their excitement to ride in a horse-drawn buggy. Joy stammered. "Oh – oh – I see…ah, no, I had no idea…really…"

"It's all right. I assumed you knew."

"But you – you aren't Amish, are you?"

"No. I was raised Amish, but I met a Mennonite girl and left the community before adulthood. I never officially joined the Amish church." Jacob paused to look around

81

again. "Ah, I see Titus's horses, down the street a bit. He'll be here in a moment. Joy, I'm sorry for the confusion, but you'll be in good hands with my relatives. If you need anything, here's my card."

Joy took the business card from him and read it. "You're a driver – for the Amish? And you have an apiary – so – you raise bees? What an interesting combination of jobs!"

"Children are expensive, even out here," he laughed. "But I'm not joking, contact us if you have a problem. Lily and I will pray tonight that you have a peaceful visit."

"Thank you so much."

CHAPTER 11

The children thought that the buggy ride was better than Christmas. Titus was patient and friendly with them and encouraged them to pet his horses while he helped the women with their luggage. He loaded their suitcases and car seats into the open bed in the back of his wagon and then directed his passengers into the covered sitting area. "Can I ride up front with the horses? Please?" Annie begged.

"No, I'm sorry not, little one. We will be driving for twenty minutes on fast roads, and it is not safe enough. But at my farm, there is a pony who pulls a small wagon, and maybe your ma will allow you to ride in it."

Joy helped the children into the wagon, but before she climbed in herself, she turned to the grey-bearded Amishman beside her. "Mr. Yoder..."

"Please, my name is Titus."

"All right...uh...Titus...can you please tell me why my mother is here? Your – your lifestyle is nothing like hers has ever been, for her entire life. Has she converted to – to Amishism?"

Titus smiled. "I know, but those are questions your mother must answer for you. I promise you will understand soon."

Joy winced. "I'm not sure it's possible for me to understand her." She turned back toward the wagon.

"Joy," said Titus, touching her shoulder. "Do not be afraid. This – this new journey of your mother – it is a good thing."

"Okay," Joy whispered.

Joy didn't say much to Joann on the slow, bumpy trip to Titus's property, because the triplets were shrieking every few seconds as they saw more horses. There were also two tall adults and three wriggling children crammed into two large seats, so Joy couldn't share her thoughts with Joann above the din. Joann recognized her tension, though, and squeezed her hand in support – when she didn't need both hands to keep Annie from bouncing on her stomach!

Just when Joy had begun to wonder if Titus was kidnapping them, he drove the horses down a long, gravel lane, lined with mature fruit trees, and up to a two-story farmhouse with dormered upstairs windows. "We're here!" he shouted. He jumped down from his seat and came to Joy's side of the wagon. "Your mother isn't staying here in the big house, and you also won't be, but she wants you to see her here at first, and to meet all of us."

"Oh." Joy tried to keep exhaustion and frustration from her voice, but she was unsuccessful.

"It will also give your children time to play after they see her," said Titus. "It is all right. Please, trust me. And do not worry over your suitcases. My sons will carry them to your mother's cottage soon."

As they all walked through the beautiful green grass to the house, an Amish woman with a kind face rushed out onto the porch to greet them. "Hello! I'm Hannah. Welcome to Pennsylvania!"

Hannah shook their hands, even the kids' hands, and guided them into the door of the farmhouse. The living room was the first room they entered, and Joy's eyes swam a little at the sight of what seemed to be a sea of people, none of whom were her mother. There appeared to be a dozen children in the room, give or take a couple, all of whom were dressed in the same old-fashioned style.

After several seconds of silent staring between the family and the visitors, Amelia entered the room, pushing a young woman in a wheelchair. Joy was astonished to see that her mother was wearing the same type of dress and apron as the other females, although she was not wearing a white bonnet over her hair. Also – to Joy's complete disbelief – Amelia did not seem to be wearing any cosmetics or jewelry. "Mother?" she asked, not sure she would have recognized her own parent if she'd seen her in passing on the street.

"Yes, it is I. I know these circumstances are confusing for you, but I will explain soon. I'd like to meet my grandchildren now, if you please..."

Joy conducted introductions in a daze. "How interesting," Amelia said, hugging each child stiffly. "They're triplets, but the boys look nothing like the girl. This one, though – what is his name? Micah! Micah looks exactly like you did at his age."

"I don't! I don't look like a girl!" Micah protested.

Joy shot him a scowl that promised future discipline, and Joann turned her head to hide a grin, but Amelia merely laughed. "He has your attitude too."

"Mother, could you introduce your friend?" Joy asked, smiling at the girl beside her.

"Yes, please forgive my rudeness. I will introduce everyone. This is Clara, the Yoders' oldest daughter..." Amelia proceeded to relate every person's name to her astonished audience.

"Wow, it is so good to meet all of you," Joy said. Her mind was whirling. Why had her mother bonded with these people, even to the extent that she'd learned all fifteen of their names, and that she was assisting Clara with her mobility?

After a few more moments of strained conversation, Hannah called out an order in a different language – Amish, Joy supposed – wasn't that like German or something? – and everyone, even Titus, scurried away, leaving Amelia with her family.

"I believe Hannah thinks it is time for me to explain myself," said Amelia, smoothing her hair, which was pulled back into a bun. "Joann, please take the children to play with the others." Joy frowned at her dictatorial tone. "If possible," Amelia added.

"Of course," Joann said calmly. "Come on, kiddos. Your mom is going to do some grown-up talking now with your grandmother, and it's time for us to find the – um – outhouse." She led the triplets from the big room, pausing only long enough to make brief supportive eye contact with

Joy. After so many years of a constant close relationship, words were often unnecessary between Joy and Joann.

"Well." Amelia said again. "I will avoid any more delays and go directly to the point. I am here to care for Clara, who has a spinal cord injury and is not walking again yet. I also assist her mother with household chores since the other girls are all quite young. I have been here for three months, and I will stay until cold weather comes, or possibly longer."

"Ooooooookay...but why? This type of situation is not exactly your...forte, Mother."

"Because I am the cause of Clara's injury," Amelia whispered, her voice quavering. Joy was amazed to see tears in her mother's eyes.

"What?!"

"Keep your voice down. The younger children do not know the entire story. I – I was using my cell phone while I was driving this February. I was in an urgent conversation with my bank, because my debit card number had been stolen and thousands of dollars purchased fraudulently on my account. Instead of parking the car to continue my conversation, I attempted to drive along the beach too – I was late for an important party – and I did not see Clara crossing the street until it was too late. She was in South Carolina with her friends to celebrate their baptisms into the Amish church. She was hurt seriously. The – the doctors do not know if all the damage to her spine will heal."

"Oh, Mother." Joy rested her hand on top of her mother's shaking ones.

"Her family was devastated. Her father was furious. But Clara was ready to forgive. She would not allow her father to press charges against me, as long as I agreed to stay on her family's farm for a while and help her mother. So here I am."

"What – what do you do?"

"I help with the cooking and cleaning – at first my assistance was minimal. You are aware of my lack of background in such menial tasks. Now, after staying here for three months, I believe I am helpful. I also work with Clara in her occupational therapy when her home health nurses and therapists are not here. If Hannah is too busy, I even assist Clara in bathing or dressing on the nurse's days off. Sometimes, I also take Clara on walks or wheel her outside and sit with her in the sunshine and fresh air. And on the Sundays that the Yoders have church, I sit with them and keep some of the little ones from making noise."

"Wow. That's…uh…I'm…wow…" Joy stammered.

"Strange for you to imagine, I'm certain."

"Ah…yes…"

"I have discarded my cell phone and am only using the types of technology condoned by the Amish while I am here. As you can see, I am also dressing similarly to them. Clara explained that those would be stipulations to our agreement – that it would disrespectful to do otherwise."

"Yeah, that make sense. I – I just can't – I mean, this is so much to take in…"

"I understand. And there is more I hope to say – no more crimes committed, but other things, but we have enough time later at the cottage. For now, we should allow the Yoders to reclaim their living room."

"Mother? Could I ask you one more question?"

"Yes," Amelia said, sitting down again.

"Are Clara and her parents still upset – have they forgiven you?"

"I do not know." The older woman paused, and Joy could see the strain in her eyes. "They have been generous and kind since I arrived, but my actions would be unforgiveable to many people."

Joy nodded, and they soon joined Hannah, Clara, and Joann on the porch, where the women had been sitting to watch the children playing in the yard. They all exchanged small talk for a few minutes, and then Hannah stood, stretched, and said she needed to start supper. Amelia and Joann rose to accompany her to the kitchen. When Joy stood also, Clara protested – it was the first time Joy had heard her speak.

"Please, Mrs. Graham, stay with me." Her voice was soft and her English less accented than her parents.' "I would like to get to know you, and your children were asking earlier if you could watch how high they climbed in the apple tree. Please, stay for a while."

Joy consented, but her newfound knowledge made her uncomfortable in Clara's presence. She waited until the other women were out of earshot, and then blurted out, "Clara, I'm so sorry about what happened with my mother. It was so unfair to you, and I can't believe she did that. Thank you for your – your amazing kindness in allowing her to – to make amends a little this way…it doesn't seem equivalent somehow, but…"

"Mrs. Graham," Clara began.

"Please, call me Joy."

"Ah, yes, Joy, did your mother also tell you that she is paying all my medical bills?"

Joy gasped. "Nooo…"

"All of them. My emergency room visit and hospital stay in South Carolina. My time in the rehab unit in Harrisburg. My therapies and home health care now. All the bills. Paid in full by Amelia Carnegie."

"Oh!"

"Yes. She has insisted. We Amish share our bills as a community if we cannot pay them ourselves, because we do not carry health insurance, but your mother did not want anyone in our community to pay for her mistake, so she is paying every penny herself. And, although it hurts our pride, we are allowing her to do it, because it is through this sacrifice that she is allowing herself to understand the concept of redemption."

Joy shook her head, unable to fathom both the enormity of her mother's choices and the wisdom of this young woman a decade younger than herself. "That's – that's amazing," she said. "Thank you. Thank you so much."

"You don't have to thank me. You have no responsibility in anything that has happened. I hope that you and your mother will be able to have a good visit with each other."

"Well, ah, yeah..." Joy mumbled. Clara smiled at her and changed the subject.

After Hannah's supper of enormous, hearty chicken potpies and several side dishes were assembled and ready to bake, she shooed Amelia and Joann from the kitchen and told them to take Joy and the children to the cottage to settle in and unpack before the evening meal. The three oldest Yoder boys had already taken all their suitcases and the car seats to Amelia's place.

"Why do you have two houses?" Annie asked Hannah. "Is the little one a playhouse?"

Hannah's eyes were twinkling, but she answered Annie's question seriously. "The small house is called a Dawdi Haus. It's where Mr. Titus's parents used to live – where David and Ben and Grace's grandparents lived. Many families 'round here have Dawdi Hauses."

"Okay," said Annie, still a bit confused. Joy put an arm around her daughter's shoulders. They were all a bit confused today. It didn't seem possible that she'd left her own cozy house twelve hours before.

Amelia's cottage was much smaller than the farmhouse built to shelter fifteen people, but it had ample space – a nice living room, airy kitchen, and three small bedrooms. There was also a pretty, screened-in back porch overlooking a flower garden and the pond.

"This is so nice, Amelia," Joann said after they'd been given their short tour.

"Thank you. As you can see, Joy, the largest bedroom has a double bed and a twin bed, so the triplets can sleep there. The other available room has only one double bed because I was not aware that Joann was coming in time to arrange another bed. I suppose one of you can take the couch..."

"We'll figure something out," Joy said. "We've shared a bed before in a pinch."

Amelia shrugged. "As you wish. And now, please excuse me. It has been a long afternoon, and I am going to

89

rest before supper." She disappeared into her room, leaving the others standing in the narrow hallway.

"Mama, what's wrong with her?" Micah burst out.

"She's tired, sweetie," said Joy.

"Doesn't she like us? I thought grandmas liked kids," Gideon contributed, but by that time, Joy had herded them into her room.

"Yes, I'm sure she likes you very much," Joy assured him, giving Joann a stressed glance.

"Kiddos," Joann said more loudly than usual, and all three turned to look at her immediately. "I have an idea. I have a surprise for you in my suitcase, but you can only look at it in *your* room. I'm going to take it in there and hide it for you, and once you find it, you can open it and play with it, all right? But you have to use your surprise only in your room."

The triplets jumped up and down in excitement. Aunt Joann gave awesome surprises. She disappeared with her suitcase and reappeared again soon. "Okay, you need to find a big, green box," Joann told them. "It is a surprise for the three of you to share in your room. Hurry! Go find it!"

The children scampered away, leaving the adults in peace, although they could hear a few excited shouts from the neighboring bedroom. "A big, green box?" Joy asked, grinning.

"Yes. I bought them a big kit of magna tiles, I think they're called – those colorful, thin magnetic blocks that seem to be so popular now. They don't have any, do they?"

"No, but I've considered them in the past. That's perfect."

"I thought a brand-new toy might give you a few minutes to decompress," Joann said.

"You're a genius," Joy said, sinking down onto the quilt on the bed. "I'm exhausted on so many levels."

"I can't imagine why. Relax for a while. If the kids need anything for the next hour, I can help them."

"Thank you, but...I don't know if I can rest. My mind is spinning."

"You can talk to me instead if that would be better."

"I don't even know where to start...but I want to..."

"Does it help you to know that Hannah already told me the story of Clara's accident?" Joann said gently.

Joy closed her eyes and released a huge sigh. "Yes, that helps a lot," she said.

"She told me almost everything, I believe, so you can focus on sharing anything you need to without the emotional back story."

"That's wonderful. I've been thinking for the past hour or more about how much I wanted – needed to tell you, but I was dreading the actual process. It's all so awful and weird."

"I think Hannah is rather perceptive and guessed that you'd feel the way you do. She told me the story in a matter-of-fact tone too; she didn't show any anger or have a gossipy attitude at all," Joann said.

"She's such a kind person – it's obvious." Joy rubbed her temples. "I'm just so...stressed and – confused. I don't know what to think about any of this. My mother committed a crime? And is doing penance on an Amish farm? In what universe does that even happen?"

Joann moved to sit beside Joy and put her arm around her shoulders. They sat in silence and listened to the clock ticking for a while.

Joy spoke up again. "All my life, my mother has been hurting people, in one way or another. Yeah, my father was usually worse, but she did plenty on her own too. She hurt you and Uncle John, she hurt our old cook's feelings when she fired her, she was harsh to every member of household staff we ever had, she'd had awful spats with most of her close friends, and of course, we won't even talk about how much she's hurt me. I'm not sure I've ever seen her be sorry for any of it – until now, when her reputation and freedom were at stake." Joy's shoulders collapsed as Joann began to massage her tense neck muscles. "But – she's also paying all those medical bills – going far beyond what anyone asked of her. And yet…since she has the means to pay the bills, it was certainly the right thing for her to do. How am I supposed to feel toward her? Ashamed of her? Proud of her? Angry at her? Is she sincerely desiring to help the Yoders, or is she covering her back? And if she *is* sincere, why has she never been sincere before?"

"Oh, dear heart. So many questions," whispered Joann.

"I know. And I'm sure I'm overthinking this. But I need answers!"

"Of course. That's understandable. And I think that's why Amelia chose this confusing, unusual way to update you on her life – so you would be able to find some of those answers. She's difficult and stubborn, but she's not stupid, and she must have known how nearly impossible it would have been not only to relate her story, but also to explain her thoughts, emotions, or motives via a phone call."

"She must have known I'd have hung up on her before she'd said all she wanted," Joy mumbled.

"Well, yes," Joann said, grinning a little. "In the meantime, while you're waiting on those answers, why don't you see if you can give her the benefit of the doubt? I'm not suggesting that you allow her to manipulate you or berate you, but it *does* seem that she wants you to understand what is happening here. It's certainly not a ploy to meet her grandchildren."

"Ha! No, I don't think that even my mother would risk jail time to ger her way."

"I think something is different this time," said Joann. "This has shaken her, more even perhaps than George's death. Try to hear her out this week."

"I will."

"And in between your chats with her, I will be available in any capacity that you need me – like a – a Swiss army knife!"

Joy burst out laughing. "A Swiss army knife! Does that mean you'll stab people for me if necessary?"

"Okay, okay. Maybe that wasn't an ideal analogy…"

"And what kind of bottles do you plan on opening with your corkscrew? Do you need to go forward and ask for forgiveness on Sunday?" Joy giggled.

"Oh, hush. Stop making fun of an old lady who has had an extremely long day," Joann retorted, poking Joy in the ribs.

Joy shrieked, laughed at her own reaction, and felt her burden easing. By the time Joann had prayed aloud for her, and they were ready to collect the kids and return to the big house, Joy's anxiety had been beaten into submission again.

CHAPTER 12

The next two days crept past in a surreal fashion for Joy. She spent hours watching the Yoders and her mother work and helping them when they allowed her to do so, and more hours watching her children playing and doing chores with the three youngest Amish children. She had several long phone conversations with Paul – in the primitive phone booth behind the barn, a technological exception that had been granted to the Yoder family after Clara's injury. Joy did not, however, spend much more time having profound conversations with her mother, and after supper on Thursday evening, she confronted her about it.

"Mother, I'm enjoying our peaceful time here on the farm, but I didn't leave my husband for a week to watch Amish people milk goats. Can you answer some more questions for me tonight?" Joy said. She'd rehearsed these lines in her mind all evening, determined to sound as direct and confident as possible.

"Yes. I know you must have many more questions, but I thought it would be best to give you some time to process our first conversation."

"That's true, and I have," Joy said, marveling at her mother's astuteness.

"Are you available immediately? I have not been sleeping well, and I am riding to the market tomorrow at 7 a.m."

"Let me check with Aunt Joann. If she can put the triplets to bed, then yes, I'm available very soon."

Joann was happy to oblige her, and Micah, Gideon, and Annie jumped up and down at the prospect. Within two minutes, they had bamboozled Joann into reading them three books, one for each of them, and singing their favorite church song, "Where He Leads, I'll Follow," plus a French nursery rhyme song!

Joy and Joann escorted them to the cottage, where Joy made a lightning-fast change into her pajamas. When she was ready to leave for the screened porch, the triplets had already wriggled into their pajamas and were piled around and atop Joann on the double bed in the children's room. They were squirming like a litter of puppies as Joann settled herself to begin reading the first book. They all looked so adorable that Joy snapped a quick cell phone photo before she went over to kiss them good night.

"Dear heart, if that photo ends up on Facebook like some others did recently, I may have to write you out of my will," Joann teased her niece.

Joy giggled. Joann was a disheveled sight. She'd also changed into her pajamas – the same shorts set she'd worn for years in the summertime, and the triplets had rumpled and disarranged it already. Annie was playing with Joann's braid, which was mostly undone now. And something on the farm had disturbed Joann's perpetually sensitive allergies that afternoon, so she was already wearing her glasses, and they'd slid halfway down her nose.

"You can give the picture to me, Mommy," Annie piped up. "Because Aunt Joann's hair is bee-you-tiful tonight. Look! It sparkles!"

Joy laughed again at Annie's assessment of Joann's silver hair, and Joann hugged Annie close and gave her a grateful kiss. Joy slipped from the room and hurried to the back porch to meet up with her mother, trying not to let the butterflies take over her stomach.

Amelia was waiting for her in one of the big wooden rocking chairs that faced the pond. She was wearing a pair of ivory-colored satin pajamas, something she would have chosen in the past, but she also wore a lightweight homespun shawl over them to protect her from the slight evening breeze. And her hair, which was showing a bit of dark color at the roots, was in a braid. Amelia felt Joy's eyes on her and winced. "You do not have to stare at me as though I were a zoo animal."

"Oh, sorry. I'm sorry. I was just – just remembering how much you used to hate braids," Joy stammered.

Amelia sighed. "Please sit down," she said. Joy took another rocking chair. "Where do I begin?" Amelia murmured to herself.

"Could we begin with my questions?"

"If you prefer."

"So, are you going to become Amish? To – to convert to the Amish religion?" Joy burst out.

"I am not planning to convert to anything," Amelia said.

"But you're wearing Amish dresses, and you're not having your hair done...and you're even going to church with them..."

"I told you before that these – alterations – to my appearance are part of my agreement with Clara's family. It would be culturally insensitive for me to dress in conspicuous clothing. And I attend church with them to help with the children."

"So, that's all there is to it? You'll be the same as always after you leave here?"

Amelia closed her eyes in frustration, and for the first time, Joy noticed that her mother's frosted hair, impeccable skin care regimen, and perfect figure were no longer enough to conceal that she was in her mid-50s. "I am certain I will be altered by some portions of this experience, of course. It would be impossible to avoid. I have learned how to cook, for example."

"What about how you feel, Mother? Isn't it nice to be respected and appreciated for the hard work you do instead of your social position?"

"That's quite enough on this topic," Amelia snapped. "Now...we also need to discuss finances."

"Why could we possibly need to discuss *that*?"

"Because I have changed my will. You are in it now, without conditions, even though your father would be erupting from his grave if he knew that. When I die, you will receive what is in my bank account, regardless of what strange things you are doing with your life at the time. The investments and any property I own will go elsewhere, including partially to Clara Yoder, to whom I will always feel a sense of obligation, as I am certain you can understand."

"Okay...well, I guess it will be a relief not to need to assess my worthiness each year like my father's old will required," Joy said, her voice dripping with sarcasm.

"Your attitude is unnecessary. I know that I have expressed my – disapproval – of your choices in the past, and I will never understand why you threw away your career and social standing, but I hardly expect to be able to change you now, after...how long? Six years?"

Joy bit her tongue and remembered her resolve – and her promise to Joann – to try to listen to Amelia this week and to take advantage of this opportunity to work through some things. "Okay," she said. "But why do I need to know about your will? You said in your letter that you weren't dying."

"I'm not. I do not have cancer or anything terminal. But I am fifty-five years old, and I am beginning to feel it. No one in my family lived long. My grandparents raised me, and they barely survived long enough to finish that task. My parents died in a car accident in their 20s, so that is not relevant, but I discovered recently that my father had already suffered from thyroid disease even before his early death. After my last physical, before I traveled here, my doctor prescribed cholesterol medicine for me and informed me that some of my other blood work was borderline, and I decided it would behoove me to update my will."

"I had no idea...about any of that. You never told me your parents died. I didn't even know your grandparents raised you until An – someone told me a few years ago."

"I was three years old, so I do not remember anything about my parents. Who did you say told you? Not many people are aware."

Joy winced at the slip of her tongue. "Angelique told me," she whispered.

"Ah, yes. She would know," Amelia said. "It is apparent that she knew everything about me many years before I even knew of her existence."

"I'm sorry, Mother. That must have been so humiliating."

"It was not a pleasant revelation." Amelia hesitated, then continued, sounding almost vulnerable. "Tell me about her, Joy. I have always wondered. Your father would never say anything about her other than that she was an ignorant foreigner he'd been forced to marry."

Joy closed her eyes as a wave of fury at her deceased father crashed through her. She counted to ten, opened her mouth, closed it again, and counted to ten again. "He was lying to you," she finally spat out. "He wasn't 'forced' to marry her; he swept her off her feet and brought her to the U.S. before she could even speak much English. She didn't know anyone and struggled with loneliness and trying to adapt. And did he mention that she was only fifteen when he married her?"

"Fifteen?" Amelia exclaimed. "That – that would have been illegal!"

"Yes, I guess so. The only reason she survived her four years of marriage to him was because Uncle John brought Aunt Joann home soon afterward, and Aunt Joann taught her how to adapt better."

"Is she beautiful?"

"I haven't seen her in a couple of years now, so I'm sure she looks like a woman in her 50s, but yes, she is – or, at least, was – extremely beautiful. She's also tiny, not even five feet tall. She still has a strong accent and prefers to speak French rather than English. I think she would have seemed quite exotic."

"George's description always made me think that she was stupid and ugly and undesirable," Amelia said quietly. "But – he also led me to believe that Joann was some sort of raving fanatic, and she is obviously functional at least."

Joy held back a snort. Functional!

"Does Angelique live in poverty?"

"I think so. She and her three sons – all by her second husband – are still farming Uncle John's old land, but I don't imagine it's bringing in much money. It didn't, even when Uncle John was alive."

Amelia nodded. Joy was dying to ask her why she was so curious about Angelique and her financial status, but she kept her mouth closed.

"Tell me more about my grandchildren," Amelia said after a moment. "Which one is the oldest triplet? And how did you choose their names?"

Joy complied, and they chatted for several more minutes about the wonders of Micah, Gideon, and Annie. When Joy left the porch a little while later, she realized with a shock that she'd had a civil conversation with her mother – for an hour and a half!

Joy entered her room cautiously, wondering if her aunt was already asleep, but Joann was propped up on the bed with a book and a steaming cup of peppermint tea. "Oh, hi, kiddo," Joann said. "How did it go?"

"Not too badly, surprisingly...we talked about all kinds of things – too many to repeat tonight...I'm too exhausted – but the gist of what she wanted to tell me tonight was that I'm in her will – without conditions."

Joann shook her head. "I suppose it seems strange to me how focused your family is on wills and money...my silly joke earlier notwithstanding...only because I've lived most of my life without enough money to worry about," she said, chuckling.

"It's not only strange to you. She's obsessed. But right now, she's obsessed because she had some borderline test results and high cholesterol at her last physical, so I guess she decided to get her affairs in order."

Joann smiled and looked back down at her book. "I'm so thankful it went well. I've been in here praying in between chapters. And nodding off." She took a sip of her tea, winced, and yawned.

"Too hot to drink?"

"No, I'm trying to fight off a sinus headache. Between all the congestion I had earlier, and the thunderstorms forecasted tomorrow – my head is ready to explode."

"Oh, no, you should go on to sleep. The last thing you need is to have a sinus infection or something on our flight home."

"I am tired, so I'll go ahead and try to sleep once I've drunk my tea. Hopefully, I won't snore and disturb you since I'm not breathing through my nose tonight."

Joy giggled. "Your snoring wouldn't disturb me as much as your cover snatching does! I keep waking up without even the sheet over me."

Joann blushed. "That has been a – ah – recurring complaint from both Alex and John," she admitted. Joy laughed again, kissed her good night, and left to go brush her teeth.

The wind was whipping the trees around the next morning when Joy awakened, and the air felt heavy with the weight of the upcoming storm. She dressed, shut the bedroom window, checked on the still-sleeping triplets, and then went in search of her aunt. Joy passed through the kitchen, which still smelled of tea and oatmeal, and went out to the screened porch, not surprised to locate Joann there.

"Good morning!" Joann said cheerfully. "I hope I didn't wake you when I got up. It's hard to slip out of a double bed discreetly."

"No, I think the wind is what woke me," said Joy, leaning down to hug her. "This is going to be quite a storm."

"Yes, it doesn't feel like one of our Vermont storms. I wonder if there's a threat of tornados," Joann said.

"Oh, man, I hope not." Joy sat in the rocking chair beside her. "How's your head?"

"Still sore. It will be until the storm breaks, I think."

"Poor head! Would you like me to rub it for you?"

"Oh, well, yes, that would feel good if you don't have anything better to do."

"I am free of responsibilities at the moment," Joy said. She stood up and stepped behind her aunt's rocker. "Should I unbraid your hair too?"

"You can do whatever you'd like."

Joy was struck with a powerful sense of déjà vu as she gently undid Joann's heavy braid and began to massage her scalp with her fingertips. She said nothing for several minutes, lost in her memories of the last time she'd done anything like this – when Joann was in the hospital years before, too weak to care for her own hair.

Although she was silent, and Joann could not see her face, her aunt was perceptive, and to Joy's dismay, guessed some of her thoughts. "Come back, kiddo," she said, putting her hands over her niece's shoulders for a second. "You're a million miles away."

"Oh, yeah. Sorry," Joy said. "Were you talking to me?"

"No, but it seemed like you might have been thinking about the last time you played with my hair – and fretting a little…"

"Good grief, Aunt Joann, are you a psychic or something?" Joy snapped. At that moment, three small figures dashed onto the porch, though, and they did not continue their conversation. Joy kissed the triplets and began to re-braid Joann's hair.

"Don't do that, Mommy," Annie begged. "Leave it like that, all long and wavy and sparkly. She looks like a fairy queen."

Joann laughed a bit self-consciously. "But I always braid my hair, Annie," she said.

"Please?" the tiny girl begged again. Joy grinned and watched Joann squirm. She knew that her low-maintenance aunt was a bit sensitive about her long, grey locks, which she kept long mostly for Alex's benefit.

"Okay, for a little while. For you," Joann said, hugging her shadow.

"Yay!" cheered Annie.

Suddenly, a distant clap of thunder sounded. "We'd better get the kids' breakfasts before the lightning comes too close," Joann said, standing up, her wavy bush of hair bouncing around her shoulders. She hurried to the kitchen, Annie trailing her like a puppy as usual, and Joy grinned again.

CHAPTER 13

The triplets had almost finished their scrambled eggs and multi-grain toast when the rain arrived with a blast. Sheets of rain beat the side of the house, and the lightning flashed all around them. The wind howled. "I think we should find a closet or an interior room," Joann began, and then the back door banged open, and Amelia blew in. Or – at least, she thought it was Amelia under the big blanket and streaming hair.

"Get the children to the cellar," Amelia gasped out. "There's a funnel cloud headed this direction! Hurry!"

Joy grabbed Gideon and Micah by the hands as Annie sprang into Joann's arms. Amelia led them a few feet into the driving rain and began struggling with the heavy door of the old-fashioned underground cellar. Joy ordered the boys not to move and added her strength to her mother's, and the door swung open at last. They scurried down the steep concrete stairs, dodging jars of canned food and a few cobwebs.

"Mommy, I'm scared!" wailed Annie.

"What's happening?" Gideon said, grasping Joy's hand so tightly it hurt.

"It's going to be okay, babies," Joy said, trying to sound more confident than she felt. "There's a big storm, and we want to make sure we are safe."

"The grandma said it was a funno cloud. Is it a tor-mato? Is it going to swallow us and eat us?" Micah wailed.

"Nothing is going eat us down here," Joy said. "Let's sit down over here on these benches and wait until the storm is done." She directed them to the benches, and all six of them huddled together, shivering a bit from their soaked clothing and the dank air of the cellar.

"Mother, thank you for running through the storm to warn us," Joy said. "I had no idea the shelter was out here."

"I was not going to let you all be swept..." Amelia began, but Joann placed her hand on the other woman's arm and hushed her, indicating Amelia's already-terrified grandchildren.

Before anyone else could speak, they all heard a steady roar in the distance, quite like the sound of an upcoming train. Joy glanced at her aunt in the glow of her cell phone flashlight, and Joann nodded. Neither of them had ever lived through a tornado in the past, but it was obvious that one was approaching – fast.

Dozens of thoughts barreled through Joy's mind with the force of the oncoming tornado – were they safe enough down here underground, or would they die there, together? Would she ever feel Paul's arms around her again? Were the Yoders in a cellar too, and would Clara be able to reach safety in time? And, if everyone did survive, would the farm and buildings be destroyed? Of all the ways harm could befall her, Joy had never expected to worry about perishing in a tornado...

The roar of the tornado grew louder, and the children all began to cry. Joy could feel her heartbeat pounding in her head. She reached over to hold her aunt's hand and discovered that they were both shaking. Joy could barely see her mother's profile in the dimness of her phone light, but she could tell that Amelia wasn't moving. Joann began praying aloud for their safety and the safety of the Yoders, but her voice was so hoarse and wobbly that Joy could hardly hear it above the tornado. Then, the wind threw open the door above them, and an avalanche of canned goods rained down the stairs, breaking into a million pieces. Joy and Joann pulled the children closer to shield them with their bodies.

After what seemed like hours, but was only a few moments, the wind's fury abated, and everything was quiet again, except the torrents of rain falling overhead and the whimpers of the triplets.

"M – mother, are you okay?" Joy whispered, her throat as dry as the Sahara.

"Yes," Amelia said in a monotone.

"Kids, are you hurt anywhere?"

The boys shook their heads, eyes still wide with terror, and Annie said she was okay, but she began listing off all her possessions that she was worried about.

"How about you, Aunt Joann?"

Joann didn't answer at first, so Joy repeated her question and discovered that her aunt was using her inhaler. "Yes, yes," Joann said as soon as she was finished, gasping a bit. "The air down here is terrible."

"Okay, no one move yet," Joy said. "There's broken glass everywhere, and it could hurt us if we touch it by accident in the dark."

"One of us needs to investigate," said Joann. "We can't stay down here much longer with the rain pouring in like this. Give me a second longer to – to catch my breath, and I'll go."

"No, I can," said Joy. She stood, ordered the children once more to stay where they were, and inched toward the streaming stairs, pushing the shards of glass aside with her sneakers. She climbed the slick stairs, one at a time, legs shaking, terrified of what she would see at the top. To her amazement, a shaft of sunlight broke through the clouds and blinded her as she left the dark cellar, but rain continued to fall through the sunlight.

Joy's grew weak with relief when she saw that the Yoder family's house and barn, as well as the Dawdi Haus, were all still standing. From her vantage point, she could see some shingles blown off the roof of the farmhouse, a few broken windows and at least one huge downed tree, but she was certain their new friends were safe. Then she turned around on the stair and cried out.

The farm across the two-lane road at the bottom of the hill was – gone. Completely leveled. Joy couldn't see details, for it was an eighth of a mile away in the steady rain, but she knew there had been a nice, two-story home and big barn there – and now – there weren't. The tornado must have passed that near them – they'd been spared by only a few hundred yards.

She turned and hurried to tell the others, descending the stairs faster than she should have.

"The Yoders' land and buildings are mostly undamaged," she called down. "But the farm across the road is just – just gone! It looks like a war z…" Joy lost her footing on the wet step and crashed down the final five stairs, landing on her hands and knees – and a broken mason jar under her right hand. She shrieked, once, as she felt the sharp pain and the blood begin to flow, but she did not allow herself to make any more noises afterward to keep from scaring the children.

"Mommy!" Annie shouted. "Are you okay?" She tried to scramble toward Joy, but Joy screamed at her to stay still.

Annie collapsed against her aunt, sobbing.

"I'm sorry, baby, but it is so dangerous down here. Mommy hurt her hand, but she'll be okay later," said Joy, crying.

"Amelia, I've got to help Joy with her hand, and then we *must* get these children out," Joann said. "Hold their hands and don't let go." She crept toward Joy and lifted her phone flashlight, berating herself for its low battery and dim light.

"Oh, dear heart," she murmured. "That's quite a lot of blood." She pulled two clean tissues from her pocket. "Okay, hold pressure on it with this." She removed one of her shoes and a sock and then used the sock to tie the tissues into place onto Joy's hand. "Stay right here," she commanded. "Are you all right for a minute? Not too dizzy?"

"Maybe a little," Joy said, gasping at the pain.

"Then we need to get you out first. Come on. Amelia, I'll be right back."

Joann piloted Joy up the stairs, kicking each stair clean before she guided Joy up it, until they'd reached the limb-littered yard. "I'll lie down on the grass," Joy said. "Just please, get my babies. My mother has no idea what to do with them!"

"Stay here," Joann repeated. She hurried back down the stairs as Joy began sobbing. She had no idea how the two ladies would get 110 pounds of child safely out of that ghastly place, but she was still bleeding around her makeshift bandage, and her head was swimming too much to help. She suspected she needed several stitches at least. She prayed for God to help the rest of them to stay unhurt.

Joann appeared again almost immediately at the top of the stairs carrying Annie, who she deposited unharmed onto the grass beside her mother. Joy covered Annie in kisses between winces of pain. Joann took a deep breath and went right back down, appearing again soon with Micah, staggering a bit under his greater weight.

"Aunt Joann, let Amelia help you!" Joy screamed.

"She can't lift them," said Joann, breathing hard. "And there's still too much glass for them to walk in those sandals." She descended once more to fetch Gideon, the heaviest triplet.

Suddenly, Titus Yoder came running across the yard toward Joy, shouting her name. "Are you all safe?" he screamed.

"Except my hand, but come quickly, please! My aunt is carrying all my kids out of the cellar, and they're too heavy for her!"

Titus asked no questions but ran directly to the cellar stairs. He did not go far down them, though, because Joann met him on the stairs with Gideon. He lifted Gideon from her arms and carried him to Joy as well.

Joann dragged herself up the final stairs and lay face down on the ground in exhaustion.

"Joann, are you okay?" Titus asked.

"I will be," she gasped. "But – help – Amelia. I think – she's in – shock." Titus obeyed.

As soon as she had kissed the boys, Joy half-crawled, half-dragged herself toward her aunt, her head still swimming. "Are you sure you're okay?" she whispered.

"Yes. Just – so – tired."

107

"I'm sorry. I'm so dizzy I can hardly hold my – my head up."

"It's okay. I'll be – fine," Joann said.

A commotion behind Joy alerted them both. The triplets were all chattering at once at the sight of Titus staggering up the stairs, carrying Amelia, whose face was grey.

"Mommy, is our grandma okay? Why is her face a funny color?" asked Annie.

"She's making weird noises," said Gideon, hearing Amelia's breathing as she hyperventilated.

Titus laid Amelia onto the grass and began trying to take her pulse. Joy crawled to her mother's side and tried to ask her what was wrong, but Amelia could only answer by clutching her chest. Her facial expression was almost catatonic, except for her open mouth.

"Does she have heart disease?" Titus said. "Her pulse is quite fast."

"I don't know!" Joy explained. "I don't think so, but I don't know!"

"I'm going to the phone shack to call an ambulance," said Joann, standing unsteadily. "I think she's in shock, but we'd better have her checked out. And Joy needs stitches soon!"

"I'll take them in the buggy. The ambulances will be in use with the tornado casualties."

Titus headed at a run to get his buggy, but he'd only gone a few paces when his oldest three sons met him in the yard. They'd gone to check on the neighbors across the road. "Papa!" they screamed, shouting several frantic sentences in Pennsylvania Dutch.

Titus gasped. "Ach, no! Our neighbors are trapped in their house!"

"I can drive the buggy," Joann said. "I've plenty of experience with horses."

"You are sure?"

"Yes, I'll ask one of your sons to hitch them up and give me a few tips, and we'll be fine. Go to help your neighbors!"

Titus yelled out a few orders to his third son, who said, "Please come with me," to Joann and took off running for the barn. Joann followed him at a jog.

In the meantime, Hannah had reached the frightened group on the grass. Joy told her their plan, and Hannah hugged her and led the triplets back to the safety of the farmhouse. They resisted, but she promised them cookies, and they complied.

Joy waved to them and blew kisses with her good hand, trying to smile, and then she was alone with Amelia. She couldn't do anything to assist her physically, because although her dizziness was abating a little, she could not use her right hand at all. She began reciting the 23rd Psalm and then Philippians 4:4-8 in a quiet voice. She wondered what she'd recite next – because Scripture memorization still was not her talent – but Joann and Isaiah reappeared in the buggy before she needed any further verses.

Isaiah and Joann half-lifted, half-dragged Amelia onto one of the bench seats in the back of the buggy. "Joy, sit with your back to her, on the floor between the seats," Joann said. "I know you can't hold her in place with your hands, but your weight will help to brace her on the seat. Here, lean on me as you climb in."

Joy climbed in shakily and did as her aunt commanded. She overheard Joann asking Isaiah for directions to the hospital and thanking him before sending him on to assist the neighbors. "Aunt Joann, are you okay? You were so exhausted," Joy whispered.

"Yes," Joann said. "Hold pressure on that hand, dear heart. Here we go!"

109

CHAPTER 14

The fifteen-minute ride to the hospital was something Joy knew she'd never forget. The first mile or so was frightening as Joann learned how to control those horses. They wove back and forth all over the road even after that, dodging debris and fallen branches. Joy bit her lip to keep from shrieking in pain several times as her hand banged against the seat when the buggy swerved. She braced her back against her mother's torso as hard as she could to try to keep Amelia from rolling off. Amelia didn't react to anything; she stared into space, barely blinking, and wrung her hands.

They had passed a blue hospital sign, indicating that they had almost arrived, when Joy's cell phone rang. She pulled it from her pocket with her left hand, planning to ignore the call to save her battery, but when she read Paul's name on the screen, she winced and answered. Her poor husband was going to be frantic.

"Joy! I got you! Are you okay?" Paul said.

"I will be…"

"Alex just called me and told me the area you're in had been hit by a major tornado! He saw it on the news in his hotel room! Was it nearby? Are you all safe?"

Joy filled him in on the past hour of their lives, attempting to downplay her own injury. Paul sounded beside himself with worry. "You're on your way to the hospital in a *horse-drawn carriage*?" he shouted. "Seriously?"

"Seriously. But we'll be there in a couple of minutes. And I'll be fine. And the kids were afraid, but they're safe."

"How close did the tornado come?"

Joy closed her eyes, shivering at the memory of the destruction. "It leveled the house across the road, sweetheart. It was only a few hundred feet away."

"Oh, good grief." Paul's voice was husky.

"I know. It's horrible."

"I'm flying down there. Tonight."

"But, Paul! How can we afford it?"

"We'll figure out something. It's your right hand, isn't it? How are you going to take care of the kids and the luggage on your flight home on Monday? Joann can't carry everyone's bags!"

"No...she can't..."

"Where is she anyway? With the kids?"

"No, she's driving the buggy."

Paul was quiet for several seconds, and then he sighed. "Wow, Joy. Just...wow."

"Yeah, but I have to go now. We're about to pull up to the emergency entrance, and Mother is still in shock or whatever. Text me what you're doing about tonight, okay?"

"Okay. Please, Joy, be careful! I love you!"

Joy said it back and began to ease herself from the buggy. The fast-moving air and conversation with Paul had diminished her dizziness. Joann had already run inside to ask someone to come out with a stretcher or a bed for transporting Amelia.

Since one of Amelia's symptoms seemed to be chest pain, she was immediately taken back to triage. Joy went along, still holding pressure on her hand, while Joann found a place to park the horses.

The nurses asked Amelia a series of questions, but she was only able to give her name. Joy provided them with her mother's age and a description of what had happened, but she knew nothing else – not Amelia's address, phone number, current doctor, medications, or medical history. "I – I'm sorry," she stammered. "My mother and I don't – don't see each other much."

"It's all right. It happens often. We're going to take your mother back to a room now. We'll put you in the room next door so you can check on her."

"Oh, thank you!"

As soon as they asked Joy the same questions, she was also escorted to a room. She felt another wave of dizziness hit her as she climbed onto the hospital bed, and she sent up a prayer of thankfulness that the hospital had not been as busy as they'd expected. A TV was on in her room, and a local news station was on, covering the tornado. From their broadcast, Joy learned that the tornado had only been on the ground for less than half a mile, and that only ten injuries were being reported. She said a silent prayer that the Yoders' neighbors were uninjured.

To Joy's surprise, the doctor came to her room within ten minutes. "How is my mother – Amelia Carnegie?" she asked before the doctor could speak.

"She's in shock, but her vitals aren't bad, except some high blood pressure and an elevated pulse, which isn't surprising under the circumstances. We're treating her for shock and a panic attack at the moment, but we'll run all the necessary tests once she's calmed down and can converse with us about any medications she may be on."

"Oh, good," said Joy. "She kept clutching her chest – that was my biggest concern..."

"We'll do an EKG and check out her heart, but our hope is that she was experiencing chest pains connected to her panic attack. And now, Joy, let's see your hand..."

Joy couldn't hold back a shriek of pain as Dr. Morgan removed Joann's sock and the tissues and touched Joy's cuts with her gloved fingers. Joy took one look at the bloody gashes, gulped, and closed her eyes tight.

"We will need to put in some stitches," the doctor said. "But first, I'm going to have to remove a few splinters of glass and clean it thoroughly."

"It was too dark to see if there was any glass in it in the cellar," Joy said, shuddering in anticipation of the pain. "And once we got out, there was no time to check."

"It will hurt, but I can remove them with no trouble," Dr. Morgan assured her. She gave Joy a clean cloth to hold on her hand and promised to return as soon as possible.

Joy texted Paul an update and tried to rest, but she was still too stressed. Dr. Morgan and a nurse came back in soon, bringing their instruments, an update on Amelia, and a visitor – Joann. "I'm sorry it took me so long!" Joann said, breathing hard. "It wasn't easy to find a safe place for the horses, and then Alex called me, and then I took the wrong turn in the hospital hallway while I was trying to console him!"

"It's all right, Aunt Joann," Joy said. "Please sit down and rest! Have you been running?"

"A little," she admitted, sinking into the chair beside Joy's bed. "I was worried about you – and Amelia."

"Well, Amelia is much more stable now," Dr. Morgan said. "You can go visit her after we clean you and stitch you up, Joy. We gave her a bit of a sedative, and she's sleepy, but she can make conversation now, and she remembers what has happened and who her doctor is, so we've called him to get a list of medications. We'll begin tests on her in a few more minutes, but if they all come back well, she can leave later today. And you'll be free to go as soon as we finish your stitches."

Dr. Morgan then began to probe Joy's hand for specks of glass. Joy didn't scream, but she cried big tears and squeezed Joann's hand as hard as she could the entire time. The doctor removed three sharp bits of jar and then gave Joy an antibiotic shot and a numbing shot to prepare her for her stitches.

"I'm sorry, Joy. I didn't see the glass shards," Joann said as Joy wept through the excruciating clean-up process. "You know my eyesight isn't wonderful, even with contacts, and it was so dark down there. It must have been awful to have been holding pressure on bits of glass!"

"You did everything anyone could have possibly done!" Joy protested.

"Yes, Mrs. Martin," the nurse said. "I've heard about your heroism this morning – pulling five people from a cellar and then driving to the hospital in an Amish wagon!"

Joann smiled, blushing as usual.

"Doctor, do you think you should check my aunt too?" Joy said, wiping her eyes. "She's totally exhausted herself, and she's had some health problems before…"

The doctor was waiting the three minutes for Joy's numbing shot to take effect, so she asked Joann some questions, despite Joann's insistence that she was unharmed. "I know you aren't checked in here, but I would like to listen to your heart and lungs, Mrs. Martin," said Dr. Morgan. "As long as they're clear, there will be no reason to admit you – or to charge you."

Joann gave her consent, glaring at Joy. Despite her pain and anxiety, Joy met her eyes and stared right back at her.

Dr. Morgan listened to Joann's heartbeat – "nice and strong and even" – and her lungs and told her to cough. Joann complied, sounding a little congested even to Joy's unassisted hearing.

"Do you have a cold?" the doctor asked her.

"Allergies and sinus congestion since yesterday, but since the storm, it's been improving, and moving – ah – down and out," said Joann.

"Well, I can hear it, but your lungs are clear, so I see no reason for concern, unless you start feeling worse," said Dr. Morgan. "And you should attempt to relax for a few days so your body can rest from the allergies and unexpected strenuous exercise."

Joann nodded and thanked her, and the doctor began Joy's stitches. Joy felt no pain any longer, merely an odd sense of pressure when the needle entered her hand. The process did not last long, although she needed ten stitches between the worst two gashes.

The doctor left then, promising that a nurse would return soon with her discharge papers, and Joy lay back on the bed in exhaustion.

"I'm glad that's over with," she said. "And I'm so thankful you're okay."

"Joy…" Joann began, sounding frustrated.

"I know, I know. I'm sorry. I know you didn't want any attention on yourself. But I had to be sure. You did so much – pushed yourself so hard. I had to be sure."

"I know."

Joy discovered, to her dismay, that she was going to cry again. "It's because I love you, and I want you to stay healthy," she said. "You – you are always risking your own health and safety for others, and I needed to be

certain I was taking good enough care of you too. Please –
don't be angry."

Joann stood stiffly and bent to hug Joy. "I'm not
angry now," she said. "I'm sorry I was at first. Thank you
for taking care of me, even though you are hurt yourself.
You know me well – I hate to be conspicuous – but that's
no excuse to be rude."

Joy hugged her again. "I love you, Aunt Joann.
Thank you for rescuing us – again."

"I love you too, dear heart. And I'm thankful to God
you weren't hurt worse."

By late afternoon, Joy, Joann, and Amelia were en
route back to the Yoder farm, this time in Jacob Fischer's
van. Hannah had contacted him and arranged for him to
take Isaiah to the hospital to get the horses and buggy and
to take the ladies home in a more comfortable vehicle than
the one in which they had arrived. Amelia had been
released with a prescription for blood pressure medication
and another for anxiety and strict instructions to follow up
with a local doctor as soon as possible.

Jacob greeted them warmly and assisted each of
them into the van. He asked them about their health and
safety, shuddered at their story, and shared the sad news
from Hannah that the woman who'd been trapped in the
house across from the Yoders was in ICU in Harrisburg
and was not expected to live.

"Oh, no," said Joy, covering her mouth. "How
horrible!"

"She's only about forty-five years old, also –
younger than I am," said Jacob. "It really makes ya think
about life – how we don't know how long it will be. Life's
like a vapor, you know, as the good Book says."

"Mr. Fischer," Joy began.

"Please, call me Jacob," he interrupted her.

"Oh – ah – Jacob, you've mentioned that you're not
Amish now, but it's obvious that you believe in God and
the Bible. What is your religion now? Are you a
Mennonite?" Joy could hardly believe her own boldness in
asking this almost-stranger such a question, but something

about Jacob's kind and unassuming ways gave her more courage than usual.

Jacob chuckled. "No, not a Mennonite either, although we were for several years, and you'd maybe assume that by the looks of our clothing and vehicles. We don't have an official religion now – we're just Christians."

Joy glanced at Joann from across the back seat. "Where do you worship?" Joy persisted.

"We worship with a small group of Christians who meet in our barn," Jacob said. "For a long time, we didn't have a name or anything, but we chose recently to call ourselves the Bird in Hand church of Christ. We have an answering machine in the barn now with a recording of our service times, and last year, we even paid to be listed on the internet. But we aren't a denomination, and we work hard to preserve that independence, because almost all of us left strict religious groups when we were baptized."

"Joy, that is the name of your church, is it not?" Amelia spoke up. "The church of Christ? I did not know there was more than one of those."

"Uh – yes, Mother, it is! I had no idea you'd remember that. Jacob, my aunt and I are members of the church of Christ in East Montpelier, Vermont."

"Well, hello, sisters," Jacob said cheerfully.

"Hello!" Joy answered. "This is so exciting."

"It is for sure," said Jacob. "And so, now that we know we're on the same page...would you ladies like to join us for worship tomorrow morning? There are a few congregations in this area, and maybe you already planned to go somewhere else, but we'd be glad to have you visit..."

"I think we can do that, Joy, eh?" said Joann. "Assuming everyone is well in the morning..."

"Oh, definitely," Joy said. "And – Mother, you know you're welcome to come with us too." Amelia only nodded, but, at least, Joy thought, she didn't refuse.

"Bird in Hand church of Christ on Lilac Lane," said Jacob. "Bible study is at 8:30, and worship is at 10, and then we have a simple meal together at 11:30 or 12. Call me later tonight if you need a ride – it's only three miles away, but none of you should be walking that far after the day you've had."

Amelia snorted, and Joy hid a grin. She knew her mother, despite her changed lifestyle, wouldn't dream of a three-mile walk over country backroads at 8 a.m. "I must admit that three miles sounds exhausting at the moment," said Joann. "I've had hours to rest now, waiting in the hospital, but I'm still so tired."

"I can't imagine why," Joy laughed at her. She was about to continue when her cell phone rang – it was Alex. "Why is Alex calling *me*?" she muttered, fumbling to answer it with one hand.

Joann dropped her eyes to her lap. "Because my cell phone is dead," she whispered.

Joy rolled her eyes and answered the call. "Hi, are you trying to reach Aunt Joann?" she asked.

Alex chuckled. "Actually, no, but I suppose she's forgotten her phone again, right?"

"It's dead."

"I was trying to reach you, Joy. Paul asked me to call you for him because he's in the air at the moment and didn't have time to call you ahead of time."

"Oh, wow, okay..."

"He's flying to Newark so he can meet up with me, and we can drive over in my rental car. I've canceled my flight home, so I will also drive him home on Monday."

"Thank you," said Joy. "That does make sense."

"If everything goes as planned, we'll arrive by about ten or eleven tonight."

"Good – that's wonderful," Joy said, thankful they were coming, but still anxious about the money. "Do you want to talk to your wife too? She's right here, listening."

"Oh, she is? Please, Joy. Thanks."

Alex and Joann spoke for several minutes, or, rather, Alex spoke, and Joann listened almost meekly. Joy couldn't understand Alex's words, but she could hear his concerned, almost insistent tone. "I know," Joann was saying. "Of course...yes, dear..."

117

Not long before they returned to the farmhouse, Joann finished her call and handed the phone back to her niece.

"He's worrying about you too, isn't he?" Joy said.

"How did you ever guess?" Joann said, rubbing the bridge of her nose.

"You listened to *him*, though," Joy teased her. "How did you manage that?"

Joann gave her the ghost of a smile. "Because I am suddenly too tired even to argue."

Joy nodded and laid her head gently on her aunt's shoulder.

The Yoder property was in chaos when they arrived. Hannah was supervising their neighbors' youngest two children, making her in charge of 18 children, although Clara was helping her as much as possible from her chair. Titus and his older sons were still assisting all their neighbors in whatever ways they could while the middle boys handled all the typical farm chores alone. Amelia went directly to bed as soon as she entered the Dawdi Haus, apologizing in a perfunctory tone, and Joy and Joann collapsed side by side onto the couch as the triplets piled around them, bounding with their typical energy despite their scary day. They'd only sat for five minutes when Joy noticed Joann had fallen asleep sitting up, even though Annie was bouncing in her lap.

"Aunt Joann, go to bed," she whispered. "You can't keep your eyes open."

Joann woke with a start. "Ah – I'm sorry," she said. "I never do this."

"Please, go on to bed and take a nap."

"But how will you manage them with a hurt hand?"

"We'll be fine, and you'll be nearby if I need you. Please."

Joann gave in at last, kissed Joy's forehead, and went to lie atop the quilt in the bedroom, leaving the door ajar.

"What is she doing?" Annie asked.

"Taking a nap, so we should try to be quiet."

"Why? She doesn't take naps. Is she sick, Mommy?"

"No, I don't think so, baby. Just really tired."

When Joy hadn't heard a sound from Joann in two hours, she peeked through the door at her, and her aunt was lying so still that Joy went on inside to be sure she was all right. She watched her breathing for a few seconds, the same way she did sometimes at night with the triplets, and then left, convinced that all was well.

Paul and Alex came at 10, not long after Joy had persuaded the last triplet to go to sleep at last. To Joy's humiliation, she crumpled straight into Paul's arms, sobbing quietly. The numbness from her hand had worn off, and ibuprofen wasn't touching the pain. Joy had a two-day supply of stronger pain medication in her bag, but the doctor has warned her that it would make her drowsy, so she'd been afraid to take it until Paul arrived.

Joy cried herself dry in Paul's embrace on the couch while Alex checked on Joann. Joy recounted the entire story to her husband, detailing her pain and fear and frustration. Paul listened without interruption, except to make her swallow a pain pill, stroking her hair and keeping her secure. When she had finished talking, Paul began to reassure her. He reminded her that everyone she loved was safe now, and that she'd be going back to her own happy house in less than 48 hours. He praised her for keeping the children safe and for staying calm at the hospital for Amelia. And then he told her that Alex had bought his plane ticket.

"Oh," said Joy, crying harder. "It must have been outrageously expensive at such short notice!"

"Almost $600 for the very back middle seat. I was nearly eating my knees."

"Oh, Paul. He shouldn't have."

"I know, but he insisted, and when I still hesitated, he said that you and I were like the kids he'll never have. What was I supposed to say to that other than yes?"

"Wow," Joy sniffed.

Alex stepped into the living room a moment later. Joy sat up straight. "How's Aunt Joann?"

"Asleep! She opened her eyes when I came in, kissed me, and went back to sleep immediately."

Alex questioned Joy a bit about her injury, and then she shared their plans to attend services at Jacob Fischer's barn in the morning. Alex returned to the room then to lie beside Joann atop the covers for the night – he wouldn't disturb her even to climb under the quilt.

Joy's pain medicine had suddenly taken effect. "Paul, I'm...so...sleepy," she mumbled. "I'm going to sleep here, okay? Can you squeeze in with one of the kids?"

"I'll figure something out," he assured her, and they said good night. Joy was almost comatose in a minute.

CHAPTER 15

When Joy awoke to her 7 a.m. alarm, she felt groggy, but her pain was still better. She sat up cautiously, and jumped when she saw Paul, who was sound asleep on the floor, an afghan draped across his middle, and a towel folded under his head for a pillow. Her heart flooded with love for this unselfish, generous man she'd married. She stepped gingerly over his form and tiptoed to the kitchen, where she grabbed a small bottle of orange juice from the refrigerator and carried it to the back porch. Ever since Joy had given up caffeine several years ago, she'd relied on cold juice to help her wake up in the morning.

To Joy's delight, Joann was already outside as well, drinking tea. "Well, good morning!" Joy said, hurrying to give her a hug. "I thought you were going to sleep forever!"

"I almost did," Joann laughed. "I slept for twelve hours, until 6 a.m. I don't think I've slept that long in my life."

"I'm sure you needed it. How do you feel today?"

"Still tired, but not like yesterday." Joann took a deep breath. "And I can breathe again!"

"Yay for breathing!" Joy cheered.

"How's your hand? Your numbing shot must have worn off long ago."

"Not too bad right now. It began hurting so badly last night that I had to have a big pain pill, but that was supposed to have worn off hours ago, and the pain is still some better."

"What time did the boys get in last night?"

"Around 10:00."

"Mercy, that late? I left you alone with the children for four hours?"

"We were okay. There were the ingredients for sandwiches in the fridge – Annie made me a sandwich with a slice of ham, four slices of cheese, a few whole cherry tomatoes, and about two tablespoons of mustard. And

121

even though they were filthy, the boys got to skip their baths, which made them happy."

Joann laughed again. "Oh, good," she said. "I was afraid you'd been miserable while I slept away the evening."

Joy didn't answer, and she chugged half her bottle of juice instead.

"Joy…" said Joann sternly. "*Were* you miserable?"

"Stink, Aunt Joann! How do you always do that?"

"Do what?"

"Read my mind, or figure everything out so quickly. It's like trying to keep a secret from the FBI!"

"You didn't answer my question."

"Yes, okay? I was miserable by the time Paul got here. But you didn't answer *my* question!"

"I'm a detail person. I notice things. But, dear heart, you should have awakened me."

"You needed that rest. I survived."

"Well, now I've rested, I intend to do whatever I can to make your life easier, kiddo. No more being miserable in secret, do you hear me?"

"Okay, okay," Joy said, finishing her juice. "I'll try to complain on the hour, every hour."

Joann snickered and stood up slowly. "I'd better get ready for church. I need to wake Alex too."

"And I'm going to check on my mom and get the kids ready and then take a shower."

"I can dress the kids, Joy. I'm sure you're anxious for that shower."

"Oh, would you? I'd like to let Paul sleep as long as possible, and helping them dress one-handed would take forever."

"Of course. Do you care what they wear?"

"If you can find clothes that don't smell and aren't stained, that's enough. They're nearly out of clean clothes."

"Matching isn't important?"

Joy snorted. "They're four. They don't have to match!"

Joy hurried to her mother's door after that, and she was trying to decide whether to knock, call her name, push her ear to it and listen, or shove a note under it, when the door swung open. Joy shrieked and jumped backward. "Ah, hi, Mother," she said. "I – I was planning to check on you, but I was afraid to wake you."

"I'm awake and fully functioning, thank you," said Amelia. "I was going to eat breakfast."

"Oh, good," said Joy. "Do you feel all better now?"

"I am still extremely tense," said Amelia. "In my body and in my mind. I will call to make an appointment with a doctor tomorrow."

"That seems best," Joy said. "I'm headed to the shower. Do you need anything?"

"I would like to know what time you are leaving for church at Jacob Fischer's barn, and if I may attend with you." Amelia fixed her gaze on an embroidered sampler hanging in the hallway as Joy sputtered and stammered.

"Why – I – I guess about 8:15...and yes, yes, of course," Joy said.

"Thank you. I will see you then," Amelia hurried to the kitchen.

Joy waited until her mother was busy at the refrigerator, and then she ran to the room where Joann and Alex were staying and rapped on their door.

Alex answered, still barefoot.

"My mother is coming to church with us!" Joy stage whispered.

"Really? Today?"

"Yes! Can you believe it?"

"No – but I'm so thankful!" Alex said. "But – oh, no. We only have seven seats, and no one can share in the back because of all the car seats we have to put in..."

"Blech! Car seats!" Joy said, groaning. "I forgot about needing to install those. What are we going to do about Mother? We have to make this work. But we leave in 45 minutes – it's too late to call Jacob for a ride..."

Joann had come to stand behind Alex. "I'll ride a horse," she said. "Or borrow a buggy..."

123

"Sweetheart, I'd rather you hold off on any more escapades for a few days," Alex said.

"I'll do it," Paul said. Joy jumped again. He'd awakened, followed the sound of her voice, and was directly behind her.

"You're awake!" Joy said, kissing him.

Paul put his arm around her shoulders. "I'll do it," he repeated. "I'll borrow a horse and ride to church."

"You will?" Joy said, staring at him as if he'd become a horse himself.

"Sure. Why not? I'm sure the family will loan me a horse for a few hours if they have one to spare."

"They have about ten, so I know they will. But – how many times have you ridden horses?"

"We had horses ourselves until I was in college, remember? Don't forget I'm still your big old woodchuck, even though I pretend to be more civilized these days."

Joy giggled. "Okay, Paul, but you'd better hurry and go ask for one – in case you aren't ready to gallop again right away."

Taking a shower with her hand wrapped in a plastic bag was a slow and infuriating process for Joy, especially when it came to washing her long hair. She would be counting the days until her stitches were removed, that much was certain. After spending ten minutes getting into her own simple clothing, she also breathed a prayer of thanksgiving that Joann was dressing the children. It was amazing how much she'd taken her right hand for granted until now.

Joy was the last person in the minivan, but they had saved a bucket seat for her so that she would not have to crawl into a back seat with her injured hand. "Did Paul find a horse?" she asked as Alex drove away quickly.

"Oh, yes," Amelia spoke up from the front passenger seat. "He went thundering past a few moments ago, looking ridiculous. He's going to be filthy and smell terribly for church." She smoothed her own pristine.

Joy felt her temper rising, but Gideon answered for her. "It's okay, Mrs. Grandmother. Church is gonna be in a barn, 'member? It will be all stinky anyway."

Amelia scoffed and said no more, and Joy covered her eyes and then thanked God for her wonderful, honest, blunt children. She looked up again toward her aunt, but Joann was staring out the window, shoulders shaking. Joy smiled then. It *had* been pretty hilarious…

They reached Jacob's property with only a minute to spare since Joy had delayed their departure. The triplets unbuckled themselves and clambered from the car, running across the muddy driveway to where Paul was tying up a huge black horse. He let them each pet the horse once and then guided them back toward the car.

All eight of them managed to get inside at last, and then they all stopped short immediately as twenty-five quiet men and women turned on their handmade wooden benches to look at them in surprise. Joy felt herself blushing – they might as well have been a herd of stampeding elephants. And were there *no* other children? Didn't Jacob and his wife have, like, thirty children too?

"Welcome!" Jacob exclaimed, breaking the silence and hurrying to shake their hands. "I didn't think you'd come. I'm so glad to see you!"

After Jacob had directed the adults to seats on the benches and explained that the children were having Bible class outside under the apple tree, and made sure that Joy could see them through the window from her seat, he introduced them to the rest of the congregation. Joy received many smiles and kind nods in the few seconds before Jacob cleared his throat, took a deep breath, and began the Bible class on the book of James.

Joy did pay attention – most of the time – but she also couldn't help sneaking a few peaks at the people crowded around her…five adult visitors had maxed out their class seating space. A few of the members were dressed in modern, casual clothing – the men in polos and jeans or khakis like Paul, and the women in floral blouses or short-sleeved summery dresses. The great majority of them, however, still wore old-fashioned, unadorned clothing – almost as plain as what the Yoders did. And at least half of the women still covered their heads, although with discreet, dark veils in back instead of the Amish caps. Joy felt conspicuous once more in her black capris, nice blouse, sandals, and wet braid.

Jacob was a good teacher – thoughtful but also humorous occasionally to maintain interest. He kept the pace of the class moving enough that Joy's attention returned to him soon after her clandestine observations of the people around her. She also noticed that her mother had not brought a Bible, so she let her use hers and looked on with Joann, whose larger print edition could be shared by two people.

Class lasted a solid hour, and then the church members talked and fellowshipped together for thirty minutes. The triplets dragged Joy around by the hand, introducing her to their new friends from Bible class, all of whom had come from Plain backgrounds and were dressed accordingly – but none of the children seemed to care. The women seemed a bit shy toward Joy, but they all greeted her warmly. Joy glanced at Amelia whenever possible, wondering what was going through her mind, but her mother smiled artificially and nodded whenever necessary and remained silent. One thing her mother had learned here in Pennsylvania, Joy reflected, was how to hold her tongue and be aware of others' viewpoints, at least until she was well-acquainted with the people...

The worship service was unlike anything Joy had ever experienced. After an opening prayer and a solemn song, they took communion, and then they began to sing – hymn after hymn after hymn – some old, some newer, some fast, some slow...some familiar to Joy and her family, and some known only to the ex-Amish. One song was even in German, although the song leader directed the English speakers to a sheet of paper pasted in the back of the old hymnal, where someone had written a rough English translation of the hymn so they'd have some idea what the others were singing. Joy sang until her voice began to break, and she could even hear Paul miss a note every now and then from the strain of the unusual amount of singing. Amelia sat in perplexed silence. Alex was smiling from ear to ear. Joann was going through cough drops like candy to be able to continue singing. Two of the triplets fell asleep, Annie in Joann's lap and Gideon in Paul's.

After an entire hour of singing, Jacob got up again to preach the sermon. While he had been a good teacher, he was an outstanding preacher. And Joy was thankful that Micah was absorbed with his toy trucks, because she soon forgot everything but Jacob's words. He referenced so many different Scriptures that Joy wondered how many hours it had taken him to prepare his lesson – or if he had so much Bible knowledge that he remembered them off the top of his head. His topic was simple but powerful – Paul's conversion to Christ. Joy had heard the Bible verses a dozen times at least over the past several years, but Jacob's lesson helped her to see them with new eyes. He didn't have a booming voice or a "preacherly" speaking cadence or even use perfect grammar – once in a while, Joy could hear that his first language had been Pennsylvania Dutch. But he was somehow the most eloquent evangelist that she had ever heard – his sincerity in his faith overflowed from him.

When the sermon was finished, Joy took a glance at her aunt's watch and was shocked to realize that another entire hour had passed. They all sang one more song – an invitation-themed song, although it was never called that, had a final prayer, and then the service was finished. Joy stood up, her body complaining a bit from over two consecutive hours on a wooden bench, and shook her head, feeling as though she'd been in a trance. It was so rare for her to be able to focus during the whole sermon, and rarer for her to hear a lesson so compelling. Paul was a good speaker, but his style was less arresting, and his sermons were shorter and more concise. And when Wilson had been their full-time preacher, he'd presented briefer, laid back ones as well. Joy was dying to ask her mother her opinion of the service, and especially the lesson, but she knew she didn't dare do so until they were alone.

The rest of the day, Joann and Joy spent time in the farmhouse keeping an eye on the younger Yoder children as well as the triplets while Hannah and Clara cooked and baked food for their neighbors. There was no Amish church service that day – they only met on alternating Sundays – and their usual schedule of visiting family and friends had been suspended in favor of storm cleanup, so Titus and all his sons over age eight spent the full day across the road, assisting their neighbors too. Paul and Alex joined them for several hours. Amelia helped Hannah and Clara in the kitchen for a while, but she soon returned to her room, claiming exhaustion. Joy watched her go, wondering if Jacob's sermon had exhausted her mother's mind as much as the storm had exhausted her body.

Monday morning came too soon for all the tired adults. Paul and Alex left right after a quick breakfast in the Dawdi Haus to guarantee they returned to Vermont before their wives and the children.

"Please, please be careful," Paul pleaded with Joy as he hugged her at the door. "You'll hurt your hand again if you try to carry anything."

"I know, sweetheart. I'm sure it will be fine," said Joy, kissing him. "I'll be home safe and sound before dark tonight."

"I know. But when I think about how much danger you and the kids have been in without me..." Paul's voice cracked. "Titus showed me – across the street...that woman...she was basically blown through a – a wall...you could still see where it happened. I've never seen anything...anything like it. And you were only a few hundred yards away!"

Joy held onto him for a long moment. Her husband could certainly be emotional and passionate – he was daily, in fact – but she had rarely seen him so shaken by the sight of a tragedy. She was anxious about the return trip too – three children and all the luggage and car seats had been plenty to keep up with even when she had the use of her right hand, but she knew God would protect them one way or another, so she tried to keep her fears to herself in front of Paul so he would worry less.

Jacob arrived in his van to drive them to the airport around noon. The children counted him as a good friend now, especially after having seen him the previous day, so they chattered to him non-stop as he helped load their suitcases. Joann loaded the smaller items as Joy and Amelia stood nearby, with Joy trying to figure out what else to say to her mother. To her surprise, Amelia spoke first.

"Thank you for coming," Amelia said. "I wish your visit had not ended with an injury."

"Oh, I'll be as good as new in a few days," Joy said, her mind still whirling over her mother's first words. "I hope you feel better soon yourself. And...and...thank you for inviting me. And for explaining some – some things. It was good to understand more."

"Yes, well, that was my goal. And I also appreciate your allowing me to accompany all of you to that – extremely peculiar – church yesterday. I am glad I went."

"I'm glad too," Joy said. "And – if – if you ever want to know more about what I believe now, and what those people believe – if you want to study the Bible together sometime, like over the phone..."

Amelia interrupted Joy's uncertain stammers. "A phone Bible study? How frustrating! I can read it myself if I have the urge – that will not be necessary."

"I know you can. I wanted you to know I'd be willing..." Joy said.

"Your ride is ready to leave, and Joann has buckled the children. You should go so you will not miss your plane," Amelia said, walking away toward the van. She hugged each of her grandchildren as if they were made of hot lava, spoke briefly to Joann and Jacob, and stepped back inside the Dawdi Haus before Joy had even managed to buckle her own seat belt.

Joy was dismayed to discover tears in her eyes as Jacob drove away. At the end of the day, no matter what happened, her mother was still the same abrasive person she'd always been. A few civil conversations and one Sunday worship service wouldn't cause her to change. Joy resolved then and there on the road to Harrisburg, as she wiped her eyes, that she would pray specifically for God to help Amelia to change, because it definitely wasn't going to happen any other way!

The plane trip was almost uneventful. Jacob parked the van and came inside the airport with them, staying with them to assist with the luggage until they were ready to go through the security checkpoint. Joann had repacked her own suitcase so she could fit most of her carry-on items into it so that she only had a small purse to keep up with, and Joy had condensed her own luggage so that she and the children only had one carry-on among the four of them. Joann wore that backpack and her purse and held a triplet's hand in each of her own, leaving Joy to manage only her ticket, ID, and the remaining child. Most of the flight was smooth, and all three children fell asleep.

Some thunderstorms near Burlington delayed their landing by half an hour, but, after a bumpy descent, they were met at baggage claim by Paul and Alex, who had only stopped at home long enough to trade Alex's rental van for Paul's own van.

"Daddy!" Annie said. "How did you get here?" Joy laughed as Paul tried to explain the intricacies of air travel and U.S. geography to a four-year-old.

Joy had assumed they'd drive straight to their homes and scrounge for sandwiches or something, but the men announced that their wives needed to relax and drove to a popular family pizzeria instead. The triplets, energized from their long naps, crammed down pizza and played at the indoor playground to their hearts' content while the adults enjoyed their meals. On the hour-long trip back home, Paul and Alex suggested that Joy and Joann rest in the back of the van, where they couldn't be reached by any small hands or feet. They complied, although Joann insisted that she wasn't sleepy.

Joy's hand was aching by this time after their long journey, and her eyes were so tired that she knew she would fall asleep almost immediately. She nestled against the side of the vehicle, using a wadded-up jacket as a pillow, but even despite her exhaustion, she struggled to stay comfortable.

"Come on, dear heart, put your head here," Joann said, patting her own shoulder. "I know I'm bony, but it's bound to be better than a plastic wall."

"If you're sure I won't be too heavy..." Joy murmured, flopping over to try it out.

"Of course not," Joann stroked Joy's head for a few minutes, and despite her aching hand, Joy relaxed and slept the rest of the way home. She awakened when Paul pulled into Alex and Joann's driveway to drop them off.

"Uhhh..." she groaned, raising her stiff neck. "We're here? Already?"

"Already!" Joann laughed. "We even ended up behind a slow truck and added ten extra minutes to the trip!"

"*Thank* you," Joy said, hugging her aunt tightly. "For your shoulder, for your presence on the trip, for – for being *you*. For everything." Joann hugged her back, squeezed her good hand, and climbed out to help Alex with her luggage.

Five minutes later, Joy was home at last, and, at Paul's insistence, she stretched out on the couch to rest while he unloaded their van and herded the worn-out triplets to their beds. Joy sank into the cushions in gratitude. It had been a difficult trip, but she was home again, and for once, her mind was willing to put off all her concerns and responsibilities until tomorrow.

CHAPTER 16

The week afterward was a frustrating time for Joy. She had all the typical post-trip tasks to complete – mounds of laundry, other unpacking, and additional household jobs that Paul had not gotten to while she was away – but none of those things were easy to do without the use of her right hand. Paul helped her nearly every moment he was home, but he also had previously committed to several jobs away from the house, and Joy knew she couldn't keep him from weeding his mom's garden or mowing her lawn or assisting Wilson in moving home from rehab at last. Even tiny things like buttoning the top button of Gideon's shorts – something he still struggled with – were almost impossible, though, and Joy felt like throwing her hands up in despair many times a day.

Joann came over as often as possible. She cooked, prepared ingredients for other simple meals, scrubbed bathrooms, and swept floors. She washed dishes until her fingers were pruny and played outside with the triplets when Paul was away. Joann was at Joy's stove, baking cookies, in fact, when Joy got a phone call from one of her tenants; he'd accidentally left his window open in the thunderstorm and long downpour the previous night, and all the paint and carpet below that window was ruined.

Joy held back her frustration until the phone call was over and promised to come and take care of the situation soon, but after she hung up, she did burst into tears. She lay down on the couch, put her head in her arms, and let out the past few days' frustration and pain – and some of the stress of the time with her mother as well. The kids were napping, thankfully, so she didn't have to worry about distressing them. And Aunt Joann was in the kitchen – busy – so maybe she could experience this moment of weakness in peace.

It wasn't Joann who caught her bawling her eyes out, but Paul, who'd finished Katie's yard sooner than he'd expected and hurried home to shower. "Sweetheart, what is it?" he said once he saw her. "Did you hurt your hand again?"

"Nooo..." Joy said. She couldn't explain yet, but she did allow herself to be comforted as he massaged her shoulders.

Once Paul was sure that everyone was safe, he didn't prod her with any other questions but continued to rub her back and stroke her head as her sobs diminished. Finally, she began to speak, telling him the entire story of her phone call, and expressing her frustration about falling behind on other work and feeling helpless. She didn't realize that Joann had entered the room until her aunt placed a small plate of chocolate chip cookies on the table beside the couch and then disappeared.

"Joy, you don't have to worry," Paul began. "I'm sure I can do the repairs to the apartment in an afternoon. It doesn't sound too serious at all..."

"You're so busy right now, though, and I want to handle it myself so you don't have to. Some women work full-time outside the home *and* keep house *and* raise kids. Shouldn't I be able to manage a property?"

Paul kissed her. "Don't worry about 'some women.' I don't care about them and what they do. I do care about my wonderful, capable wife, and she needs to allow herself to rest up and give herself some grace." Joy rolled her eyes at him, but she also cracked a smile.

Paul continued. "I have something for you. I'd been wanting to wait to show it to you until I finished it, but your little tornado adventure kept me from working on it this weekend. I want to go ahead and let you see it now, though. I think you need it."

"Oh?" answered Joy, sitting up straight. Paul had many talents – he could make almost anything when he had the time and energy. But time and energy had been in short supply recently...

Joy had been expecting some handmade item – a new cutting board, maybe – so she was surprised when Paul pulled his phone from his pocket and began typing into the Google search bar. He tapped his phone a few more times and then handed it to her. Joy shrieked and then laughed. Paul had made a website, a vibrant, intuitive, amazing website, for her book! She navigated through its features – an author contact page with a flattering recent photo of her, photos of the book covers and some of the places mentioned within its pages, pricing information, and even a photo of her reading aloud from it at the one and only official "author appearance" she'd made after their wedding.

"You did all this?" she croaked, hugging him tight.

"Yep. I had to do something in the evenings while you were gone."

"It's perfect!"

"No, it isn't perfect. You'll probably want to make some changes and add some things. I haven't done any web design since right after college, and that world has changed during a decade. I've forgotten stuff I used to know too. But I think it's a good start for you."

"It's perfect. Thank you so much!" Joy repeated.

"I should have done it a long time ago, sweetheart, but now you have something fun to work on while your hand heals. I think you'll be able to manage well enough with your left hand to tweak what I've done until it's ready for the public."

"Oh, yes," Joy said. "It's going to be a great distraction. I love you. Thank you for all you do for me."

Paul smiled. "Nothing you don't deserve, Joy. I love you too. But – I don't love the way I smell right now, so, if you're feeling a little happier, I'm going to get my shower…" Joy laughed and shoved him toward the bathroom.

Joy was in the kitchen, awkwardly splashing warm water on her salty eyes, when Joann came in with a basket of dirty laundry. "Here, let me help you," Joann said, dropping the basket. She rinsed the washcloth in tap water and handed it to her niece. Joy thanked her and wiped her face briskly, feeling embarrassed. "No, no," said Joann, taking the cloth back from her. "You'll hurt your poor eyes.

Here, sit down." She led Joy to a kitchen chair and began dabbing away Joy's eyes herself.

"I'm such a baby today," Joy muttered.

'Not at all dear heart," her aunt said. "I overheard what you told Paul about the rental house repairs – I didn't mean to, but I did – and that would make me frustrated if I were you too, especially on top of the stress of your trip and injury."

"Everything has been piling up the past few week – I'm stressed about the rental, worried about Katie, stressed about starting Pre-K with the kids, even if we do a small amount of school each day, and I've hardly had a moment to process how it went with Mother because of the chaos at the end of the trip."

"Well," said Joann. "I can't heal Katie, or your hand, and I can't help you choose how to homeschool, but I *can* paint a wall, or at least drive you into town to assess the damage at the house."

"Oh, would you take me? Tonight, if Paul can stay here with the kids? It would make me feel so much better to know what all I'm dealing with. My tenant was pretty vague about the damage."

"Of course…let's see, if Paul says yes, I'll run home and talk to Alex, but I doubt he'll mind. I'll also grab my crockpot – I threw together a huge vegetable beef soup before I walked down here – and we can eat supper here together, a bit early maybe, before you and I go town. How does that sound?"

"It sounds beautiful."

"I'm afraid the children won't enjoy the soup, though, so I'll put together something else as well…"

"They can eat cold cereal or peanut butter and jelly sandwiches," Joy said firmly. "There's no need for you to go to even more work. In the meantime, I'll ask Paul as soon as he's out of the shower. Do you want to see what he made me?" Joy began to show Joann her website, her stress dissipating again for the time being.

Joy and Joann were in Montpelier long before sunset that evening. Joy's tenant was not home but had agreed on her coming over to check the wall and carpet while he was away. As soon as Joy opened the door of the third-floor unit, which she had not entered for several months, she wrinkled her nose. The apartment smelled musty – or possibly mildewed. It was a bit cluttered, but did not seem dirty, so she wondered if the wet carpet could already be souring in the warm, humid air.

Joy knew which wall she was looking for, but she would have been able to distinguish it regardless. The entire area under one of the living room windows was covered in pale grey and pink mildew spots, and the carpet underneath it was a different color than all the other carpet because it was so saturated.

"What a mess," Joann said, coughing.

"I know. I'm not going to disturb the carpet with you around, but I'm afraid the pad and possibly even the flooring underneath has been destroyed."

"I'm afraid so. I'm also afraid this young man hasn't been straightforward with you. I've never seen mildew like this grow in 24 hours. This is Vermont, not the tropics."

"Oh, you're definitely right about that. I'd say he's left this window open during *every* rainstorm since he moved here. This is going to be an involved repair – and a really, really unpleasant conversation."

"And an expensive repair, because I'm not going to be able to help you with it myself," her aunt said, moving to the other side of the room. "I don't know how he can tolerate the mildew in here."

"I'm sure Paul will still be able to fix it," Joy said. "Mildew doesn't bother him if he wears gloves and a mask. But the supplies and labor will be much more than I'd hoped. And I can't help but wonder if this guy has been hiding any other damages. I guess after more than five years of good tenants, my luck may have run out." Joy looked at Joann, who was coughing again. "Let's go," she said. "You don't need to breathe this junk. Nobody does." Her aunt did not argue, and they returned to Joann's jeep as fast as possible.

Paul had every intention of handling the repairs himself that week, but all his plans came to a screeching halt two nights later with a call from Katie that a tree had fallen through their living room, landing with one large limb across Jennifer's right arm.

"Oh, good grief, Mom!" Paul exclaimed. "Is she okay? Are you okay?

"I think something's broken because of how much it's swelling, but she doesn't want to spend the money to call an ambulance. She doesn't have health insurance right now, but if she goes to the ER, the bill will be reduced because of her low income."

"Will she go?" Paul asked.

"Yes, even if I have to drag her by her hair. But I don't think I'm quite up to driving yet...that new medicine makes me so dizzy I almost passed out yesterday."

"I'll take her. I'll be there in ten minutes. I have to get dressed again."

"It's also starting to rain in the living room," said Katie. "I'm coming with you."

Paul hung up and told Joy what had happened as he threw on some old clothes – it was nearly 10 p.m., and he'd been lounging in some disreputable shorts.

"Oh, no, and their house is going to be destroyed too," Joy said. "All that hard work you put in!"

"I know, but it sounds like it's amazing that they're still alive," said Paul. "The tree fell between them as they were sitting in the living room. One branch hit Jennifer's arm, but otherwise, they weren't touched. And if I'm not mistaken, it was that enormous pine that fell – it *is* almost the size of the living room!"

As soon as Paul had sped away, Joy called Joann to share the news and ask her to pray.

"Mercy! We certainly will," Joann said. "And we can do more than that. We have several old tarps in the shed from when we remodeled this house. I'll wake Alex, and we'll go see if we can keep the floors and furniture from being ruined."

"Thank you!" Joy said, sighing in relief. "This is the last thing Katie needs right now – her righthand helper injured and her house destroyed!"

"I agree. We'll do what we can. Be sure to let Paul know so he won't be fretting. And keep me posted about Jennifer's arm!"

"I will. Please be careful too! I looked at my phone, and there are storms forecasted off and on all night. I feel so helpless." Joy tugged on her braid in aggravation.

"Keep those babies safe in bed and that hand protected," Joann said. "You're doing the biggest job of all of us and doing it beautifully."

Joy read and dozed and prayed on the living room couch as everyone else scurried around with their midnight activities. Paul sent her a report on Jennifer within an hour – fractured right wrist, no surgery required, so Joy passed along word to her aunt.

"Ouch! But not too serious for someone so young and strong," texted Joann. "We're still at the house. It could be much worse too."

By the early-morning hours, they all had a plan. Jennifer (who was being released the next day) and Katie would crash at Paul and Joy's house for the rest of the night and the next day. Alex and Joann, who had returned home after two hours at Katie's place, would get a little sleep, and then would pick up the well-rested triplets and bring them home with them so the rest of the adults could sleep. And once Paul woke up, he would go to Katie's house to view the damage and contact the insurance company.

It was 7:30 when Joy crawled into bed beside Paul and set her alarm for noon. She'd seen the triplets off to go home with Joann, who had arrived at the time the children usually awakened, despite having been out until 1 a.m. herself. Katie and Jennifer were asleep on the spare room bed, thanks to their respective pain prescriptions, with strict instructions to wake Joy if they needed anything. *"Please help me to sleep until noon,"* Joy prayed to God as she drifted off.

Alex brought the children back not long after noon as Paul and Joy were staggering sleepily around the kitchen, trying to prepare themselves a quick bite to eat. When Alex heard that Katie and Jennifer were still asleep, and that Paul hadn't gone to check the house yet, he offered to stay for a while so that Joy could go with Paul. "I'd take the kids back home with me," Alex said. "But Jo-Jo has finally gone to bed. She didn't fall asleep until sunrise, and then she watched the kids until noon."

When they drove up to the little house Paul had built for his mom, Joy could see that the immense pine was indeed the culprit, as it had broken in a gust of wind, and a tangle of huge branches and piles of needles lay across what was left of the roof on the right side of the house. Most of the tree, however, was obviously inside the house – as they walked up to the front porch, they could see the massive trunk lying on the living room floor. They both stood and stared for a long time, thanking God that their loved ones had been spared. "That recliner was where Jennifer had been sitting right before the tree fell," Paul said. "And look – there's nothing left of it." Joy shuddered.

The living room was indeed destroyed, but Joy was confused by how bare it appeared. Yes, here was the rest of the furniture, pushed to one side and covered by a tarp. But where was the TV? The rug? The photos and décor? And all the small debris from the tree?

"Joy!" Paul called from his mom's bedroom at the opposite side of the house. "Come and see!" Joy tore herself away from the disaster scene. She stepped into Katie's room and stopped short, puzzled by the mound of plastic storage totes along one wall. Paul handed her a sheet of notebook paper. "Read this," he said. "You have to read this."

"Dearest Katie," the paper read, in what Joy recognized as her aunt's handwriting. "Everything from your living room has been packed up inside these containers. Don't worry, they are clean and were only used to hold our things the last time we moved. It didn't rain much at your house, but we dried all the drops we could see. There were a few frames knocked from the wall and broken, so we discarded the glass but saved the frames in these containers. The photos are inside gallon Ziploc bags. We love you and are so sorry for your troubles. Alex and Joann."

"Oh, my," Joy said. "They saved it all!"

Paul was lifting the lid from one of the top totes. He pulled out a Ziploc bag that held his parents' wedding photo as well as the frame it had been in. "I thought she'd lost all of this," he said. "There was an absolute downpour at the hospital."

"There was at our house too," said Joy, her eyes filling.

They replaced the tote lid, pocketed the note, and closed Katie's door against the moisture of the rest of the house. "Paul," said Joy. "Where's the debris from inside the living room?"

"That's a good question," he said, poking into the damaged area again. Except for the covered furniture and the tree that was far thicker than he was, the room appeared nearly clean. Joy continued to explore.

"Paul!" she yelled. "It's out here! They brought it all outside!"

Paul stared at the mound of branches in the backyard. "How did they do all this – in the middle of the night?"

"I know they were here for two hours, but this is an entire day's worth of work!" said Joy.

"Yeah, and the roof's been covered too, with more tarps, and even tacked down so the wind can't blow it loose. For the life of me, I can't imagine how Alex pulled that off at midnight."

"Paul," said Joy, her eyes wide. "Alex couldn't have done that. He's terrified of heights. He told me once that he feels shaky on a three-foot step ladder."

"Surely your aunt didn't..." Paul whispered, appalled at the thought of Joann climbing the sloping roof like a nocturnal monkey.

"There's no way Alex would have let her…I don't think…" Joy murmured. "I have to call him, though. This is all just…just too much to take in."

Joy had her answer soon after Alex had laughed loud and long at the idea of his sending his wife up to cover the roof. Alex had cleared the debris from the house while Joann had meticulously packed up and stored the living room items, and then they had paid Jack to drive over to climb and cover the roof.

CHAPTER 17

That evening, after everyone had rested, the Grahams had a family meeting in Paul and Joy's living room. "We have some things to figure out, gang," Paul began without preamble. "First of all, we need to decide on a timetable for the home repairs. The insurance company will pay for the repairs, but with the flooding there was earlier this year, the adjustors are running behind, and no one can come out to look at the house for about two weeks. I could do most of the repairs myself for the cost of supplies, but I wouldn't be done sooner than two weeks, and a new roof is an expense none of us need right now…"

"I definitely think you should wait on the insurance company, Paul," Katie said, patting his arm. "We can make do for a few weeks, and I don't want you to have to spend your time off from teaching doing all that work again."

"You've brought up the second point, though, Mom. You and Jennifer don't need to stay in the house for weeks, waiting for the repairs, and although you are always welcome here, I know that the stairs are still difficult on your joints, Mom, and Jennifer needs a quiet place to study…"

"But all those nights in a motel would be wicked expensive!" Jennifer protested. "I'm sure I could find somewhere quiet to do my courses…"

Joy snorted. "I doubt it, at least during the daytime. It's a circus around here, Jennifer, and the doors don't lock, and the triplets follow you around like puppies…"

"Puppies?" shrieked Micah. "Where?"

"Can I have a puppy, Mommy?" said Annie. "Please? Please?"

"Do you see what she means?" said Paul, chuckling, as Joy tried to explain that there would be no puppies around tonight.

"Could I sleep in here on an air mattress?" asked Katie. "I know it would be an expense to buy one, but they aren't too costly…"

"No!" answered Paul and Jennifer in unison. They laughed at each other, and then Paul continued. "Mom, *I* am sore after a few nights on an air mattress, and I'm not suffering from Lyme disease."

"Hey, could we bring the spare room mattress down here instead?" asked Joy.

"That's not a bad idea," said Paul, rumpling his hair...three weeks post haircut, and his waves were wild once more.

"It puts you through a lot of trouble," said Katie. "Surely I can do a flight of stairs a few times a day. My joint pain won't last forever..."

"No, Mom, it's not too much trouble at all," Paul said. "But it doesn't solve Jennifer's problem...unless...maybe Jennifer could study at Alex and Joann's house...I doubt they'd mind..."

"Oh, that would be amazing," Jennifer said. "And the walking back and forth would be good too. I've been turning into a lump again this summer from a lack of strenuous exercise."

"It's still early – why don't you call Aunt Joann and ask her?" Joy said, offering Jennifer her cell phone. "It would make everyone feel better to know what we're going to do..."

"I – I don't know," Jennifer stammered. "I'm supposed to be an adult now, and adults don't usually invite themselves to someone else's house daily...for weeks...and I've hardly spent time with her for years now...can – can you ask her, Joy?"

Joy smiled kindly at Jennifer's awkwardness. Their beloved Brat had grown up, but she was still unsure of herself, and Joy understood that feeling so well. "Sure," she said. "I'll go do that now."

Joy stepped onto the front porch into the cooling evening air and pressed down the number three on her speed dial – her aunt's cell phone – and then settled onto the porch swing to let it ring. She expected to have to dial number four as well – the house phone – but Joann answered her cell quickly instead.

"Hey, I got you – on your *cell phone*!" Joy said.

"Yes, yes." Joann rolled her eyes. "We've been having so much excitement in the family lately that I've been making a better effort to keep it charged..."

"Good!" Joy laughed. "It's about time!" She could almost see Joann rolling her eyes from a quarter mile away.

"What's going on, kiddo? I don't think you've called to lecture me about my phone."

Joy explained Jennifer's dilemma and mentioned Paul's idea. "Jennifer felt a bit nervous about inviting herself to your house," she added.

"I certainly don't mind, and I know Alex doesn't either. We'd love to be able to help her out in any way possible."

"I thought that's what you'd say, but I didn't want to presume."

"What else can we do to make things easier on all of you?"

"I don't know, Aunt Joann...you and Alex have already done so much!" Joy thought for a moment. "Well, there might be one other thing. Could Alex come over long enough to help Paul move the mattress and box springs from the spare room down into the living room? I still can't lift much with my hand, and Jennifer is out of commission...I know Paul says he can move it himself, but I don't want him to..."

"I'll ask him, but why do you need that...oh, is it for Katie?"

"Yes, the stairs are painful for her, and we don't want her to stay in her house. And motels are so high, especially in tourist season..."

"Hold on a second, please, dear heart, and I'll speak with Alex."

Joann was back on the phone so fast that Joy was startled. "Joy? Alex is available this evening, but we would rather invite Jennifer and Katie to stay with us instead. We have two extra bedrooms, you know, and the bedroom on the ground floor even has clean sheets tonight. There would be no reason for Katie to climb stairs – and if we have the urge to shout and bang pots and pans, we'll come to your house."

Joy giggled. "And we'd never notice the difference! But – are you sure? They may need to stay a month. And the ground floor bedroom is yours…"

"We're sure. We're fortunate enough to have both the extra space and the health to climb stairs. Would you let me speak to them and invite them myself?"

"I'll take them the phone. Thank you so much. I think this will be the perfect solution."

Katie and Jennifer were delighted – but overwhelmed – by the Martins' generosity. "I feel terrible to think of kicking you out of your own bed," Katie said. But Joann continued to assure them that they would be welcome, and they finally agreed to come. Alex promised to drive over to pick them up in thirty minutes, and Paul suggested that Joy ride with them to assist in the relocation process while he put the children to bed.

Joann's house guests arrived as she was running up and down the stairs, transferring items from the master bedroom and bath to one of the guest bedrooms upstairs. "Make yourselves comfy!" she called out. "I'll be done soon." As soon as Katie and Jennifer were settled in on the couch, and Alex was in the kitchen pouring them cold fruit tea, Joy hurried to assist her aunt. She found her in the master bathroom, switching out the nicer guest towels so that Katie and Jennifer could use the softest, newest ones.

Joy hugged her. "What can I do?"

"Mmmm…I'm almost done for tonight," Joann said. "I'll change over most of our clothes tomorrow. Let's see – here's a grocery bag. Would you empty my medicine cabinet into it for me? And here's another bag – you can bring down the contents of the upstairs medicine cabinet in it."

A few minutes later, Joy and Joann joined the others in the living room. Alex had poured them glasses of tea as well, but after asking Jennifer for more details about her arm, he said his good nights and jogged upstairs to bed.

The women shared grins as they watched him go. "I think my children wore him out," Joy giggled.

"Oh, there's no doubt about that," Joann said, laughing too.

"Not to mention all that work he did at my house," Katie said quietly. "All the work that *both* of you did. I can't thank you enough for saving everything."

"I'm thankful we got there in time," said Joann. She changed the subject. "Jennifer, if you'd like a bit more privacy, I do have a third bedroom, you know. I can rearrange it a bit tomorrow – I have to confess, it's a little junky right now, and then you could have a bed to yourself too."

"Oh, I'll be all right," Jennifer assured her.

"Think about it after you've rested a little," Joann said, patting her good arm. "It would give me a good excuse to do some decluttering I've been putting off."

Katie left them soon to head to bed herself as well. "I hate to be a party pooper," she said. "And I realize it's only 9:00, and I've slept all day, but I can't seem to get enough sleep."

"That's what your body needs right now," Joy said. "Do you need help with anything?"

"Nothing at all. Thank you, sweetie." Katie kissed Joy's head and limped toward the bedroom.

"Are you sleepy too?" Joann asked Jennifer.

"No, not at all. Those strong pain meds they gave me made me sleep until 6 p.m., and they're worn off now."

"What are you taking now?" Joy said.

"Ibuprofen and extra-strength Tylenol – oh, and some of Mom's turmeric."

"Is that enough?"

"Not quite," Jennifer said. "I may have to take another zombie pill tonight."

"I'll probably regret this offer – but would you like to play a game of Scrabble?" asked Joann.

"Why would you regret it? You'd stomp us both," Joy laughed.

"Because I only slept from 5:30 until 7:00 and noon until 3:00," Joann laughed. "I'm not sure I remember how to spell my own name – but I'm not sleepy either."

"That sounds great," Jennifer said.

"I think so too, but I'd better text Paul to be sure the kids went to sleep well," Joy said. She tapped a quick message to him right away.

Paul answered within seconds. "They're fine. Go ahead and stay all night if you'd like. I'm about ten minutes away from falling into an utter coma myself, but there's no reason why you can't have a fun girls' night."

"He suggested that I stay all night if I want to," Joy said. "He thinks we're having a big sleepover or something."

"Well, I suppose we are," said Joann. "Do you want to stay?"

"I – I guess so. It feels strange to randomly leave him with the kids all night, but I do want to play Scrabble with you…"

"Aw, slip out in the morning and go make him a huge breakfast and call it even," said Jennifer.

"Okay, good idea," Joy said, laughing.

"If we're going to be having a pajama party, we should at least be comfy," Joann said, standing up. "Joy, do you want to borrow some pjs?"

"Sure, if you don't mind. Or even a t-shirt and shorts are fine."

"I'll find something when I put on my own pajamas," Joann promised. "Do you have pjs with you, Jennifer?"

"Yes, Paul and Joy packed suitcases for Mom and me when they were at our house today, but I think I'll stay in these clothes. Changing is too complicated at the moment."

Joy glanced at Jennifer's jeans and fitted t-shirt. "Are you sure? I can help you…"

"With only partial use of your right hand?" Jennifer giggled. "We'd be like the blind leading the blind!"

"Riiight," Joy grumbled, scowling at her hand. Two more days of stitches. Two.

"I can help, Jennifer, if you'd like," Joann said gently.

Jennifer blushed. "That's more than you bargained for. I'll be okay."

"I don't mind at all. Come on, kiddo. There's no reason for you to be uncomfortable all night."

It took a while, but finally they were all in pajamas and sitting around the table at the Scrabble board. Joy had experienced many such girls' nights with her aunt years before, but she realized that Jennifer had never spent this type of time with Joann before. Joy looked down at her outfit and chuckled to herself. Joann's spare pajamas were all hanging on the clothesline outside, so Joy had ended up in her aunt's only pair of sweatpants and an almost threadbare t-shirt instead. The pants were red, and the shirt was neon orange. If she went out on the road tonight, she'd stop traffic!

The game dragged on forever, because they tangled up the board almost from the beginning. Joy was keeping score, and to her amazement, she was beating her aunt for most of the game. Jennifer played a strategic match, but her spelling was still her weakness, so her score lagged a little. At last, near midnight, Joann went out with the word 'qoph'.

"No, no, no," Jennifer protested. "That can't be an approved word. What is it, a Swahili form of cough or something?"

Joann laughed. "No, I promise it's a word, a real Scrabble word. I think it's a letter in a foreign alphabet – I can't remember which one, but I looked it up years ago when I memorized all the 'q without u' Scrabble words."

Jennifer grabbed her phone and began googling furiously. Joy watched anxiously. If Joann were correct, she would move into first place, but if she were mistaken, Joy would go out on her next turn with "at" and win. But Joy was pretty sure her aunt was right – it *was* Scrabble.

"Awww!" Jennifer dropped her phone on the table in disgust. "It *is* a word, a letter in the stinkin' Hebrew alphabet. What in the world?"

"Stomped again," Joy groaned, pushing the score sheet toward her aunt. "But I shouldn't be surprised. You always win, Aunt Joann."

"That's not true! You've beaten me before, dear heart."

"Twice! Twice in six years! And one those times, your glasses were broken so you played half-blind!" Joy rolled her eyes.

Joann grinned at her and began to gather the tiles back into the box. "I'm glad you love me enough to play with me anyway," she said.

Jennifer snorted. "Love has nothing to do with it! We only play Scrabble with you because we know we'll slaughter you in Monopoly!" They all began giggling so hard then that they had to stuff their faces into couch pillows to keep from waking Katie. Joann was as notoriously awful at Monopoly as she was notoriously amazing at Scrabble.

By the time Joy went to bed on the comfy living room couch, she was too tired to worry about anything for a change. She set her phone alarm for 8:00, planning to text Paul at that time to tell him she'd be home soon afterward to cook breakfast for everyone. She fell asleep almost to the subdued sounds of Joann helping Jennifer brush and braid her tangled hair.

CHAPTER 18

The next few weeks flew by in a whirlwind of activity. Joy's stitches were removed at last, and her hand healed with only a little stiffness around the scars to remind her of her injury. She stayed busy with the kids and with helping her aunt care for Katie and Jennifer. She also found herself in charge of locating a temporary rental house for Luca and Marie and their girls, who would be arriving the last day of August. They trusted Joy to find a place for them that they would rent, sight unseen, until they could buy a house. Joy cringed at the thought of touring the scarce local options again and wished she could evict her troublesome tenant and let them live on her rental property...the tenant whose wall and floor covering were still covered in mildew. Joy cringed some more.

Paul was far too busy to replace the damaged areas himself. The insurance company had unexpectedly sent someone to view Katie's house after only three days, but none of the local construction guys that Paul trusted were available for weeks, so he ended up doing most of the work instead. With school beginning again the day after Labor Day, and his teaching responsibilities the week before, he only had about three weeks to finish the repairs. Paul awakened at 6 a.m. six days a week, worked all day, came home for supper and an hour of play with the triplets, and then returned to work, sometimes even hammering by lantern light or moonlight. He slathered himself in sunscreen several times a day, but he kept a perpetual sunburn – and doubled his freckle quantity – from all his hours on Katie's roof. He also burned so many calories that he finally lost the last ten pounds he'd been trying to lose for years – and then ten more.

"Good grief, Paul," said Joy, late one night as she added some stitches in the waistbands of his dress pants. "You're getting positively thin!"

Paul grinned at her between bites of his midnight snack – a peanut butter sandwich. "Skinny and grey-haired in one summer! You'll soon hardly recognize me!" he teased.

Joy glanced up at him. With his sunburned cheeks, hundreds of freckles, and mop of hair, he could still pass for a teenager, especially in lamplight. "I think I'll manage," she said. "But you need to be careful. You're pushing yourself hard."

"Oh, I'll be fine," said Paul, chugging half a glass of milk. "I'll be done in another week, Lord willing. I just hate that we've had so little time together this summer. And I hate that I've had to neglect the repairs for your rental. I guess you'd better hire someone."

"I'll look into it first thing Monday morning," Joy said. "I hate it too – mostly the not being with you part, but I know we haven't had much choice." She kissed Paul on his milk mustache, and they trudged up the stairs together.

Joann was busy during the month of August as well. She went to her GED classes with Jack, studied with him on the phone when he got stuck, and spent plenty of time with Joy and the kids while Paul was working. The rest of her time was filled with caring for her patients, as she called them. For the first week, while Jennifer was still in a good deal of pain, Joann did everything for her, because Katie was too weak to do anything except barely care for herself. Joann even washed Jennifer's hair for her, much to the young woman's embarrassment. Once Jennifer felt better, Joann spent an entire day and a huge amount of energy decluttering and rearranging her seldom-used third bedroom so that Jennifer could have some privacy. Jennifer sat and watched her, assisting whenever possible, protesting all the while at how much trouble she was causing, and hurrying to recruit Alex to help when she could see that Joann intended to move a huge wooden dresser by herself.

Joann also read up on every health food and natural remedy she could locate online and dosed Katie with the most credible ones. Katie had been a healthy eater for most of her life, but she put her foot down one day when Joann served her a plate of calf liver and flaxseed omelet. Slowly, however, the rest and extra nutrition began to replenish Katie's exhausted body, and after two weeks, Katie and Jennifer were able to take care of each other again, so Joann quietly stepped back and let them.

Alex was hardly idle either. One evening, wearing clothes he planned to throw away and a mask, and tore out the soaked carpet, padding, and sheetrock from the apartment Joy owned. He also replaced the sheetrock and laid down some cheap carpet squares until Joy had the presence of mind to decide if she wanted to replace all the flooring in that room. He did it all with the help of DIY websites and YouTube videos, and he paid every expense himself. Then, he snapped a photo of the finished result and texted it to Joy's cell phone. Joy cried from relief for ten minutes that night.

Paul's first day of teacher in-service was the Wednesday before Labor Day, and on Monday of that same week, he completed repairs on Katie's house in early afternoon. He went home, showered, and fell asleep before 4 p.m. – and slept until 7 a.m. He spent his final day off watching the children most of the day while the women cleaned Katie's house, moved Katie and Jennifer back into it, and took Katie to a follow-up appointment with her doctor. The following evening, after Bible study, Paul was scheduled to drive to Burlington to pick up Marie and her family, even though he was due at the high school at eight on Thursday morning.

Joann had originally planned to deep-clean Katie's house while Joy drove Katie to the doctor, but both Joy and Jennifer over-ruled her. "The house will be covered in dust – sawdust and normal dust, and maybe even some mildew," Joy protested. "There's no reason for you to do the dirty work. Seriously. And it feels so good to have the use of both my hands again that cleaning actually sounds kinda fun."

"Let's not get crazy here," said Jennifer. "Cleaning is never fun, but neither are doctors' offices. I'll help Joy. I can do an awful lot with one arm now."

"And, Lord willing, by next month, I'll be able to drive myself again," said Katie. "I could today, I believe, if my right leg weren't still so wobbly."

After Joann and Katie had driven away, Joy and Jennifer tackled their task. Their goal was to remove as much construction residue as possible before the others returned, to sanitize surfaces, and to move belongings back in last. Jennifer insisted that unpacking the bins of décor could wait – she would help her mother do that later.

Joy and Jennifer were sitting on the porch, taking a short break to cool off from the humid day, when Joy received a text from Joann. "Doctor wants to do more blood work. We'll still be a while." She read the message aloud to Jennifer.

"Oh, good," Jennifer said. "I was hoping they would. Now maybe we can finish our work completely before they're back."

"That would be wonderful. Just give me five more minutes here..." said Joy, fanning herself with her hands.

They sat in companionable silence for several seconds, and then Jennifer spoke up quietly. "This has been such a weird month – well, really, the entire summer has been strange, but especially this past month."

"I'll say!"

"It hasn't been all bad, but it's been – unsettling, I guess. I haven't said this to Paul, but I really think Mom was becoming depressed again before the tree fell on the house. Sometimes, it almost seemed like she didn't think she'd ever recover, and that she was tired of trying. I was going to suggest that she discuss it with her doctor today, but I don't think it's as important now. Her attitude – or – outlook on life – seems almost normal again."

"What do you think has made the difference?"

Jennifer sniffed and wiped her eyes. "Your aunt," she said simply. "She's held us together. I – I was realizing yesterday that she gave Mom jobs as soon as possible – she made her feel needed. With all that we've been doing to help Mom, it took your aunt Joann to see that what she needed most was to be useful again."

153

"I'm not surprised," said Joy. "She's incredibly observant."

"She listens too, and she remembers what is important to people and what makes them tick. She knows that Mom is a great cook, so she would consult her about seasoning for our meals, or later, once Mom was a bit better, she'd ask her to prepare one dish for a meal – not enough work to exhaust her, but enough for her to feel that she was contributing. She also remembered how good Mom is at interior décor, so she consulted her about where to hang things on the walls when she rearranged that bedroom for me." Jennifer pushed her bangs off her sweaty forehead and sighed. "I want to be like that. I want to be able to – to intuit how to help people in the ways that are the most beneficial. But I'm too impulsive; it's still such a struggle for me to keep from blurting out everything that crosses my mind."

"I wish I had Aunt Joann's gift with people too, Jennifer, believe me, but something she's always telling me is that she can do more for others and has more time to think and plan than I do – and the same goes for you, with all your school work. When we're in our 50s and retired, we'll have more opportunities and time to serve too, Lord willing."

"That's true…but I kinda feel like she's always been like this."

Joy recalled her days on her uncle and aunt's farm nearly two decades back and smiled. "Aunt Joann was already crazy perceptive and all that when I first met her," she said. "But I didn't know her yet when she was your age, or even mine, and I've heard some pretty interesting stories about some impulsive choices she made and hot-tempered discussions she had when she was young. She'd tell you about them herself, I'm sure, if you asked. Maybe there's some hope for us yet!"

"Not if we don't get back to work," Jennifer grumbled, as they both stood up to head back inside.

"Hey, we're making good progress!" Joy encouraged her. "Would you rather try to use the hand-held vac left-handed or wipe down the living room walls?"

"The vacuum. The loud noise makes me feel like I'm doing something important."

Joann and Katie pulled into the driveway as Joy began her final planned task – washing the few dishes that were left in the sink. She was elbow-deep in dish water when they came bolting in the kitchen door – Katie, bolting! "What in the world is going on?" Joy said.

"I'm clear, Joy! I'm clear! I'm testing negative for Lyme now," said Katie.

Joy flung her arms around her mother-in-law, soap suds forgotten. "Oh, Katie, I'm so thankful!" she said. Jennifer had been taking out a bag of garbage and overheard her mother's last sentence as she returned to the house.

"You are? Really?" she shouted.

"Yes, sweetie. Really!"

Jennifer's eyes welled up. "Oh," she said. "Oh, Mom." Mother and daughter hugged as well.

"What's your next step?" Joy asked after they had all sat down together in the tidy, renovated living room.

"I'm going to be changing to maintenance antibiotics," Katie said. "I'll take them for one week a month for six months or so unless the disease comes back. I'll keep taking all the homeopathy for at least a year – it won't hurt me."

"What about the pain and weakness you're still having?" Jennifer questioned.

Katie grinned sheepishly. "It's arthritis," she said. "Lyme has made it worse, but the doctor has checked my legs, and that's why the pain isn't gone. I'm going to be trying to continue to reduce my inflammation, but basically, I'm getting old. The doctor told me to take Aleve."

"And will you?" Joy asked.

"If nothing else works. I'm not ready to sit around all day."

Joy hugged her again. "I'm *so* thankful. Have you called Paul?"

"No. I want to tell him in person. I want to see the look of relief on his face."

"Well, we'll be finished in about ten minutes here, and then you can ride back with me to tell him…"

"And I'll bring you back home," Joann added.

"Okay, thanks," Katie said. To Joy's delight, she noticed her mother-in-law's eyes were sparkling again. Amazing what hope could do for a person!

When Katie shared her news with Paul later, he broke down and sobbed like Joy hadn't seen him cry since shortly after his father's death. Joy gently shooed the children into the kitchen, where she and Joann assured them that their daddy was happy, not sad, and fed them each an irresponsibly large scoop of frozen yogurt. In a few minutes, Paul and Katie came in and had some frozen yogurt too, and then Joann drove Katie home as she had promised.

Joy put Micah, Gideon, and Annie to bed a few minutes early that night so she and Paul would have a longer stretch of time to enjoy the last night of Paul's summer together, and to discuss Katie's recovery. With all the windows open, they could sit on the front porch and still hear if a child called out, so they sprayed themselves from head to toe with Joy's new eucalyptus oil natural bug repellent and sat down on the swing.

Paul leaned back and closed his eyes. "What a summer."

"No kidding," said Joy. "It feels like we've done about two years of living in two days that has actually happened over two months!"

"Something like that," Paul groaned.

"I'm sorry you had basically zero time to relax," Joy said, taking one of his hands.

"Ah, well, I suppose I've had a good look at what *your* job is like," Paul said. "You know, pretty much 24/7 work."

Joy nestled closer to him. What a good, good man she'd married...Paul wasn't finished talking.

"You know, my faith hasn't been strong enough this summer," Paul said slowly. "I'm ashamed to say that I didn't believe God would heal Mom. I didn't know which I expected – that she'd be ill for years, or that she'd get worse until she died, but I didn't think she'd recover. I spent this entire summer resigning myself to – to losing her, or at least to losing her personality."

Joy hugged him close. Tears from her husband again – twice in one day! "Awww, sweetheart."

"I never doubted that God *could* heal her, but I didn't expect that he *would*. I – I didn't know why until tonight, but...but now I think I do." Paul sniffed and blew his nose on the random napkin from his jeans pocket. Joy waited, holding him.

"I don't think I've ever stopped wondering why Dad had to suffer so long, and why he never recovered, despite modern medicine and all our prayers for him. I prayed for Mom, of course, all the time, but I – I put God in a box. I expected the answer to be 'no,' like it was with Dad. I'm ashamed of myself."

"Paul, I don't know what to say except that I love you," Joy said. "And I'm sorry you've been going through all this inside, and that we've been too busy for me to even notice or talk about it."

"It's not your fault. I was too upset to talk about it until tonight."

"I also know that your faith is stronger than you think. It's one of the reasons I respect you so much, and one of the reasons I married you."

Paul smiled slightly. "Thank you, honey," he said.

"You know, I do think I can relate in some way too," Joy said. "I'd never want to play the comparison game with your pain, but I felt a bit like that the first year or so I lived up here. I felt so alone, and even when you and I became close, I kept expecting we'd break up because I didn't think God gave me good relationship opportunities. And let's not even talk about how neurotic I was when Aunt Joann was

157

sick – I was so sure I was going to lose her. Sometimes, I still am. It's been so, so hard to cultivate faith that God will say yes about my getting to hang on to anyone I care deeply about."

"I know," Paul said. "I know that the lack of loved ones can hurt as much as grief over the loss of a loved one." They swung quietly for a while, and then Paul asked,

"How are you doing in processing all that happened in Pennsylvania?"

"I don't know," Joy said, rubbing her forehead. "It still hurts my brain to think about – possibly because my brain has been *so* full of everything else since 3.7 seconds after we got home.""

"That's understandable."

"I still don't know whether to be angry at my mother, proud of my mother, grateful to my mother…or what."

"The answer might be "or what," said Paul. "You had a strange, intense, confusing time with her. She's the queen of mixed messages."

"Pretty much…" Joy's sentence was interrupted by the ringing of her cell phone.

"I don't know this number," she said, frowning.

"Sales call?"

"At 9:15 p.m.? Surely not. The area code is not local, but it looks familiar…oh, maybe it's my mom!" Joy hurried to accept the call, her eyes wide.

"Hello, Joy, this is Jacob Fischer from Pennsylvania," said the accented voice she remembered. "I'm calling with good news, so please don't worry."

"Oh! Ah…okay, thank you…" Joy stammered, mouthing his name to Paul, who was as surprised as she.

"I hope I didn't wake you or frighten you, and I apologize for bothering you…"

"No, no, please don't apologize. I'm awake, and it's nice to hear from you…" Joy said.

"I called to tell you that I baptized your mother in Titus's pond about two hours ago," Jacob continued.

"Whaaaaaaat?" Joy shrieked. "You – you did? Really?"

"It's true. I – I would have let her tell you herself – and perhaps I should have – but when I suggested that she call you right away, she seemed embarrassed and mumbled something about writing you a letter eventually, and I thought you'd want to know – that you *needed* to know – sooner than that."

"Yes, yes, of course! Thank you so much!" Joy exclaimed. "Please – please hold a second. Paul is right beside me, and he's beside himself to understand what's going on..." She covered the speaker with her finger and managed to explain to Paul. His mouth dropped open.

"Thank you – thank you, Jacob," Joy said again. "But how – when, I mean – did she *understand*?"

"She for sure understands. She's been to worship every Sunday this month – once Clara Yoder heard that Amelia had found a church, she insisted that she be able to attend services with us instead of helping with the children at the Amish assembly. My wife and I have also had five or six study times with your ma – just her and us. She knows God's plan for salvation as well as we do now."

"I – I still can't believe it! So she just got baptized without any warning on a random Tuesday night?"

"She went out to the phone booth and called me up after supper tonight. She saw a doctor today, finally, and he told her that if she didn't reduce her stress and anxiety and lower her blood pressure, she'd be in trouble. And ever since the tornado, it's been hard for her to rest. She knew what she needed to do to be right with God, and she was scared to wait."

Joy and Jacob talked about the details of Amelia's decision for a couple more minutes, and then they said good night. Joy promised not to let on to Amelia by letter that she already knew the joyous news.

Joy fell against Paul's shoulder, nearly paralyzed with shock and racing emotions. "I'm – I'm so relieved, and so, so confused," she whispered at last. "Why now? How did a little bunch of Plain people reach her when no one else could, not even her own daughter?"

"There's nothing wise or original that I can say about this one," said Paul. "Just – it was God. We don't know how He works sometimes – obviously. But it could only have been accomplished by Him."

"Paul, I don't know how much more excitement I can take – good or bad," Joy said. "I seriously think my brain is going to explode."

"Mine too," he said, stroking her head. "Mine too."

CHAPTER 19

It was late before either Paul or Joy could fall asleep that night, so by the time Paul had worked a full day of in-service and attended Bible study, he was ready to fall over from exhaustion. Joy wished she could go to the airport with him to pick up Marie and her family, but there weren't enough seats in their van for her and the triplets, and the kids turned into pumpkins after 10 p.m. anyway. As they were leaving Bible study that evening, Jennifer caught Paul in the middle of a head-splitting yawn. "Do you need me to ride with you?" she asked. "Mom is fine alone for a while now, and you look too sleepy to be driving alone."

"That would be awesome if you don't mind being super squashed in a small space with jet-lagged toddlers..."

Jennifer laughed. "Let's face it, no one wants that, but I'll survive. I'm going to be staying in the same house with them for a few days regardless."

"Thank you," Joy said. "I was concerned that he would fall asleep at the wheel."

The flight from New York City was delayed, so Paul did not get home until 1 a.m. Joy had not gone to bed, but she dozed off on the couch with an alarm set to wake her if Paul was not back by 1:30. He stumbled through the doorway, kissed Joy, and climbed the stairs to fall into bed, his alarm set for 6:45 a.m.

That afternoon, Joy and the triplets picked up Joann and headed to visit Luca and Marie and meet Eva and Lucia. "I hope no one is still asleep," Joy said as they drove the short distance to Katie's house. "My kiddos will wake them up for sure if they are."

"We can take turns watching them outside, maybe, if they are," Joann suggested. "Or – it's such a nice day – the adults might even want to chat on the porch while the children play."

"Oh, yes, maybe so. I can't imagine dealing with jet lag with little ones. It felt like mine lasted forever after our trip overseas…but then again, I traded jet lag for morning sickness like two weeks later."

Joann chuckled. "I'm sure that made your experience a great deal harder than most people's."

To Joy's relief, everyone at Katie's house was awake, except Jennifer, and they all knew that Jennifer could sleep through a hurricane. Just the same, they all migrated to the front porch while the cousins all got to know each other by running around the yard. Joy discovered that she had missed Marie much, much more than she'd realized, and the shared experience of having small children drew them instantly even closer than they had ever been before Marie had left for Italy. The two women jabbered so quickly to each other it only took them ten minutes to close half the five-year gap since they'd last seen one another.

Eventually, Marie had to get up to go comfort Lucia, who was distressed by a fresh mosquito bite on her tanned little nose, so Joy sat back to observe the weary travelers. Marie hadn't changed much in five years, except to look a little more tired and to sport a short "mom haircut." Unlike Paul and Jennifer, Marie had always been fairly slender, but she was even thinner now after half a decade of walking almost everywhere.

Joy had only seen Luca in person once before, when she and Paul had spent their honeymoon in Venice, but she was pretty sure he hadn't had grey in his hair then like he did now. He was tall and had a dark complexion and a serious manner. When Luca smiled, though, his whole face lit up, and it was obvious that he was kind and gentle. When he spoke English, he had just a trace of an accent.

The girls were petite and adorable and as dark as their father, but with long curls. Although Eva was only nine months younger than the triplets, they towered over her, even Annie, who was not tall at all for her age. Eva was fully bilingual – her English was excellent, and according to her father, so was her Italian. Lucia didn't say much yet at fifteen months, but she could understand many words and simple sentences in both languages also.

Joy focused on Eva and the triplets for a moment longer. They were playing a game – a toddler version of hide and seek – and counting – in Italian! Marie rejoined the others on the porch, holding a still-whimpering Lucia, and Joy told her to listen to the children's game for a minute.

"My bossy little girl," Marie laughed.

"But she's already being educational for the triplets – they're learning how to count in Italian!" said Joy.

"Yes, except for the number five," Luca spoke up, laughing also. "My Eva omits the number five every time she counts, in either language!"

After an hour, everyone loaded up to make the short journey to Joy and Paul's house, where they would have a big family supper that night. Joy had planned the meal – a roast turkey with many simple side dishes – but Joann agreed to help with the food costs and the cooking since they would be feeding thirteen people. The gang all arrived as Paul was coming home from in-service, half asleep but thankful to see them.

Amid all the hugging and excited chatter, Joy and Joann slipped into the kitchen to begin cooking. Joy prepped the turkey first, seasoning it but not stuffing it since the stuffing was not gluten free. "Whew," she breathed as she slid it into the oven. "I'm glad that's going. I had a nightmare during my tiny bit of sleep before Paul got home last night that I'd accidentally put the turkey to cook in the dishwasher instead of the oven – and it was stressful!"

"But you don't even have a dishwasher!"

"Exactly!" Joy said, giggling.

The women had agreed ahead of time that Joann would make the desserts, a pie and a cake, both of which would be gluten free, since the recipes were complex, and Joy rarely made desserts. Joann began the cake first so it would cool in time to be iced and chilled.

"Aunt Joann," said Joy, after she'd washed her hands. "Things have been so hectic the past few days that I've hardly had a chance to talk with you one-on-one."

"I know, dear heart," murmured Joann, squinting at the tiny print of her smudged cake recipe.

"Something – ah, something wonderful – but very unexpected happened on Tuesday," Joy continued, still struggling to wrap her mind around Jacob's news.

"What's that?" Joann asked, giving Joy her attention.

Joy told Joann about her phone call from Jacob in full detail. "Why – why, that's – that – is wonderful," Joann said. "I would have never expected it to happen, especially so soon after she began attending…"

"I know. I was shocked. Still am shocked. I'm glad and thankful, of course, but my mind is pretty much blown."

"It is shocking, but it proves that God can do anything," her aunt said.

"That's true," Joy said. "I feel like a horrible person for saying this, but I'm kinda…scared, though." She abandoned all hope of accomplishing any other tasks at that moment and leaned against the counter, wringing a dish towel. "I – I know I need to – to have a different attitude toward her now – now that she's a Christian. I need to encourage her – and to think of her as my sister in Christ – and – and probably to try to talk to her more. But I don't trust her, Aunt Joann. I don't trust that she's not going to hurt me, or the kids. I can't believe that she's changed that much."

"So that's why you're worrying?" Joann said gently. "It's okay, kiddo. It's natural to be afraid of being hurt when it happened so deeply and so often." She paused, choosing her words carefully. "I think you can love your mother, and encourage her as a new Christian, and continue forgiving her, without – ah, jeopardizing your own emotional health. You don't have to spend time with her in person if you can't handle it or don't want the kids around her much. You can write letters or cards or make phone calls. You can pray for her and for her growth…because remember, changing our lives and our habits can take some time after we become Christians." She smiled wryly before continuing. "It certainly took me many years after I was baptized before I had control over my hot temper and sharp tongue...and you would still be appalled by all the things I *want* to say when I get angry. Your mother may not seem much different until she can retrain her heart and mind and speech to be more considerate and kinder. And it's not wrong for you to limit your exposure to her until that happens at least."

"So...you don't think I'm horrible, I guess?" Joy said, sniffing.

"Never!" proclaimed Joann, hugging her tight. "Now, tell me, does that recipe say two teaspoons of vanilla, or three?"

"Two, Aunt Joann. Definitely two. Would you like a magnifying glass...or a microscope...so you can see the rest of it?"

Joann stuck out her tongue at her impertinent niece, and they proceeded with their huge cooking job.

CHAPTER 20

The month of September was one of adjustments for everyone. Marie and her family moved into the tiny two-bedroom rental house that Joy had located for them, planning to search for a house to buy as soon as Luca could judge how successful his practice would be. They busied themselves with other tasks in their new American lives too – buying a good used car, finding furniture at secondhand stores and the last few yard sales of the season, and seeking out all the best gluten free foods Vermont had to offer. Luca began preaching for the East Montpelier congregation the first Sunday after they arrived, and, although he seemed a bit nervous, it was obvious that he would be a good fit until Wilson either recovered or knew he would not be able to resume his position.

Joy began unofficial preschool with Micah, Gideon, and Annie in the middle of the month. Especially after all the craziness of the summer, she had decided to take Paul and Joann's advice and skip curriculum, so they did 15-20 minutes of "sit-down" work each weekday morning – working with letters and numbers in simple, colorful ways – and then spent some time whenever possible in hands-on learning. Joann often helped with the hands-on part of their education – she was teaching them gardening and nature study, piano, and cooking. Katie did arts and crafts with them on a weekly basis. Alex taught them the names of their bones with the skeleton that had hung in his office. Paul taught them sports and games in the evenings or on the weekends, as well as a little more French. And they were picking up bits of Italian from spending time with Eva. To Joy's surprise, they did not complain at all about their short school time, and most of the rest of the time, they thought they were playing.

Katie had nearly recovered at last by the end of September. She had more energy than she had had in over two years, and her pain was gone except for in her knees; a sugar-free diet with plenty of green tea and turmeric was keeping it manageable without medication except on her busiest of days. Best of all, Katie was so relieved to feel like herself again that she was also happier than she had been since before Jean's death.

One of the most beautiful things to happen in September that year was that Joy and Marie were able to re-connect. The good friendship they had cultivated before Marie moved to Italy had been rekindled, and their shared experiences and similar stages of life gave them much more in common than ever before. Joy found herself with a close female friend her age again for the first time in half a decade, and Marie's reverse culture shock after so long overseas was eased significantly by having Joy nearby. They were at each other's houses as often as they could justify the eight-mile drive, and they helped each other with chores and errands and laughed and cried while the cousins played. The rest of their family watched them and smiled, thankful.

Jennifer returned reluctantly to South Carolina mid-month, no longer able to take all her required courses online. She was sad to leave so soon after Marie had returned, but she was so relieved by her mother's increasing health, and she knew it was time to get on with her own life again. Her arm was healing well and was scheduled to be cut out of her cast in two more weeks, much to her excitement...after all, Christmas vacation wasn't that far away, and she needed to be fully recovered in time to visit for some sledding and ice skating!

One afternoon the last week of the month proved to be unpleasant for everyone and provided Joy and Joann with memories they would wish they didn't have for long afterward. Paul was still at work – he was staying late for parent-teacher conferences that night, and Joy and the kids had gone to Joann's house for a quick gardening lesson before the forecasted first frost that night. Alex left not long after they arrived to grab a few items from the hardware store, so only Joann and Joy and the triplets were at the house when an unfamiliar red sports car sped into Joann's driveway.

"Do you know that car?" Joy asked, looking up from the basket she was helping to fill with tomatoes.

"No," said Joann, standing up and brushing dirt from her hands onto her ancient blue jeans. "It's probably some lost tourists."

"Kiddos, why don't you take a break from gardening and go play on the slide?" Joy said, feeling a bit uneasy without knowing why. They complied, running to the back yard, several yards away, to the small swing set that Alex had set up for them.

Joy breathed more easily when she saw that the car was only occupied by one middle-aged woman who appeared to be sober and unarmed. All kinds of awful scenarios had flown through her mind in the past thirty seconds – something about the speed and aggressiveness with which the driver had arrived had spooked her. The woman was dressed in a revealing, trendy blouse covered in sequins and skin-tight leggings and high-heeled sandals. She minced toward the front door until she caught sight of the women in the side yard, and then she lurched across the lawn toward them, her shoes puncturing the lawn.

"Helllooo!" she called out. "Is Alex home?"

"Ah, not at the moment," Joann replied. "But I can take a message for him if you'd like."

"No, no, that will never work," the woman said. "I haven't seen him in decades. I won't leave him any old note."

Joann smiled at her quizzically, waiting for her to explain herself, while Joy marveled at her patience. She'd have demanded their visitor's name, address, and social security number by now!

"I suppose you don't know who I am. I'm Melinda Anderson – I was Melinda Turner when Alex knew me. We were quite an item back in the 80s, you see, so I'd like to stay and wait to see him. You may not understand since you're just the gardeners, but we were too special to each other for me to miss the opportunity to look him up since I'm in the area. He's a lot older than I am, of course."

Joy nearly spit out the gum she'd been chewing. This was too much to take in – and – the gardeners? Was that this Melinda person's assumption of who they were? She turned to her aunt.

"You should definitely see him after all those years," Joann was saying. "Would you like to sit on the porch and enjoy this lovely day, or would you prefer to come inside?"

"Oh, inside," Melinda said. "I'm freezing. I can't believe how much colder it is here than in Boston." She rubbed her exposed shoulders and shivered.

"I'm afraid we've had the windows open, so it's not much warmer inside," said Joann, leading the way onto the back porch. Joy followed her, beckoning for the children to move to the screened porch to play. Melinda flopped onto the couch, and after she requested something hot to drink, Joann went into the kitchen to make tea. Joy followed again, keeping a careful eye on Melinda as well as the children through the screened door. "How do you know she's not an ax murderer?" she hissed to her aunt as Joann started the teakettle.

Joann shrugged. "I have heard Alex mention her name a couple of times. I think she worked with his brother. But other than that – I'm as clueless as you are, kiddo. I'm fairly certain that we could beat her up if we need to, though."

Joy snickered. "I think so!"

Soon, all three women were sitting in the living room with their tea, waiting anxiously for Alex's return for vastly different reasons. Annie came inside not long afterward. "Oh, what a beautiful little girl!" Melinda said. "How old is she?"

"I'm four," Annie piped up.

"Do you go to preschool?" asked Melinda, addressing Annie directly at last.

"No, I go to homeschool."

"How strange!" Melinda stared at Joy. "Aren't you worried that their development will be delayed?" Joy blinked, shocked at her rudeness, but her attempt to answer was interrupted by Gideon, who came barging into the room, shouting.

"Mommy!" he yelled. "Micah's being mean. He took my helicopter, and when I took it back, he kicked me in the femur!"

Joann snorted, although she disguised it well with a cough, and Joy told Melinda, "No," before she hurried out to the porch, seething, to speak to her son so he would grow up to be nicer than the woman in the living room. She returned to her aunt's side after threatening Micah with an extended time-out if he did any more kicking.

After several minutes, Melinda sighed, dramatically checked the time on her bejeweled phone, and said, "Ladies, don't let me keep you from your jobs. I can amuse myself just fine if you need to go back to work."

"Our jobs?" Joy asked. She'd tried so hard to stay quiet and let her aunt run the show, but the question popped out anyway.

"Yes, your gardening – or housekeeping – or whatever it is the two of you do here. If Alex would ever get a wife, he wouldn't have to keep hiring so many people to take care of him and his house."

"Melinda, Alex had a wife – has had one for over six years," Joann said finally, her eyes twinkling over her teacup as she took a sip of her drink.

"You can't be serious! That's impossible – none of the old Boston crowd has heard anything like that about him!"

"I don't think he told many people from Boston, other than his family," Joann said. "Since he's retired, Alex has mostly focused on the simple life – family, church, his hobbies – things like that. He doesn't stay in touch often with anyone else from Boston."

"How do you know that?" Melinda's voice was rising.

"Because I'm his wife."

Melinda slammed her cup down onto the coffee table. "Don't lie to me to get rid of me," she snapped. "There's no way Dr. Alexander Martin would be married to – to someone like you."

"I can assure you I'm telling the truth," Joann said, her voice quiet but steely. She had gone pale under her tan.

"What did you do to make him marry you?" Melinda said. "He was one of the most prominent pediatricians in Boston a decade ago, and it's impossible to believe that he would choose someone like *you* to hook up with, much less marry!"

"What do you mean?" Joann said, even more quietly.

"Look at yourself, girl! You're covered in dirt, in clothes from, like, another century. Your hair's a mess, and grey, for pity's sake – have you never thought of coloring it? And you're as brown as a Mexican! You're the wife of a prestigious doctor, and you're in this cabin in the wilderness, grubbing in the garden, instead of being in society. And I'll bet you have no background or pedigree or education either. I don't know what he was thinking – or not thinking – getting caught by a hillbilly out here who looks old enough to be his mother. Why, I…"

Finally, Joy found that she could use her tongue again as the utter shock of Melinda's vitriol continued to rain down on Joann, who sat still except for her hands, which were shaking. "Get out," Joy said at last. "Get out of this house right now, and never come back."

Melinda blew a raspberry from her brilliantly painted lips. "Right. Like I'm going to listen to some backward fundamentalist wacko who doesn't believe in school. This is not your house, it's Alex's, and I'm not going to leave until I've seen him."

Joy took a deep breath. "Then I'll call the police, and they'll make you leave. You're trespassing now. This is my aunt's house too, and you have no right to sit here and – and rip her to shreds."

Melinda began cursing but made no move to leave. Knowing that there were six innocent ears on the other side of the screen door made no difference to the furious woman. Joy pulled out her phone, unlocked it, and began to dial 911, and only then did the intruder stand up and move toward the door, still spewing venom all the way. Joy followed her with her call screen facing out, planning to tap the call button if Melinda did not continue to march toward her vehicle. Joann followed but remained on the porch as Joy herded Melinda across the yard.

"This is outrageous!" Melinda snapped, out of breath from her brief walk. She slammed the door of her convertible and revved the engine.

"It certainly is. Get a life, Melinda Anderson," Joy said, still holding her finger over the send call portion of her phone screen.

Melinda reversed from the driveway so fast that she missed by inches catching her back wheels in a ditch, much to Joy's unholy disappointment, and roared back down the gravel road at double an appropriate speed. Joy considered calling the police anyway to warn them that an unsafe driver was on the road, but didn't, sure they'd never catch Melinda and afraid she'd return for vengeance if she got a ticket before she reached town.

Joy hurried back to the porch as soon as she could no longer hear the departing vehicle. Her heart was pounding from the stress of the confrontation – oh, how she hated confrontation – but most of all, her heart was hurting for her aunt. She knew Joann wasn't sensitive about most things, but who wouldn't be crushed by such an unprovoked, vile onslaught of abuse about almost every aspect of her identity? She dashed up the stairs, prepared to throw her arms around Joann and hug her close, but to her surprise, her aunt reached her first and did the same to her.

Joy hugged back, too startled to begin the sympathetic speech she'd planned during the fifteen-second walk back to the house. When Joann released her, Joy saw that there were tears in her eyes, and she tried to start her spiel, but her aunt stopped her mid-sentence.

"Thank you, dear heart," Joann said. "Thank you so much for – for protecting me...for standing up for me."

"Of course, Aunt Joann! But I didn't protect you very well – I was so shocked that I didn't get rid of her until she had already, like, torn you to pieces with her words…"

"You were amazing – you did a perfect job," said Joann, hugging her again. "I – I would never allow someone to say such garbage to anyone else in my house, but…I suppose I still revert to being passive when someone is insulting me…a hang-up from my childhood, unfortunately. I should have kicked her out myself, but I couldn't, so thank you – so very much – for taking care of me."

"Are you okay?" Joy asked anxiously. "I mean, you turned awfully pale…"

"No worries, dear heart. You know I turn all sorts of colors so easily when I'm upset or surprised or embarrassed, despite my – ah – extremely brown skin."

"Oh, Aunt Joann. "You know that she was just – just pouring out a bunch of prejudiced insults and lies!"

"Not entirely – it *is* true that I have very little formal education, and my background is about as unimpressive as they come – I would have been considered homeless by some standards when I was a teenager. And yes, my clothes are old and dirty, and my skin is tanned – that's inevitable – both of my parents were always as brown as nuts, even in wintertime, as soon as they got the slightest hint of sun exposure…"

"There's nothing wrong with any of that! And you didn't finish school, sure, but you're smarter and know more than most other adults I know! And you were *gardening*. In the dirt…and…"

"Whoa, slow down, kiddo. I know. None of those things bother me, nor do they bother Alex. I'm not going to lie awake tonight fretting about being mocked for wearing old clothes to dig in the garden."

"I'm glad. She was so – cruel. I was hoping she didn't hurt you too much."

Joann smiled slightly and then shivered. "It's getting colder," she said. "Let's go back inside."

173

They checked on the children, made them put on their jackets since they insisted on staying on the back porch, and warmed up their neglected mugs of tea from earlier. They sat down again in the living room as though nothing had happened, except neither of them had much to say.

After several minutes of silence, Joy sat down her cup a bit too forcefully. "Aunt Joann, are you *sure* you're okay? It's all right if you're not, you know. That was horrible."

Joann leaned back and sighed. "You know me well, Joy. One part of what Melinda said is bothering me – did upset me, I'm ashamed to say."

"Why should you be ashamed? She's the one who deserves all the shame!"

"I'm embarrassed to admit it because it's so superficial," said Joann. "But I did hate hearing that I look significantly older than Alex."

"That was a lie too – you absolutely don't look old enough to be his mother. Surely you know that! I mean, his mom would have to be 85 or something if she were alive!"

"I know I don't look 85. But – humor me for a minute in my pride, dear heart...do I look that much older than my age – and do I look a lot older than he does? Can you give me your honest opinion? I know you'll be kind – don't be afraid of hurting my feelings."

Joy obligingly took a good look at her aunt. "No," she said after a moment. "No, you don't. You look like someone who is probably fifty, give or take a couple of years, and so does Alex. Mostly, it's because of your hair, but your hair suits you...I don't think you'd look like yourself if you colored your hair. You don't act your age most of the time, but I know that's not what you were asking..."

"Thanks for your perspective. I know that appearance doesn't matter, especially compared to what's inside, so I shouldn't care...but I'd hate to think that – that people who see me with Alex are wondering why he's with such a slouchy, old hag or something."

Joy bit her lip to keep from spitting out an angry rant, the likes of which she rarely indulged in these days. She knew it was a sin to hate anyone, but it was difficult to avoid hating Melinda as she watched her typically confident aunt stammering out the pain their unwanted visitor's words had caused her.

"No, Aunt Joann, I can assure you that no one is thinking that – at least, no one who isn't insane – and insanely jealous," Joy said tightly. There was more she wanted to say – so much more – but she couldn't form the words through her anger. And, before she could calm down, Alex drove up.

"Hi, girls," he said, hurrying inside and dumping his purchases onto the dining table.

"How was the hardware store?" Joann asked from across the large room. Joy marveled at her aunt's even voice.

"Pretty busy, but nothing unusual," he said, coming toward them at last. "I did see quite a sight on the way home, though, outside Woodfield...a slightly-wrecked Maserati in a ditch! Someone's having a bad day..."

"Oh, could you tell if the driver was injured?" Joann said, color rising in her cheeks.

"Not injured, but in handcuffs, swearing at an officer," Alex said, shrugging. "Like I said, she's having a bad day."

"Didn't you recognize the driver?" said Joy.

"Should I have?" asked Alex, staring at her.

"It was Melinda Turner Anderson," Joann said quietly. "She came here while you were gone, looking for you, and was terribly upset when she left without seeing you."

"What? Melinda Anderson? Well...it couldn't have happened to a better person," said Alex, wrinkling his nose.

"Alex!" Joann scolded.

"I'm sorry. That was unnecessary. But she's not exactly my favorite person – and why in the world would she have come to see me?"

Joy and Joann shared glances, and Joy knew despite her frustration that she had to let her aunt handle this discussion. "I think she may be – ah – available again, and was assuming you were as well," Joann said. "And she had a lot to say about how much you meant to her in the past."

"That's a pile of junk," said Alex, rubbing the bridge of his nose. "We went to one dinner together – a formal banquet – that required a date. My brother had heard she was interested in me and set us up. I despised every moment of the entire experience. I wouldn't form a relationship with her if she were the only woman on earth."

"She seems to feel much more positively about you," Joann said, grinning a little at her flustered husband.

"Disgusting," Alex said, and Joy was surprised at the energy her aunt's mild husband was displaying. "Is she as petty and vulgar as she was thirty years ago?"

"Ah...you might say that," Joann murmured.

"Well, I'm thankful I missed her. I would have never recognized her, though. She's about your age, Jo-Jo, but she hasn't grown older gracefully from what I could tell as I drove past...not like you at all, sweetheart."

To Alex's utter shock and alarm, Joann burst into tears and then hid her face behind a cushion. Alex stood to go comfort her, stopped mid-stride, turned to Joy, opened his mouth, closed it again, and then stared at his wife again...his normally rational, articulate wife. Joy took a deep breath and took him by the arm, pulling him into the kitchen. He had to know – she had to put him out of his misery – but she didn't want Joann to have hear again about all the hurtful things Melinda had said. She spoke softly but spared no details.

When she had finished, Alex's face was blood red, and his knuckles were paper white from squeezing the counter as she'd talked. "I want to go and kill her," he whispered, but his eyes were blazing. "I won't, but at this very moment, I want to."

"I feel the same way," Joy said. "It was all so – so senseless and – and cruel. And unprovoked. Aunt Joann was being so kind and hospitable to her – you know how she is."

"Yes, I do. Thank you, Joy, more than I can tell you, for chasing her away. Your aunt has always been much more able to protect others than she has herself."

"I only wish I had done it sooner...but it was like watching a – a horror movie or something, and I felt paralyzed at first."

Alex shook his head. "I have to go back over there," he said.

Joy stayed in the kitchen for a few minutes to give them some time alone, trying not to listen, which was difficult because of the house's open floor plan. In a few minutes, though, she saw Joann leave and go into her bedroom, so she returned to the living room to check with Alex.

"She's okay," he whispered. "She's washing her face and getting her glasses and such."

"Oh, good," said Joy, and sure enough, her aunt was back soon, her eyes red, but with her hair re-braided and wearing clean clothes.

"Hi," Joy said uncertainly.

"Hi, dear heart. Don't worry. I really am okay now. Alex's sweet and unprompted compliment just did me in."

"I do that too," Joy said. "Cry more when someone is nice to me *after* I've been hurt."

"Yes, well, I don't usually bawl my eyes out like that at all, as you know," said Joann. "That woman hit a nerve, I suppose. But – I'm moving on now – the show's over, folks."

"And we want to kill her for hurting you," Joy said.

"I suspect you aren't the first people to feel that way, eh? But – imagine how awful it is to be Melinda Anderson, Joy...to be so – bitter and spiteful."

Joy and the triplets left soon afterward so they would be home when Paul arrived. In front of the children, Joy only explained that she had had a tough afternoon and would give him more details later. Paul could tell that Joy was upset, though, so the moment the children were in bed, he peppered her with questions.

"Are you okay? What's this about a loud, sparkly lady with a mean voice and a fast, red car? Did someone bother you or the kids?"

For the second time that day, Joy repeated the terrible story, her blood boiling. Paul was furious too, of course, but he praised Joy for her actions.

"You're always wanting to do things for your aunt, Joy – to help her, since she's done so much for you. Sticking up for her today, and actually running that – that creature off her property – well, that's the best way you could have shown your appreciation for her right now."

"I hope so. I'm so thankful Alex was able to reassure her with his words, because I have such a hard time telling her how special she is."

Paul kissed Joy. "She knows how you feel, honey. She knows."

CHAPTER 21

On October 1st, Joann and Jack took their GED tests at last. The test was scheduled for early morning, and then Joann planned to take Jack out for ice cream afterward to congratulate him for his dedication, regardless of his score. Joann promised to drop by the farmhouse after that to discuss everything with Joy.

It was about noon when Joann arrived, and the children were finishing their cheese quesadillas. Joy waved her into the kitchen, her mouth full. "Want one?" she asked when she could speak.

"Yes, thanks. I'm starved!"

"So...how did it go? When will you know your score?"

"I felt good about the test – it seemed easy, but that doesn't necessarily mean I did well," Joann said, munching her lunch. "I won't get my score for a while – several days at least. Instead of taking the test on the computer, as we've been expecting, we took the old paper version, which is mailed in and scored. Someone hacked the GED website a few days ago, and it's still under repairs."

"Oh, no! So you'll be in suspense for that much longer?"

"Yes. I especially hate it for Jack. He was so nervous about the reading part of the test, and he has a lot at stake if he can pass. If I don't pass, the only consequence will be a tiny bit of hurt pride."

"I don't see how you can be so patient! I'm impatient on your behalf!" Joy whined. Joann laughed at her.

The following week, on Thursday, Paul came home late from work. "Hi, honey," he said, dumping his bag on the kitchen counter and planting a kiss on Joy's lips. "Sorry I'm a little late."

"I was getting a bit worried," she said.

"The principal called me into his office as I was about to head home," Paul said.

"Oh?" Joy scrutinized his face. He was trying to conceal his emotions, but his eyes were sparkling, and the dimples even his recent weight loss couldn't remove were showing.

"He told me I have to work late tomorrow night too – until 8:00 at least..."

"Awww, on a Friday night?"

"Yep. There's an awards ceremony at 7:00 tomorrow evening, and I have to be there."

A light bulb switched on in Joy's brain. "Paul, did you win an award?" she asked.

"I did," he said. "I won Teacher of the Year – just for the school, but I have to show up tomorrow regardless."

Joy bear-hugged him. "I'm so proud of you!" she said. "Let's invite everyone to the ceremony before they make other plans!"

"Everyone?" Paul said. "Wait a minute here...are we talking...our children...our family...the church...the universe? I'm not going to make a zillion phone calls tooting my own horn!"

"The family, you goofball. And you don't have to make any phone calls. I'll make them all. I can toot your horn all I want since I'm your wife."

"Okay, okay. Toot away. In the meantime, I'd better go invite the kids before they make weekend plans."

Joy swatted his backside with her dish towel as he escaped the kitchen.

All of Paul's local family members made it to the ceremony the next night, and they had a big, wriggling, noisy cheering section in the front row of the high school auditorium. He received an attractive wooden plaque, a gift card to Barnes and Noble, and such glowing praise from the principal and superintendent that his face stayed the color of a fire engine for a solid half hour. Afterward, to celebrate, Joy suggested that they go to the nearby Friendly's restaurant for ice cream, but only Alex and Joann took her up on the offer – Katie's knees were hurting, and Lucia was cutting a molar and keeping everyone awake all night. So the seven of them squished into an over-sized booth and ordered ice cream all around, despite the 45-degree temperature outside.

"Mercy, restaurant ice cream twice in less than two weeks," Joann said. "Such extravagance!" They all laughed.

As they were waiting for their orders, Paul slapped his forehead. "I can't believe I forgot to tell you," he said. "I got a text from Jack before the ceremony! He passed his GED – every portion – so he'll be promoted immediately at work."

"How exciting!" Joy said. "I know he's so relieved and proud." She glanced at her aunt. "But didn't Jack tell you too?"

"I left my cell phone at home," Joann confessed, "I'm sure he texted me too. Oh, I'm so relieved for him!"

"Wait...did all the scores come out at once today, or are they mailed out in bunches or something?" said Joy, giving Joann the fishy eye.

"I don't know," Joann answered mildly, but her eyes gave her away.

"You got your score, didn't you?" Paul said. "Did you pass?"

"Yes," Joann said, grinning.

"Why didn't you say so hours ago?" Paul scolded her as he and Joy jumped up to hug her.

"She didn't say anything because she didn't want to steal your thunder tonight, Paul, and put any attention on herself," Alex spoke up. "Because, you see, she didn't simply pass." Joann tried to shush him, but he persisted. "She got a perfect score."

"A what?" Joy said, her mouth dropping open.

"A perfect score. She answered every single question correctly. She'll receive a special high honors GED."

"Aunt Joann! That's incredible!" Joy exclaimed.

"Shhh..." Joann said. "Don't tell the entire restaurant!"

"We need to celebrate your accomplishment too," Paul said. "What should we do?"

"Nothing involving ice cream," Joann laughed. "Or I'll be too full of sugar to remember any of the information from the test!" She thought for a moment. "Actually, in celebration of a major life milestone that has finally happened for me, I'd like to do something else I've always wanted to do...hike Mt. Mansfield."

"The whole thing?" Joy said.

"Yes," Joann laughed. "The whole mountain. It's not that high. I've hiked some of the trails before, but never the entire mountain. And I'd like to go before winter arrives."

"I'm afraid that's out for me," Alex said, wincing at the idea. He had broken his pinky toe a few days before and was still having some pain when he wore shoes. "But that's a long, tough hike – you shouldn't go alone."

Joy took a deep breath. "Okay, okay. I'll go. I'll also probably die. When do you want to go, Aunt Joann?"

"Are you sure, kiddo? It's more intense than any hikes you've done recently or...ever, actually..."

"I'm sure I don't want you to go alone, or to have to wait until next year."

"Well...Paul, what does your schedule look like for next weekend? Could you spare Joy all day Saturday?" Joann asked.

"I can make it work," he said. "If I'm behind on anything, I can ask Marie or Mom to watch the kids for a couple of hours."

"Will next Saturday be okay with you dear?" Joann asked Alex. "Is there anything you were needing me to do?"

"Saturday is fine, but Jo-Jo, please, take it easy. Have you ever climbed a mountain that high before?"

"Once or twice, but don't worry. It isn't a technically difficult climb – it's just very steep."

"I'm surprised you don't want to climb Mt. Washington," Paul teased her.

"Shhh...don't put any ideas in her head!" said Alex.

"Oh, I do want to, but I'll save that to celebrate turning sixty."

Joy and Alex both shuddered, for different reasons, and Paul laughed at them until the children begged to have the joke explained to them.

Joy spent the next week preparing herself for her upcoming hike. She pulled out the moisture-wicking layering clothing she'd bought years before for cold-weather hikes with her aunt, washed it, and tried it on, and rejoiced that it all still fit – sort of. She bought healthy, high-protein trail snacks and a new pair of low-temperature socks. And she took a good, hard look at her thoroughly worn hiking boots from five years before, and sighed.

When Paul came home on Tuesday, he was grinning from ear to ear. He handed Joy an Amazon package. "Hurry and open this and put them on right away!" he said.

"Whaaaat?" said Joy, hurrying to open the box. She could think of nothing – except maybe a strait jacket – or deodorant – that was urgent for her to "put on."

"Just open it! You'll understand," Paul said.

Joy obliged and found a beautiful new pair of hiking boots inside. They were an excellent brand and a soft grey-blue color.

"How did you know?" Joy squealed, kissing him, and hurrying to try them on right there in the kitchen.

"It occurred to me when I was thinking about your hike that your old shoes were about shot, so I checked the closet the other night. I don't want you to attempt the most strenuous hike of your life in pathetic shoes – so Merry Christmas – in October! But you'll have to wear them every day until then to break them in, so you don't end up with epic blisters. I asked Joann about a good brand to buy."

"They're perfect," Joy said, standing up and clomping around the kitchen. "The fit is great, they're sturdy and stabilize my ankles, but they don't feel heavy. Thank you *so* much, sweetheart!"

"You're welcome. I hope they help to keep you safe. I'm kinda nervous about you doing a big hike like this, you know, especially since you haven't had the opportunity to hike often in so many years."

"I know. I'm nervous too. But the trails are fairly busy – I googled them – and we'll get there early in the morning so we can hike for, like, nine hours if necessary, which is almost twice as long as the route is supposed to take. And we should have decent cell phone service when we're the highest things around."

"That's good. And I know Joann knows what she's doing and will advise you well. It is a bit nerve-wracking, though."

"I'll be super careful. There aren't many people I'd do this with – or for – but I do trust Aunt Joann."

"Just remember too that despite her strength and enthusiasm, she is pushing sixty, and she may not be able to pull you out of ravines or drag you down mountains anymore."

Joy nodded. That thought had crossed her mind too, but she didn't want to dwell on it. She wasn't sure which idea she hated worst – that she might not be able to be rescued as quickly, or that Joann might not be strong enough to rescue her anymore.

Joann dropped by on Friday evening once the triplets were in bed to help her finish packing her backpack. They weren't carrying much – food, an extra layer of clothing and pair of socks, basic first aid supplies, a Swiss army knife, a flashlight, a map, their phones, and a water filter so that they could refill their water bottles at any mountain stream. Joann was also bringing a dose of her daily medications and her glasses in case they were stranded overnight, but she emphasized multiple times that she really, really doubted that would happen.

"Whew!" Joy said, sitting back on her heels after she put the last item into her backpack. "That's that!"

"It shouldn't be too heavy," Joann said, lifting it with one hand. "Mine isn't – no, not bad at all. Much lighter than our packs were on our overnight hikes."

"Ironically, my arms are stronger than they were back then, thanks to lifting triplets all day. But I think my leg muscles are made of jelly, so you're still going to have to be patient with me."

184

"The arm muscles will come in handy for part of the trail," her aunt assured her. "There are supposed to be some scrambling portions."

"You mean – rock climbing?"

"Yes, but not like you're thinking. More like crawling on all fours up slopes of smaller rocks, if I'm understanding the blogs and maps correctly. We won't need ropes or any other technical equipment, though, so don't worry about that."

Joy gulped. "That's good."

Joann placed a hand on Joy's shoulder. "Dear heart, you don't have to go with me, you know. As much as I'd love to go on this adventure with you, I don't want you to feel forced into it. I know you aren't quite as enamored with the whole hiking experience as I am, and that tomorrow will be an exhausting day for you…"

"But – if I don't go with you, who would?" Joy protested.

"I could wait until next year, and that would allow me the time to find someone willing to go. I'm not hiking it alone, even though I'd expected to, because Alex has asked me not to. He's worried enough about my plan to go at all, even though I've been hiking all my life."

Joy was quiet for a moment. She was afraid of the idea of scrambling up rocks, in particular, since she had a fear of heights, and the thought of postponing or canceling her part of the trip was appealing, especially since Joann had promised not to climb the mountain alone. Maybe she could train for the hike this winter – do some snowshoeing or something – so that the intense exercise would not be quite such a shock to her body…she almost made that suggestion, but something stopped her. Her aunt was sitting there on the couch, eyes sparkling and foot tapping in anticipation, so excited at the prospect of sharing this journey with her. And, despite Joy's best intentions, there would be no guarantee that she would actually have time to prepare herself any more during the winter…and there were her lovely new boots from Paul…and, although

Joann was the picture of health today, who knew what the future held?

"I'm going," Joy said before she could change her mind. "This is important to you, which means it's important to me. Let's do this."

Joann grinned at her. "That's my girl," she said. "Now, go to bed, kiddo. I'll see you at 7:30."

The next day dawned cloudy and cold, unseasonably cold. Joy stepped onto the porch as she drank her juice and shivered, making a mental note to add another layer of clothing and her gloves to her backpack. This autumn was early and chilly – the coldest they'd had since she had first arrived in Vermont seven years ago.

The children were still asleep when Joann drove up, so Joy blew them kisses from their doorways, said her goodbyes to Paul, and slipped out to her aunt's jeep.

They chatted about light and pleasant subjects for most of the 75-minute drive to the base of the mountain. When they were still a few miles from Stowe, they caught their first glimpse of the day of Mt. Mansfield through a brief break in the clouds. "Oh, there it is!" Joann breathed. "We're going to the top of that today! Thank you, Joy. I've wanted to do this since I was a teenager."

"You're welcome, Aunt Joann. Why haven't you before, though, with all the hiking you've done?"

"I've made plans to go several times, but something has always come up," Joann said. "The first time was when I was very young – I had convinced Angelique to hike it with me, the first and last time she ever agreed to a hike, but George left her that week, so of course, we didn't go. I think the next time was the year that a huge storm hit the day before, and I had to help John repair the barn. Another time, I planned far in advance, and John even said he'd go with me, but I wasn't strong enough after – after my miscarriage to go – that was the year before you visited the farm. The last time I tried was almost 4.5 years ago."

"What happened that time?"

"We got the call that you were having the babies early," said Joann, smiling at her.

"Well, I can promise you I won't hinder your adventure by childbirth today!" Joy laughed.

"What's on your 'bucket list', Joy?" Joann asked.

"Ahhh...um...you know what, I – I don't guess I've really made one," Joy said. Something – a tiny prickle of pain – niggled at her as she realized how practical and mundane most of her current goals were – keep the kids alive, eat healthier, exercise more, etc. Goose bumps rose on her arms. She'd forgotten, somehow, how to daydream lately...a tragedy for a creative person. She determined to sit down the first chance she had – if she lived through this hike – and compel herself to make a bucket list. "But I'm going to," she added belatedly, taking a deep breath. "What – what are some more things on yours?"

"Oh, mine is pages and pages long...to hike Mt. Washington, to go skiing in the Alps, to study the genealogy of my mother's family, to visit the Grand Canyon and the redwood trees and the other famous landmarks out west, to see the aurora again, to learn another language, to hike the entire Appalachian Trail...and on and on. Pretty outrageous list for an old lady, eh?"

"No," Joy said firmly. "I believe you can do whatever you set your mind to do, Aunt Joann, and your list sounds wonderful."

Joy and Joann found their trailhead easily, thanks to Joann's extensive research. They planned to hike a difficult trail on their way up the mountain and a more moderate one on their way back down when they were more tired.

Joy was exhausted before they'd traveled half a mile, and as soon as the elevation gain started in earnest, her calves were screaming for mercy. The trail marched relentlessly upward the entire way except for a few bone-crushingly cold stream crossings. To Joy's frustration, she was forced to ask her aunt to stop often so she could rest her legs and catch her breath. "This is ridiculous," she fumed to herself. "I can't even keep up with someone over two decades older than I am!" Joy vowed once more to improve her endurance in exercise...because she felt every single one of her extra fifteen pounds and every single muscle that she didn't use often enough. She was grateful for her aunt's perpetual patience.

The women stopped briefly for lunch once they were about two-thirds of the way up the mountain, because it was noon, and they both were starving. "I think the most difficult portions are ahead of us still," Joann said, finishing up a protein bar. "There's a jump, and then the rock scrambling."

"A jump?" Joy almost choked on her mouthful of almonds.

"It seems to be a wide crack on the rocks that we'll have to leap over. The drop under us is only around six feet, though, not the entire height of Mt. Mansfield."

Joy nodded and began to gather up her garbage to repack, since there were no trash cans along the trail. Of course, there was a leap across space, since heights weren't her favorite. Because she wasn't already dying. But what could she say? She could hardly give up now, and she wouldn't dream of telling Joann how sore she was.

"We'd better get moving again if you're able," Joann told her gently. "We're growing a little tight on time."

"I'm sure," Joy said, trying not to groan as she got to her feet and shouldered her backpack again.

They reached the crevice a few minutes after lunch. Joy eyed the gap with butterflies in her stomach. Of course, she should be able to jump three feet, but she hadn't tried recently, and the thought of missing her footing and splatting on the rocks below made her shudder.

Joann noticed her hesitation. "Let's toss our packs over first so their weight won't throw off our balance," Joann said. They then checked to be sure their boots were securely tied. "Would you rather jump first, last, or together?" Joann asked Joy.

"I – I have no idea," Joy said, wondering if her legs would move even if she tried...her fear was beginning to paralyze her.

"Okay, I'll go first, and then I'll catch you," Joann said. Joy nodded again. It was all she could manage.

Joann took several steps back and ran forward, sailing over the gap in the rocks and landing without stumbling. She made it look simple and hardly frightening at all, but Joy's brain and legs weren't inspired. Finally, Joy breathed a quick prayer that she wouldn't impale her spleen on a boulder and took a running jump, endeavoring to copy her aunt's motions. As she was two inches taller than Joann, she cleared the crevice with plenty of room to spare, but her shaking legs didn't support her on her landing, so she tripped and fell up against her aunt, knocking both of them onto their knees on the other side. "I'm sorry," she gasped. "Are you hurt?"

"Not really," Joann said, standing carefully. "I thought you'd made it, so I didn't try to catch you. Are you all right?"

"Yeah, give me a minute," Joy said, taking deep breaths. Her knees were bruised, but she was so grateful to have jumped over successfully that she hardly felt the new pain. Surely the rest of the hike would be less intimidating. Surely.

CHAPTER 22

The last leg of the trail took them above the tree line and into an area of rocks interspersed with small patches of vegetation. The hiking from that point until the summit involved scrambling up the side of the mountain over a series of sloping boulders. Joy felt the fear returning when she saw how far they'd climbed, but fortunately, she could not continue to hike while looking back, so she gritted her teeth and focused on finding safe places for her hands and feet.

It was almost three p.m. when they finally reached the top. They hugged, and then Joy lay down full-length on the ground to rest for a while before she could even appreciate the views. Joann sat down beside her, not asking her any questions once she verified that Joy was only tired. When Joy sat up at last, she gazed in awe at the panorama of beauty surrounding them. Layers upon layers of mountains, some blue, some still emblazoned with fall foliage, windswept evergreens, and straggling clumps of arctic plants…there were natural wonders on every side. She struggled to her feet, and they took dozens of photos with their phones. After they had failed repeatedly to take a good selfie of themselves together, a nearby hiker offered to snap their photo instead. He took an excellent shot that included some of the incredible scenery as well.

"I hope you plan to head down the mountain soon," he said as he returned Joy's phone to her. "It looks like thick fog is rolling in." He pointed to a bank of clouds on the nearby horizon. "These rocks are treacherous when you can't see where you're going."

"We'll leave right away. Thank you," said Joann. "I should have paid better attention to the weather instead of the views alone."

"I've climbed this peak at least twenty times," the man said. "And I'm still shocked by how quickly the weather can change. Everything looked fine ten minutes ago. You should be okay if you hurry."

They thanked him once more, located the easier trail on their map, and began their descent. To Joy's relief, the rock scrambling was much less technical, but she did not enjoy being required to look down. She spent most of her time staring at her boots.

The fog swept in soon and obscured their visibility with breath-taking suddenness, and Joy realized that seeing their location was scary, but not as scary as not being able to see at all. Joann stopped often to consult both her map and her compass, and she urged Joy to pay close attention to every step she took, for safety and to be sure they stayed on the blazed trail.

They had seen quite a few other hikers along their way, but no one else had spoken to them except an occasional mumbled greeting. When they were not quite halfway down the rocky area, Joann murmured, "Joy, that's the third time I've seen that man since we left the summit."

"What do you mean?"

"He's gone past us three times now, twice going up, and once going down. I think he's lost in this crazy fog. I'm going to flag him down. Stay right here – don't move!"

Before Joy could protest, Joann was jogging back up the mountain, shouting. She disappeared for a moment, and although Joy could still hear her voice, it was one of the longest minutes of her life as she stood there on a rock, alone, 2,500 feet up, unable to see more than about two yards in any direction. She prayed, focused on not hyperventilating, and felt no shame at all about the goosebumps of relief that rose on her arms when her aunt reappeared after only about 60 seconds, followed by a tall, slender man.

"Oh, I'm so thankful you're back," said Joy, hugging Joann.

"Yes, I am too, but I'm also so thankful I listened to my hunch. This is Clark Campbell, and he *was* lost. He tripped going over that jump on the trail we took and wrenched his ankle and smashed his glasses, so he's struggling to find his way in this fog."

"Hello," Joy said. "I'm glad you're all right." Her stomach was churning again. What if Joann hadn't noticed him – but what if he was a criminal or something? And at least she hadn't been imagining the dangers of that stupid rock crevice!

As if he could read her thoughts, Clark spoke up. "I'd appreciate it if I could follow you down, at least until we leave this fog, but I know it can be risky to travel with a stranger." He removed his wallet from his jeans pocket and handed it to Joy. "I can't see well enough to take it out myself, but if you'll look in here, you can have one of my business cards, and maybe it will set your mind at ease a little."

Joy fumbled in the worn leather wallet, her fingers trembling from exhaustion, until she located the card. "Dr. Clark Campbell, Professor of English Literature, Johnson University," she read aloud.

"I retired last year, but I hope you can trust me that I'm a respectable fellow to travel with," he said.

"Thank you," Joy said, and Joann murmured her agreement. At least he was a prominent, well-respected person, Joy thought, so even though it went against her instincts, she felt a bit better about him.

"We need to get moving," Joann said. "How much – how well can you see, Dr. Campbell?"

"Please, call me Clark. I'm afraid I can hardly see my own feet, although I could see the lovely scenery earlier at the summit."

"Hey, Aunt Joann, do you think your glasses could help him?" Joy said. "You see better at a distance too…"

"Joy, you're brilliant," Joann said, shedding her backpack right away. She gave her glasses to Clark, who tried them on anxiously. Although he was half a head taller than Joann, his face was thin, so the glasses fit him perfectly.

"Is that any better?" Joann asked.

"Definitely! Things are still fuzzy, but at least I can identify the difference between a log and a rock at my feet," he said.

"Mercy, you're even blinder than I am," Joann laughed. "Let's go – but slowly, so your ankle doesn't give out again."

After another hour, they dropped below the clouds at last, the trail grew far less slippery, and they all breathed more easily. "How much farther is the trailhead?" asked Joy.

"Well, to reach our car, we take this trail about one more mile, and then we join up with our original trail for another half mile," Joann said.

"I think I'm parked near you," Clark said. "What a blessing!"

Joy wondered at his terminology – not too many people in New England used such a religiously-influenced phrase. Maybe he had more in common with them than she thought. She was able to observe their new hiking partner more now that the trail was less dangerous. Clark was middle-aged, she could tell, but except for dozens of laugh lines at the corners of his eyes and grey streaks in his dark hair, he seemed quite young. He was at least 6'4" and slender but not emaciated. He was dressed in basic jeans, boots, and a heavy coat, but Joy's upbringing caused her to recognize that his clothes were expensive and high-quality. He moved quickly and gracefully, except for favoring his left ankle, and his voice was quiet but authoritative with the trace of an accent she couldn't place. She heard him speaking again and listened because Joann had asked Clark about himself.

"I'm from southern Ontario," he said. "I've lived there my entire life except for study abroad in college. I enjoy traveling, especially to mountainous places, and I like to hike, although my hikes are generally a bit – ah, shorter and easier than this one. This is my first visit to Mt. Mansfield, although I've spent plenty of time in Burlington, because that's where my wife was from. She – ah – she passed away last year from cancer."

"I'm so sorry," Joann said quickly.

"I am too, but she had been sick for many years, so it was time for her to – to go home. But I never stop missing her."

"Never!" Joann agreed.

Clark stopped in his tracks. "Are you a widow? You sound as if you understand."

Joann smiled kindly at him. "I was for several years, yes. My first husband died when I was 43. I'm re-married now, but I remember the loneliness."

"I knew it wasn't wise to continue hiking after I broke my glasses," he continued, his voice becoming husky. "But I couldn't turn around. I was climbing this mountain to scatter my wife's ashes on top. It was her favorite place from her childhood, this area, and she adored mountains...so at least I was able to complete my mission."

Joann murmured something understanding, but Joy found herself at a complete loss for words. Fortunately, Clark continued to speak soon afterward.

"Why are the two of you climbing Mt. Mansfield today, if I may ask?" he said, seeming anxious to divert the subject of conversation away from sadness.

Joy, stumbling along at the back of their little hiking party, noticed Joann's hesitation and suddenly flushed neck. She felt a flash of residual anger at Melinda Anderson for her insults from a couple of weeks back, sensing that she had made Joann self-conscious about sharing her GED success with a university English professor.

"We're celebrating the completion of an important goal in my life," Joann said at last.

Joy was afraid that Clark would pry, but he was perceptive and merely congratulated her on both her success and their climb.

It was growing dark when the parking lot came into their view, and Joy was so thankful to see her aunt's jeep that she thought for a minute she would burst into tears. She was so exhausted, sore, and hungry that it was all she could do to keep from whining like one of her four-year-olds. She slung her backpack onto the ground beside the jeep and plopped down on the gravel nearby.

"Joy, we did it! We hiked the entire mountain!" Joann said, dumping her backpack too. She bent to give Joy a hug. "Thank you *so* much, kiddo!"

"You're welcome. I'm glad I didn't quite hinder you from your summit, although I'm sure you were beginning to wonder."

Joann laughed, dropped a kiss on her head, and rose again to talk to Clark.

"Thank you again, ladies, more than I can express," Clark said. "I have to confess that I was not prepared to have had to spend a night on the trail. You rescued me from significant discomfort at the very least – or perhaps, even being eaten by a moose!"

Joy giggled at the mental picture of an herbivorous moose trying to consume someone as tall as it was. "We're glad you're safe," she said quickly.

"And now, I should drive home so I can arrive before midnight," Clark said. "I have an Australian Shepherd who will scold me if I'm out past her bedtime, and it's already nearly seven."

"You'd better continue to wear my glasses," Joann said.

"As much as I dislike admitting it, you're correct…that is, if you can spare them for a few days. If you'll give me your address, I'll mail them to you first thing on Monday."

"That will be all right. I hate to ask for them back at all, but I only have one pair with the accurate prescription lenses, and I wear them often."

"Of course!" Clark said. "I will return them as soon as the post office can manage. I'm very sorry for the inconvenience."

"Don't be sorry," Joann said, smiling. "Get home safely to your bossy dog."

Clark opened the door of his car – a Subaru Outback – and grabbed a loose sheet of paper. "Here," he

195

said, offering it and a pen to Joann. "If you'll write down your address for me…"

Joann took the paper, which happened to be a church bulletin from South Lake church of Christ, and complied. "Clark, you're a Christian, aren't you?" she said kindly as she returned the pen and paper. Joy raised her head and paid attention again.

"Ahhh…yes – how did you – oh, this bulletin gave me away, eh?" he chuckled.

"Not only the bulletin – your references to heaven and your respectful manner did too – but yes, I noticed the bulletin. It's always nice to meet brothers in Christ. Joy and I worship with the church in East Montpelier."

"What a small world it is in the church, even here in the Northeast," Clark answered, smiling at them. "And thank you both again for showing a Christian attitude to me today. Have a safe drive home!"

Joann tossed their packs into the backseat and waved as Clark drove away, and then she held out her hands to Joy, offering to pull her up from the ground. Joy accepted, allowing herself a good, long moan as she stood. Joann grinned at her but kept her mouth shut.

The dashboard clock read 6:50 as Joann turned the key in the ignition. "Ugh, look at that, we're two hours behind our ideal schedule," Joy said. "I need to call Paul. He's probably getting worried."

"I should call Alex too," Joann said. "Because I can't drive directly home – I *have* to eat some supper as soon as possible. I was nearly hungry enough to begin gnawing on a tree that last mile. And I don't want a little cheeseburger or anything, either."

"I'm starving too. Why don't you drive toward civilization, and I'll ask Paul to let Alex know that you're okay but will still be gone a while."

"Deal! Is Chinese all right with you? There's a decent buffet in Stowe…"

"I could eat all of it by myself right now. Go, go!"

"I'd fight you for it!"

Paul had grown concerned, but he was impressed by Joy's short summary of their assistance to Clark. "Don't rush," he said. "We're fine. The kids know you might not be back until they're asleep, and they're so worn out from playing with Marie's kids all afternoon that they don't even seem to mind. I'd let them stay up and wait for you, but since tomorrow's Sunday, I figured I shouldn't."

"No, they'll have a hard time getting through worship if they stay up too late. And we're going to have a buffet, so it may be 9:30 or 10 by the time we're back."

"Oh, yum. Have fun. I'll call Alex as soon as I get off the phone with you."

"Thanks!"

"Oh, and sweetheart? I'm very, very thankful that you're safe."

"So am I, Paul!"

The ravenous hikers ate and ate and drank glass after glass of water until they felt replenished – and after that, they had some ice cream. "Joy," Joann said, pushing her dish forward. "I have not eaten this much in months – maybe even years."

"I know," Joy said. "Look at all these empty plates in front of me – it's embarrassing!"

"But *so* delicious – and *so* necessary. I could hike another mountain now!"

Joy glared at her aunt. "Has anyone ever told you that your energy level is annoying?"

Joann laughed. "I'm joking, dear heart. I promise. My calves are as tight as vises, and my knees ache. I absolutely am not ready to hike another mountain tonight."

"That's more like it," Joy grumbled, trying to get out of her chair without falling back into it.

A cold rain had begun as they were inside the restaurant, and the fog from the mountains had settled down into the valleys. They had barely left Stowe when Joy noticed Joann blinking often and rubbing her eyes. "You're wishing you had those glasses back now, aren't you?" Joy said.

197

"I am," Joann admitted. "They're much better for night driving in the rain than my contacts are…someday in the not-too-distant future, I may need to give up the contacts entirely. And my eyes are getting tired too."

"Let's switch. I can drive."

"Are you sure? You're so sore and tired that you can hardly walk."

"I'll manage. There's no need in you straining your eyes."

Joann consented, and Joy swapped seats, swallowing all the noises she felt like making every time she moved. She drove cautiously around the unfamiliar curves, giving thanks for her own perfect vision in the low visibility of the weather conditions.

To Joy's relief, the fog lifted a little while before they reached the interstate, and she zipped along comfortably after that. Joann offered to drive again, but Joy told her to rest her eyes. The dark car seemed cozy, comforting, and conducive to deep conversation.

"Aunt Joann, do you think I should give up my rental property?" Joy asked abruptly.

"Mmm…" Joann said, not startled at all by Joy's fast dip into serious talk. "Tell me why you're thinking about this."

"It's impossible for me to keep up with everything right now – to take care of Paul and the kids, homeschool, maintain the house and the laundry, and serve others outside our family. Add in being a landlady, and I'm too overwhelmed. Getting more sleep has helped a little, but not enough."

"You forgot something in your list of duties," Joann said.

"Oh? I'm sure I did…"

"You forgot to include taking time for yourself – for Bible study, for exercise, for writing, for all the things you've shared that you struggle to fit in. They're important too, dear heart."

"Oh. Right. All of that too. But the money those apartments bring in – it's not that much because I intentionally price my rent so low through the foundation, but it's not something we need to lose."

"And have you decided against hiring a property manager?"

"Not completely. Paul thinks I should, but he's left the choice up to me. I hate to lower my profit margin even more by hiring someone to do something I feel like I should be able to do myself, though."

Joann did not answer immediately, but after seven years of closeness to her, Joy did not expect her to. She knew that her aunt was still focused on their conversation and was finding – and possibly even praying over – her answer.

"Whose expectations are you following, Joy? Paul's? Society's? Your own?" Joann questioned her gently.

"Ummm...what do you mean exactly? You and Paul are the only people I've consulted about this..."

"Who has made you believe you 'should' be able to juggle all these responsibilities at the same time?"

"I – I don't know," Joy admitted. "It wasn't Paul. And it obviously wasn't you. It – it probably was some combination of my own expectations – or – or ideals, I guess, and comparing myself to other people."

"Sometimes our own expectations are the hardest to fulfill?"

"Yeah, maybe so."

"Joy, I can't give you the answer, you know that. But if you're holding onto the concept of doing the work on your property all by yourself solely from a sense of obligation to your own expectations – you've answered your own question, in my opinion."

Joy sniffed. "You're usually right about these things. But – who would I hire? Most people wouldn't appreciate Looking Up or be willing to help me uphold its principles..."

Joann thought for another moment. "I wish I could do it – and for the most part, I could, but if you had any more mold issues, I'd be forced to throw the work back onto someone else again. You'd be even more successful in reducing your workload if you found someone who managed the property and did repairs as well."

"That would free up more of Paul's time too," Joy said.

"Let's see…oh, of course! Jack! You could ask Jack if he's interested. He's recently landed a new job, thanks to having a GED. The hours are better and shorter, and it's a lower management position, so he may be able to climb in the company – it's at a Stewarts. It was a bit of a pay cut, though, because he doesn't have overtime now, so he has more time on his hands but less money coming in."

"And you think he'd respect Looking Up?"

"I do. Even though Jack isn't a Christian, he respects morality and decent behavior, and he thinks the world of Paul. I believe you could trust him."

"I suppose that's what I'll try to do, then," Joy said.

Joann held up one hand. "Okay, kiddo. Listen to your old aunt for another minute or two. I'm going to make both of us squirm now. You've told me several times over the years that you admire me. Is that still true?"

"Aunt Joann! Of course!"

"For which of my accomplishments do you admire me?"

"Whaaaaat…"

"I'm serious. Do you admire me because I've won prestigious awards – and no, doing well on a GED test 40 years late doesn't count as prestigious – or do you admire me because of my advanced education, my glorious career, the stack of novels I've written – or maybe the many political positions I've held?"

"But you don't – you haven't…"

"Exactly, Joy," Joann interrupted her. "I don't, and I haven't. I am a skinny old housewife with hardly any education and no background or prestige whatsoever. No one has heard of me unless they've known me, and my family name dies with me. I'm not even on Google, except on whitepages.com and similar websites – yes, I've checked. I should remind you that I'm basically the most ordinary person ever, in case you've somehow forgotten."

"Good grief, Aunt Joann. Those things don't matter. I don't admire you because of what you've accomplished...or haven't, in the world's eyes. You know that who you are as a person is what matters to me." Joy paused. "Oh," she said more quietly. "Oh."

"Then why do you hold yourself to these expectations, ones that you'd never impose on me or anyone else you love and admire?"

"I – I understand now. I'm sorry."

"Don't apologize to me, dear heart. As uncomfortable as I am when you praise me, I love how unpretentious you are – that you appreciate me for whom I am instead of what I've done, and I am thankful – so thankful – to feel needed. But I think you'd better apologize to you – to my sweet, sweet girl – for being unreasonable and harsh."

Joy reached over to squeeze her aunt's hand in gratitude. She did feel squirmy – but also convicted. She *was* hard on herself – harder than she should be – harder than she was on anyone else. They finished their journey in silence.

CHAPTER 23

A week after Joy's epic hike, around the time she could move her legs again without her calves screaming in pain, she and Katie were enjoying a warmer Saturday afternoon on the front porch of the farmhouse while Paul and the triplets played ball in the yard. The women clapped and cheered as Annie caught the small football her daddy had thrown to her.

"I almost feel like joining them," Katie said, smiling.

"Really? That's wonderful! Go for it!"

"I haven't thrown a football since Paul was a child," Katie protested.

"It's a toy football!" Joy said. "Come on – if you feel that well, do it!"

"Okay, okay," Katie got up slowly from the porch swing and headed to play with the others, her first active playtime with the children in years.

Joy watched them with happiness in her heart. Katie's recovery was now complete, and while she did still have some pain from arthritis, she felt so much stronger and more energetic that she never complained. Not long after Katie joined the game, Joy noticed an Asian make of car driving creeping down her dead-end road. It was exceptionally clean. "Tourist," Joy muttered to herself, grinning. She stood to look at the license plate as the car passed. Ontario, Canada. "Lost tourist."

Joy wasn't surprised when the car came back down the road soon, but she did not expect to see it enter her driveway seconds later. The windows were too tinted for her to see the driver, so she stayed at the top of the porch stairs until she could be sure they were going to ask for directions. When a tall, familiar figure climbed out and waved, Joy was astonished; Clark Campbell was standing in her driveway.

"Hello," he said. "I know you weren't expecting to see me again…"

"Oh, hi," Joy said, remembering at last to close her mouth. By this time, Paul had come to the front yard, and Katie and the triplets followed him at a slower pace. "It's – it's good to see you again. Paul, this is Clark, the man we met on our hike last week."

The men shook hands, and Clark jumped into an explanation. "I was looking for your aunt to return her glasses," he said, pulling them from his shirt pocket. "It took longer than I expected to have mine repaired, but I still would have mailed Joann's back already except that our esteemed postal service decided to go on a strike this week, and we won't receive or be able to send mail until next week."

"Do you only have one way to send mail in Canada?" Joy said. "I always assumed you had FedEx or UPS like we have..."

"Oh, we do, but they're overcome with extra packages right now, and prompt delivery would have been almost as expensive as delivering the glasses myself and treating you ladies – and your spouses, of course – to dinner – so here I am. But I didn't find your aunt at home."

"That was so nice of you! What a long drive it was for you, though."

"Only about three hours, and I have nothing but time now. Except for church events, I haven't quite – found my groove again yet." Clark smiled slightly. "I'm so relieved that I recognized you, and that you live nearby so you can return these to Joann."

"I am too. I'm sure she'd want to see you and to introduce you to Alex, her husband. Would you mind waiting while I call her quickly and see if they're nearby?"

"Yes, please," Clark said. "Thank you."

As Joy called her aunt's call, and then, predictably, Alex's, Paul introduced Clark to Katie and to the children. The children monopolized him once they realized that he was the "lost man from Mommy's mountain," as Gideon said. Clark smiled at them and answered their chatter patiently, but he hardly took his eyes from Katie. Finally, once the triplets were distracted by Joy getting off the phone, Clark said quietly to Katie. "Are you certain you're Paul's mother? You look far too young."

Katie blushed to the roots of her hair. "You'd better hang on to those glasses after all," she laughed. Paul heard their exchange and struggled to hold back a snicker.

"Well, Aunt Joann and Alex have gone to town for a few errands, and they'll be back in an hour. Can you wait that long? She understands if you can't," Joy said.

"Of course. And I was serious in my offer of dinner – for you and Paul and your children, and for Joann and her husband if they'd like, and also for Katie and – and anyone she would like to bring as well. My treat."

"Good grief – you'd be feeding an army," Joy said. "And – don't you see – I have not one, not two, but *three* preschoolers! Are you sure you'd want to dine publicly with us?"

Clark chuckled. "The invitation stands. We could go to a family-friendly place – maybe get some – ah – frozen dairy confection – and then no one would be shocked by a few lively children."

Joy looked at Paul, who shrugged. "We'd be glad to," he said. "Mom, you up for it too?"

"It sounds fun," she said, smiling.

Joy texted Alex about the dinner invitation, and he and Joann accepted, promising to be back about 5:30.

Joy invited Clark to sit on the porch, and he did so willingly. Paul took the children inside to give them their baths early so that the unexpected meal out would not delay their bedtimes too much; he did their baths on the weekends since he was often grading papers during the week.

"I – I think I'm going to run home to change," Katie said, standing abruptly. She smoothed her ancient blue jeans self-consciously. "I didn't expect to go anywhere else tonight. I'll be back before Joann and Alex are." Before Joy could reply, Katie had hurried to her car.

Joy shook her head, confused by her mother-in-law's uncharacteristically fast retreat, and then looked up to see Clark watching Katie intently as she drove away.

Suddenly, Joy thought she understood. Clark opened his mouth as if to speak, and then he closed it again. Despite his sophistication, Joy was reminded of a timid teenage boy as she watched him.

"Paul's father died several years ago after a long illness," Joy said softly. "It's been difficult for Katie."

"Oh, I see," Clark said, taking a deep breath. "I wondered if Paul's father was – was in the picture, so to speak, but I didn't want to ask or assume."

"No, his father died of congestive heart failure about six years ago, after years of poor health. He was an amazing Christian man, and we all miss him." Joy paused, choosing her words cautiously. "But Katie – Katie is still so – so vibrant – so very much alive. And lonely." She made eye contact with Clark, willing him to be perceptive enough to pick up on her cues.

"Thank you," he said. "Thank you for understanding. I've only been alone a short time myself, and I don't consider myself to be 'on the market' again. But when I drove up and saw her – saw Katie – playing with the children in the autumn sunlight – I couldn't believe how beautiful she was. And when she teased me, it – it felt like that I'd known her forever." He sighed. "You must think I'm a silly, desperate old fool."

"Not at all," Joy assured him.

"I suppose Katie must be about my age, unless she had Paul as an utter child," Clark said. "I'm 58. Naturally, I'd never ask you to divulge another lady's age – but – she is at least in the same – *era* – as I am, isn't she?"

Joy smiled at his gentlemanly information fishing. "Yes, in the same era," she said. "And so are Alex and Aunt Joann. I think you could all be very good friends."

"I – I would like that very much," Clark murmured.

Katie returned, looking tidy and cheerful in nicer jeans and a fitted blouse, as the scrubbed triplets bounded back outside. Five minutes later, Alex and Joann arrived. The porch was a noisy hubbub of greetings and introductions for some time, and during the busyness, Joy slipped back into the house to brush her hair. Joann followed her soon afterward and hurried to take out her contacts to give her eyes some relief at last.

"Ahhh," she groaned. "It's been a long week. I can't believe I'm voluntarily leaving my house and going out in public with my glasses on – when I'm not even sick – but my eyes are *so* scratchy from all the extra hours of contacts!"

"I'm sure!" Joy answered. "You must have been wondering what was taking your glasses so long to arrive in the mail."

"Yes!"

They all decided to eat at Friendly's, even though the Graham/Martin family had been there so recently, because it was kid-friendly and had ice cream for the children, although Joy soon discovered that Clark was as interested in the ice cream as her four-year-olds were. Katie rode with Paul and Joy and the children in their van, and Clark rode with Alex and Joann.

Friendly's was quite crowded, so they had to sit at two booths instead of all together at a large table. Paul and Joy found themselves sharing a table with their children while the four other adults conversed in the other booth.

"Well, this is an unexpected treat – dinner with the four of you on someone else's dime," Paul murmured to Joy.

She laughed. "Right? I do feel like we're a little – cut off – from the party over there, but it's good to see them enjoying each other's company."

"They practically seem like they're on a double date," said Paul. "And Mom looks happier – and younger – than she has in years."

"How does that make you feel, sweetheart?" Joy whispered.

Paul took a deep breath. "A little sad, but mostly thankful. A few months ago, I thought I was about to lose my mom too. Seeing her like this – so – so *lively* again makes me relieved, even though the thought of her showing interest in a man other than my dad feels super weird." Joy nodded and blew him a kiss across the table.

The adults sat in Paul and Joy's living room and talked into the night after the triplets were in bed, because Paul had convinced Clark to sleep in their spare room that night and worship with them the next morning instead of driving all the way back to Ontario. He had agreed enthusiastically, called a neighbor to let his dog out, and settled in for the evening as if he belonged. The discussion encompassed all kinds of solemn topics – including politics and religion – and plenty of light-hearted ones, and it was a full two hours before Alex and Joann left to return home. Katie lingered for a few moments longer, although Paul and Joy had also said good night not long after the Martins left.

"Is Paul your only child?" Clark asked Katie.

Katie chuckled. "He's my only son…but I also have four daughters, and now, three sons-in-law. Oh, and five other grandchildren, plus one on the way."

Clark's eyes opened wide. "What a family!" he exclaimed. "Your house must be a busy place when everyone visits."

Katie sobered. "We haven't actually managed a full family reunion yet…my daughter Fiona is in Maine, Celeste is in Virginia, Jennifer is in South Carolina, and until August, Marie was in Italy. But yes, we are a big, noisy crowd." She hesitated, then continued. "How about you? Do you have any children and grandchildren?"

Clark smiled wistfully. "Not exactly. We couldn't have kids, but we did foster one teenage boy for a year a decade ago. He was never eligible for adoption, but he calls me Pop Clark – it's supposed to sound like Pop Tart, he tells me. He's a Navy Seal overseas, so I don't see much of him."

"Pop Clark! That's hysterical. How in the world did he come up with that?"

Clark dropped his head. "I, ah, seem to have a rather well-known sweet tooth, I'm embarrassed to say, and when I was a decade younger and healthier, I kept a box of Pop Tarts in the glove compartment of my car."

"Once? Or at all times?" Katie giggled.

"At all times." Clark's ears were crimson. "I don't do that anymore – my doctor convinced me that I needed to cut back on the sugar years ago – but Jared was impressed by my stash when he lived with us."

Katie could hardly contain her laughter. "I'm sorry," she said, bursting into giggles again. "You just look and seem so – so sophisticated and health-conscious. And the Pop Tart story was such a random surprise."

"Any sophistication is at least 50% city slicker – and the rest of it is a mere illusion. I had to appear that I had life figured out every weekday for over thirty years as a college professor, but that didn't mean that I actually was that person." He grinned.

"I hear you. I spent several years as a high school English teacher. If you let the students think you're not confident and put together, they'll eat you."

Clark laughed. "You do understand! I didn't realize you'd been a teacher too – that we had that in common too."

"Yes, although I can hardly compare a dozen years of teaching – not even a dozen consecutive years – to your long career as a university professor! I don't even have a master's degree."

"Ah, but all teaching is fundamentally the same, and we both taught young people who were attempting to – as they say – learn how to adult. I'm sure you can relate quite well despite your years at a much bigger job – raising your children."

Katie caught his eyes and smiled wide. "Thank you," she said. "I *do* consider that to have been my most important job – and one that I would have continued full-time if it weren't for my husband's poor health and eventual death."

"That must have been such a difficult time for you." Clark's voice was husky.

"Yes. He'd been – we'd been farmers, you see, and we couldn't keep our heads above water once his health failed. I'm a pretty tough cookie, but I couldn't farm alone with a house full of girls in school, and Paul was already on his own at that point. We ended up losing the farm in a short-sale right after Jean's death."

"I'm so sorry."

"So was I, but life is good again now too, just very, very different...but it has been much longer for me than it has for you, Clark. How are you holding up?"

Clark fixed his eyes on the clock across the room. "In some ways, I'm relieved," he said finally. "She suffered for seven entire years, and she was so ready for heaven by the end of it. I had plenty of time to say goodbye – or, at least, to say goodbye to our happy, healthy, active lives together. At the same time, though, I feel adrift. I took early retirement two months before her death, so I lost both of my primary earthly responsibilities in one summer. My friends have cautioned me to be aware of the danger of becoming depressed, but I'm – not certain what I should be doing."

"Yes," Katie said. "I'm sorry. It's so hard."

"Did your husband – did Jean suffer long too?"

"Yes, but so gradually at first that we didn't prepare well. He developed diabetes at a young age and didn't take good care of his body, mainly because he was working such long hours on the farm. He also had to combat some major genetic tendencies for bad health. All at once, within a couple of years, he had to have a leg amputated and went into congestive heart failure. He was only 61 – the age I am now – when he passed away in 2013. I – I can relate to feeling adrift as well – I still do sometimes, in fact."

Clark stood up and quickly crossed the space between himself and Katie. "Katie," he said. "This – ah – ah – today, has been the first time since Bridget's death that I've felt – felt like myself again. It seems as though I've known you for many years instead of a few hours. Would you – would you like to try to keep in contact – and help each other in our drifting stage?"

Katie stood up too. "That would be wonderful," she said.

"I'm not – not asking you for a – a dating relationship," Clark stammered. "I'm not ready for that, although you do seem to be an amazing and attractive lady. But – would you like to be friends – and see what happens down the road?"

Katie's eyes were full. "Yes. Yes, let's be friends," she whispered. She turned to go home at last, but Clark caught her arm and gently kissed her hand before bidding her good night.

CHAPTER 24

It seemed to Joy that she blinked, and the holidays had arrived already that year. Thanksgiving was a hectic time for her, because she was hosting the meal – for everyone – since Paul and Joy's house was the largest. For the first time since Joy's marriage, Paul's entire living family was going to be together. Celeste and her husband and children were flying in on the Tuesday before, and Jennifer would fly in the following day. Fiona and her family were driving in on Wednesday as well. And Alex and Joann and Clark and Jack were all invited too. The total number at Thanksgiving dinner would be 23.

Joy had intended to ask Jack, finally, on Thanksgiving, if he'd be interested in being her property manager. The same tenant who had left his window open and caused so much damage during the summer had also exploded a printer cartridge across most of one wall, and the eight hours that Joy and Joann had spent the week before, repainting the entire living room while suffering from the sneezy cold they were all passing around, were enough to make Joy throw in the towel once and for all. If she ever saw another can of white paint, it would be too soon, she thought with a shudder. She almost sneezed again remembering that day. But on the Monday before Thanksgiving, Joy changed her mind and decided that she would be far too busy to talk with Jack during the chaos of dinner, so she and Paul invited him over for dessert Monday evening to discuss her idea.

Jack accepted without hesitation. "That would be cool," he said. "I need something else to keep me busy now that my job is over so early in the evenings. I'm too young to be falling asleep in front of the TV at 8 p.m. and too old to be into some of the junk that my high school people are doing these days."

"Good for you!" Paul said.

"I can't believe you've been running that huge, old place by yourself all these years," Jack said to Joy. "It's ancient – there must be a million things that can go wrong with it."

"I've been fortunate," Joy answered, laughing. "There haven't been many repairs yet, and I've had good tenants until now. But I think this one problem guy is going to cause enough trouble to make up for it all by himself."

"Too bad he's only doing stupid stuff instead of illegal stuff, so you can't evict him," Jack said.

Paul snickered. "There's always hope."

"*Boys!*" Joy snapped at them, but she was grinning too.

By the time Jack left, they had settled on a salary, 25% of the rents plus reimbursement for all supplies. It was a higher pay rate than many property managers earned, but Jack would be performing maintenance as well as minor repairs too. The only task that Joy saved for herself was screening and interviewing potential tenants.

Joy heaved an immense sigh of relief as Jack drove away. "Thankful to be free from those burdens?" Paul asked, putting his arm around her shoulders.

"Ohhh yeah," she said. "I hung onto it far longer than I should have."

Paul, who had shared that view for most of their marriage, remained silent; he was sometimes much wiser than his years.

Thanksgiving was every bit as crazy as Joy had anticipated, and much more fun. Joy found herself bonding with Paul's other sisters in the same way she had with Marie, now that all of them except Jennifer were mothers. The cousins played together from sunup until sundown, not caring that many of them had barely met before. Only five years in age separated Celeste's oldest from Marie's youngest, so they were all still young enough to ignore their age differences. Best of all, six inches of snow fell on Thanksgiving morning and stayed on the ground through the weekend, so the children built snowmen and sledded as often as their parents allowed for three days straight. Joy cheerfully ran a load of cousin laundry – socks and coats and hats and mittens, plus an occasional stray adult's item – every night, shaking her head at the thought of separating the clothes again when everyone went home. She knew for a fact that four of the nine children wore the same size of clothes – including two of her own kids – and that Annie had been wearing snow pants for two days that belonged to another cousin!

On Saturday afternoon, Joy and Joann took kid-watching duty outside while Katie talked to all her children in the living room. Alex, Clark, and Paul's brothers-in-law had disappeared to build a bonfire for later in Alex's yard, so Katie took the opportunity to speak privately to Paul and his sisters about her growing friendship with Clark. Joy knew what was happening inside and was nervous on Katie's behalf. She paced around the back yard until her aunt asked her if she'd swallowed a wind-up toy.

"What?" Joy said, startled. "Oh. Ha. No, I have something on my mind."

Joann verified that the children were all preoccupied and leaned close. "The big conversation in the house?"

"Yes. Katie's talking to them about Clark."

Joann grinned. "I thought so. I'm so happy for her, that she's found a special friend."

"Oh, so am I, and Paul has made his peace with it too, but I have no idea how the others will react. And I know they're not officially dating or anything yet...but they're perfect for each other."

"Let's pray about it." Joann grabbed Joy's gloved hands in her own and said a quick prayer for the outcome of the conversation. When Joy opened her eyes, Gideon was standing beside her, staring at them.

"Mommy, why are you praying in the snow?" he asked.

"Ummm...we were asking God to bless Grandma Katie," Joy stammered.

"Oh. Okay. Aunt Joann, can you take me sledding down the big hill?" Gideon said. The big hill was in an empty field, and none of the children were allowed to go there without adult supervision because the field was located across the road from the farmhouse.

Joann, who had sledded, sledded with kids in her lap, pulled sleds up the hill for small children, and taken approximately 20 snowball hits to every part of her body every day, moaned. Joy giggled. "I think Aunt Joann is tired of sledding," she said. "I can take you instead."

"But Mooommmy...it's more fun when Aunt Joann goes!"

Joy laughed. Four year olds! "And why is that?"

"Because she screams really loud every time. She is the bestest screamer – more than me or Micah or Annie or the cuz-lins!"

Joy laughed again. "I guess I can't compete with that, Aunt Joann."

"Okay, okay. Yes, Gideon, I'll take you across the road," Joann said, laughing too. "Let's ask if anyone else wants to go, though, because this is my last sledding session for today."

"Are you sure?" Joy asked. "I know they've been running you ragged."

"I'll survive," Joann muttered. "But this is absolutely the last time today. And probably tomorrow. I'm about to get frost bite on my rump."

Joy watched her trudge away, tickled at her aunt's rare grumbling and also gripped with thankfulness. She was thankful that her children had her aunt to love them and play with them, thankful that Joann had great-nephews and a great-niece to fill the void of not having her own children, and thankful that her aunt had the stamina for hours of outdoor winter activities without side effects other than sore muscles.

Joy didn't have a chance to speak with Paul about Katie's revelation until bedtime that night, when they finally collapsed together in their first privacy all day. "How was it? What did your sisters think?" she demanded the moment Paul's head hit his pillow.

"How was – what – oh, yeah," he mumbled, growing drowsy already. "It was fine. The only one of us who got – ah – emotional – was Celeste, since she's been gone since before he died, y'know." Paul yawned widely. "But she said she'd get used to the idea too."

'That's good," Joy said. "I was praying – and so was Aunt Joann – that it would go well."

"Thank you, sweetheart. Tell you more 'bout it in the morning," said Paul, his words beginning to slur with sleep. Joy kissed him and turned over, willing her over-tired mind to rest like Paul's.

In the short break between worship service and Bible class the next morning, Luca came hurrying up to Joy and handed her a folded sheet of paper. "Good morning," he said, his eyes full of excitement. "I have such an interesting story to tell you. One of my clients from the Northeast Kingdom, Sheila Bellows, is an independent film producer. She's also religious, and while she doesn't typically produce religious films, her work is always wholesome and positive. I told her about your book weeks ago and directed her to your new website. Last night, she sent to me an email, so I printed it for you."

"*Seriously*?" Joy squealed, fumbling to unfold the paper.

"Mr. Vianello," the email read. "Thank you so much for recommending your wife's sister-in-law's book. It was a lovely read, and she has great talent. I'd even go so far as to say that her book could make a successful film. I'd like to continue that thought process with Joy herself by phone. Would you have her call me at her convenience, please?" The email concluded with Sheila's phone number.

Joy sat down in the nearest chair, almost dizzy with excitement. Her book. A *movie*? "Thank you, Luca," she finally managed. "Thank you so much."

"It was nothing special. I am glad she read and enjoyed your book and contacted me. I recommend your book to almost everyone – it is fun to have an author in my family – but I don't think many of my clients read Christian fiction novels."

"Thank you," Joy said again. She jumped up. "Oh! I have to tell Paul! And Aunt Joann! And Alex!"

"Tell me what?" Paul said, coming up behind her. "I heard you squeal from inside the bathroom!"

Joy repeated the news to him, and he was as excited as she. She also squeezed in an announcement to her aunt and to Katie before Bible class began, but the others would have to find out afterward. Joann hugged her so tightly she could hardly breathe and whispered that she was so proud that she'd have a hard time concentrating on the class.

Joy's news dominated the conversation at lunch, the last meal that they would all share together before Celeste and her family flew back and Fiona and hers drove back that afternoon. Jennifer was taking a red-eye flight in the morning. Everyone congratulated her and chattered about where it would be filmed and who would act in it. Annie was convinced that she would be in the movie and would become a "movie star princess."

"Okay, hang on a second!" Joy shouted at last above the pandemonium. "I haven't even talked to this woman yet. This may not even happen at all. She may tell me that all the references to God must be cut out or that I have to add things to the plot that aren't appropriate. And I'd probably have to give up some of my rights to my book, and I don't know if I should or want to do that. I'm super excited, but I'm not getting my hopes up."

"I still think you'll end up famous," said Jennifer, and Joy laughed and let the speculations resume.

Joy made herself wait until 9 a.m. on Monday to call. Joann came over to keep the triplets occupied so Joy could talk in peace, promising to let them help her decorate Christmas cookies later if they did puzzles and Play Doh quietly now. Joy took her cell phone into her bedroom, shut the door, and sank into the cushions of her window seat that Paul had built for her for their second anniversary. She took a deep breath, whispered an instant prayer, and tapped the phone number into the keypad.

Sheila answered on the second ring, to Joy's surprise. "Ah, Mrs. Graham – may I call you Joy?" she said. "I'm so glad you got back to me quickly."

"Yes, please do," Joy said. "And thank you for your kind words about my book."

"It's gold, girl. Pure gold. Got a few rough edges, but there's potential in it for a heartwarming film."

"Wow," Joy said. "That sounds so exciting."

"It *is* exciting. It's so rare for me to come across material that is this wholesome without being preachy."

"Thank you."

"Obviously, before either of us can make any commitments about collaborating, we both need to ask and answer some questions, and I've typed up some changes that I think would have to be made to increase the popularity of the storyline. I'll email you that list today. But – do you have any questions you want to ask me today right away?"

"Hmmm...I think two questions come to mind immediately," said Joy, trying to sound calm and professional.

"Yes?"

"I know you mentioned that you appreciated that my book wasn't 'preachy,' but would you be planning to eliminate all the references to God and the Bible and the church when you made the movie?"

"Not at all," Sheila said. "They would stay subtle, as you have them, but I'd keep that underlying theme. I've never made a religious movie – never enjoyed the ones I've seen – they're usually so sappy or fake, but I believe your book could change that for me."

"Well, that's the most important aspect of it for me," Joy replied, her excitement rising. "So I'm thankful we'd be on the same page there. My other question is whether or not I'd retain any rights to my book."

"Absolutely. I would not have any rights to your book itself, only the rights to create a movie from its material. I would have full rights to the movie, although naturally, you'd receive major compensation for allowing me to produce a movie from your book. I mean, I'm a small-time producer – we aren't talking about Hollywood here, but I've never bought movie rights for less than $2000."

"Oh. That's – that's good to know," Joy said. To herself, she was silently screaming, "Breathe. Breathe. Two thousand dollars. Breathe!"

"So, if we're in agreement so far, I'll send you that list, and you can read it and think about it. In a week or so, I'll have a better idea of what the film budget would be, and I'll also email you a copy of my standard contract for when I purchase rights to produce a film from a book so you have a better idea of what you'd be getting into. And I'll also have a price range for you soon – in a week to ten days."

"Ahhh...okay," said Joy. "That sounds good."

Their conversation ended after that, and Joy punched the end call button on her phone before permitting herself a crazed shriek aloud. Then she thundered down the stairs to tell her aunt. She wished so much that she could call Paul, but his planning period wasn't until after lunch. He'd said he'd text her if he was able.

Joann hugged her and chattered with her. "Now I'm nervous about this *list* she mentioned," Joy said a few minutes later, her adrenaline rush beginning to fade for the first time in twenty-four hours. "Probably she's talking about minor things – editing that I need to do, or a different order for a few of the events, or something like that. But I really have no idea what to expect."

"I've never created anything a fraction as important as a novel," Joann said. "So I can't relate completely, but I'd imagine that the thought of giving up *any* control – even creative control – of your – your book baby – is pretty daunting, eh?"

"Eh," Joy agreed, laughing, never too preoccupied to tease her aunt about one of her rare Canadian-isms.

"Mommy, are you having a baby?" Annie piped up, her eyes huge.

"Whaaaaaat?" Joy shouted, and then she remembered Joann's word choice that, while accurate, must have been confusing to a four-year-old. "Oh. Oh, no, sweetheart. Aunt Joann was just – just saying that I'm – that my book is…oh…rats…help…" she trailed off.

"Your mommy wrote her book before she had any real babies – before you and the boys were born, and she worked very hard to make her book, so she is really happy when people like it," said Joann, anxious to unravel the chaos she'd inadvertently created. "She's proud of her work on her book – but not nearly as proud as she is of you and Micah and Gideon."

"Yes, yes!" said Joy. "Yes, exactly. Aunt Joann is right, Annie."

"Oh, okay," Annie said. "I was hoping for a little sister. Or maybe a baby unicorn."

Joy took a deep breath. And then another. "No, sweetie. No sisters. Or unicorns." Joann excused herself to the bathroom, probably to laugh hysterically, Joy realized between breaths. If only she had that privilege now so she wouldn't hyperventilate to keep from howling.

CHAPTER 25

Sheila's email didn't arrive until almost suppertime. It contained a line of apology – her day had become unexpectedly hectic following their phone call, as well as the list in an attachment. Joy had set her email notifications on her phone to full volume and had been jumping all day every time one came in. When the anticipated email finally chimed through, Joy squealed, "It's here!"

"Why don't you go sit and read it?" said Paul. "I'll stir the soup and take the rolls out of the oven if I need to."

"Oh, thank you!" Joy needed no additional urging. She threw herself onto the couch and opened the attachment with shaking fingers.

Five minutes later, she was confused. The list was short, but also vague. The most difficult portion to understand was in the section marked "characters." Sheila had written, "Aunt Julia is the salt of the earth, and I can see her and hear her from your book, but she needs something more for the film. Pizzazz?"

"Pizzazz?" Joy whispered. "What is she talking about?" She returned to the kitchen to show Paul the list.

He pushed his glasses up his nose – no matter what, he couldn't keep them from slipping – and read it in an instant – lightning fast.

"Wait – what? Pizzazz?" he said.

"That's what I said too."

"That doesn't make sense. Why would she think that a farmer's wife needs pizzazz?"

"I don't know, but I think I need to discuss this list with her in person. She may be an incredible movie producer, but she writes weird lists!" Joy said, frustrated.

Joy didn't tell anyone else about Sheila's comments, merely saying that she was trying to schedule face-to-face negotiations, and she emailed her back that night, sharing her desire to discuss the deal in person. Sheila agreed, suggesting that they share dinner in Montpelier that weekend and promising to bring the contract with her if possible.

Joy moved through the rest of that week like a robot. She went through the motions of cleaning and laundry and parenting and cooking, but her mind was preoccupied with her upcoming meeting. On Friday, the day before the scheduled dinner, Joy was almost beside herself with a combination of excitement and nerves. Joann came over to eat lunch with Joy and the children because Alex was away for the day at an old colleague's funeral, so Joy attempted to whip up a pot of hearty vegetable beef soup for herself and her aunt instead of the PBJs she had planned.

They all sat down to eat together, the triplets with their preferred sandwiches, and the women with their soup. After the prayer, Joy sat in distracted silence for a moment instead of eating, but Joann tried a bite, gasped, and began coughing. Joy jumped from her chair, assuming that her aunt had inhaled a vegetable or something and prepared to try to assist her. "No, no!" Joann croaked, waving her away and gulping water. "I'm – not – choking. It's – spicy!"

"What? The soup's too spicy? I only put black pepper in it," Joy said, puzzled. Her aunt could scarf down a plate of Mexican food with the best of them, and Joy's soup recipe was not hot at all. Joy put a spoonful of soup to her lips, felt a fiery sensation almost right away, and spit out the liquid into her bowl. "Oh! What did I *do*?" she moaned.

Joann, nose and eyes streaming, was squinting at her bowl of soup. She sniffed it too. "Joy, it looks and smells like it's full of cayenne pepper!" she said.

Joy hurried over to her spice cupboard. "Ohhhh...man...seriously! Aunt Joann, you're right!"

"How did that happen?" Joann said, still coughing a bit.

"I bought some new sea salt on sale last week, and I wanted to see if it would improve the flavor of the soup, so I decided to use it today...but it was sitting beside my

221

cayenne pepper, and the container is a similar size and color. And now my cayenne pepper container is almost *empty*!"

"And you laugh at me for being blind!" Joann teased her, blowing her nose with a paper napkin.

"It had nothing to do with my eyes – just my mind. I'm losing my mind this week, Aunt Joann! I'm so excited but so afraid of making the wrong decision about this movie!"

"Dear heart, whether or not your book becomes a world-famous movie doesn't change anything about you or your abilities. You'll still be a wonderful, talented woman – wife, mommy, niece, author, Christian – regardless. And a generally decent cook most of the time these days...except for maybe today..."

"Thank you, Aunt Joann," she said. "But I *am* sorry. This is terrible. I'll throw it away. Do you want a PBJ like the kids had?"

"Yes, please, with some milk too. My throat is still on fire," Joann admitted.

Joy covered her face. "Aaaagggh!"

"No worries," Joann said. "It happens to all of us."

"But not this badly! There's enough cayenne in there for twenty pots of gumbo! Do you want, like, a Tums too?"

"I'll take some peppermint when I get home," Joann said. "Try to relax, kiddo. This – as well as the movie situation – will all turn out all right in the end." Joy took a deep breath, nodded, and tried to believe her.

Joy was not scheduled to meet Sheila until 1 p.m., but by 11:30 a.m. on Saturday, she was so antsy that Paul urged her out the door an hour early and suggested that she take a short walk in the park beforehand to calm her nerves. Joy left willingly, anxious to get away before she bit someone's head off or began wailing.

Joy slipped into a parallel parking space half a block down from the upscale downtown restaurant, only a few minutes early after a chilly stroll through the park. She tugged at her basic blouse and dress pants and scowled at her old black shoes. The simple life in Vermont was certainly her preference now, but her current wardrobe was not conducive to professionalism.

Sheila had described her appearance and told Joy that she would wait in the entryway of the restaurant, so, when Joy walked in the door, she glanced around the empty space and then sat down in a chair to wait. She attempted to relax as she observed the elegant dining area in the next room and listened to the soft music and chiming of silverware against china. She smiled as she contrasted lunch time at this establishment, one of the town's finest, with lunch time for Paul and the triplets at home. Someone at home would have already spilled ketchup or milk down his shirt by now!

Sheila was slightly late, but Joy knew who she was the moment she breezed into the door. She was of average height, slender, and dressed far more glamorously than most of the people Joy knew in Vermont. She wore tasteful cosmetics and jewelry and managed to appear much younger than she actually was – Joy knew she'd graduated from NYU in 1975.

Joy rose to greet her, they shook hands, and then they hurried to claim Sheila's reservation before it was given away, for almost every table was filled.

"Let's eat before we discuss business," Sheila suggested as they opened their menus, and Joy agreed, but she inwardly moaned at the thought of consuming any food until she had calmed down.

As soon as Joy caught a glimpse of the prices on the menu, she understood why she had never eaten there before. A bowl of soup was almost fifteen dollars, and the entrees began at $24.99. Joy was careful not to show her shock, but when she only ordered a bowl of the house minestrone, Sheila spoke up.

"Joy, I'm paying for this meal," she said. "I'd never presume to meet up at the most expensive place in Montpelier otherwise. I've been wanting to try this restaurant for years, and today seemed to be a good opportunity."

"Oh, it's fine – I mean, thank you, but I'm honestly not very hungry," Joy said.

"Perhaps you'll be in the mood for dessert later, after we've finished," Sheila said. Joy smiled, but she had her doubts that she'd be ready to eat much for hours.

Joy sipped her soup spoonful by difficult spoonful, while Sheila ate soup, salad, and manicotti, not completing any of her courses, but enjoying each portion of her meal. She set her plates aside to be taken away instead of asking for a take-away box, and Joy hid a grin as she realized yet another way her own life had changed in the past few years – she'd once done the same as Sheila without a second thought, but now she was subconsciously calculating how many triplet meals could have been made from her dining companion's leftovers.

"Now, let's talk business," said Sheila at last. Joy laid down her spoon, thankful to stop pretending to eat. "First – what do you think about the list I emailed you? Any deal breakers in there?"

"Most of it seemed fine, but I wasn't sure exactly what you meant by your comments on the characters, especially the ones about Aunt Julia."

"Mmm...yes. I remember I expressed some concern over her." Sheila took a printed copy of her list from her briefcase. "I'm re-reading precisely what I wrote...yes, I was rather vague; I apologize. I meant that I'm afraid Aunt Julia written as-is would not appeal to my typical movie patron. She's intended to be a strong secondary character – almost a secondary heroine, correct?"

"Yes," Joy said quietly, on the edge of her seat.

"She comes across as too plain – too ordinary. Not exotic or entertaining enough for the screen. She's neither young nor impressively old. She rescues her niece with hot tea and math lessons. That's very noble, and I have no doubt that there are many such women who exist, but they're not the people you see in movies."

"So, what are you proposing for me to do to her?" Joy said, her heart sinking.

224

"We need to jazz her up...make her much younger, more of an older sister relationship, or give her a stunning talent or a secret, wild past, or a side career in modeling...something that would have appealed to her teenage niece but would also fascinate our viewers."

"I understand now, but I don't know if I can..." began Joy. Sheila stopped her mid-sentence. "Don't decide now. Think about it for a while, please...and let me show you the contract."

Joy's worries shrank into obscurity when she read the contract. It was brief and straightforward and looked simple but legitimate. Sheila would purchase the right to make a movie from Joy's book over a two-year period, and if for some reason the deal fell through, or the movie was never completed, her option would expire after two years. And, Joy read with a thrill she could hardly conceal, Sheila had offered her three thousand dollars for it, not to mention the increased publicity her book would receive.

Joy's mind went wild for a few minutes over the possibilities. Three thousand dollars would update her ancient kitchen or replace their aging second vehicle or allow the triplets to take special classes and play sports or pay for all of them to take a real vacation or...the options were endless. Her family never lacked anything they needed on Paul's high school teacher salary plus her rental income, but major wants usually got postponed for months, years, or indefinitely. Three thousand dollars would change that for them for a little while.

"I can see that you're a bit overwhelmed," Sheila said, bringing Joy back down to earth with a thud. "Like I said, please, take some time to think. Don't decide today or tomorrow, or even next week. Christmas is coming up, and you'll probably be busy with your family. Give me your answer after the holidays, maybe at the beginning of the new year, all right?"

"That sounds good," Joy said.

"And don't forget – I love your book. It's refreshing and delightful. We just need to give it some more oomph in the right places to transition it into a successful movie."

Joy said her goodbyes and drove away in a daze, no less confused than she'd been before their meeting. "How in the world could I turn down thousands of dollars unless it was actually sinful?" she asked herself repeatedly as she zipped home in the growing shadows of the December afternoon. But another question always followed the first one. "How much am I willing to allow her to change such an important part of my book – of my account of my own past – for any amount of money?"

Joy waited until the children were asleep that night before she told Paul the details of her time talking with Sheila. First, she told him about Sheila's assessment of her character, Aunt Julia. Paul whistled. "She's asking an awful lot of you with that one," he said. "And I still don't get it. Making that character glamorous or mysterious would be like the covers on those Amish fiction books you see at Walmart, the ones with the supposedly Plain women covered in makeup."

Joy giggled, and he continued. "Okay, so that was an odd comparison. But I still don't see why she's so determined that your character has to change."

Joy expected Paul to jump up and down – or at least cheer – when she told him the amount Sheila had offered her for the rights to produce the movie. After all, as the primary wage earner in the family, he felt the most stress about managing their finances. Instead, when she told him, he took off his glasses and rubbed his eyes. "Well, that would be helpful," he said. "But you'll have to decide if it's worth it to you to let her re-vamp your book entirely like that."

"Don't you think that much money would be worth almost anything?" asked Joy.

"How I feel really doesn't matter, honey. I think your book is wonderful, and I'm super proud of it, but it's not my creation, and I wouldn't be the one doing the work of changing it. The decision has to be yours."

"Aaagh!" Joy wailed. "I don't want to have to decide!"

"Then take her advice and wait. Don't even think about it anymore for a few days, at least until I'm out of school for Christmas vacation."

Joy didn't think she would be able to push the dilemma from her mind at all, but the flurry of activities of the Christmas season took over soon. In the course of the next three weeks, Joy and the kids and sometimes Paul wrapped presents, went to a Christmas parade, welcomed Jennifer back again from grad school, brought home and decorated the Christmas tree, attended the annual church holiday party, went snow-shoeing with Joann, built more snowmen, went sledding several more times, baked gluten free Christmas cookies with Marie's girls, and taught Eva how to ice skate. Having three small children in the house, they also passed around a case of strep throat, so they spent three days in total quarantine until the triplets and Paul took enough of their antibiotics to stop being contagious and feel well again. Joy stayed well, somehow, despite the sleepless nights and fevered children coughing in her face, but by the Monday before Christmas, she had cabin fever so badly that Paul sent her out of the house, proclaiming himself recovered plenty to supervise the kids watching a movie.

"Are you sure?" she protested. Paul's fever had been higher than the children's, and he was still quite tired.

"Very sure! If I weren't on break, I'd be back at work tomorrow. I don't want you to end up sick after all from sheer exhaustion. Go get some fresh air."

"Oh, I almost never get strep for some reason, you know that..."

"Go!" Paul said. "We're fine. Go find someone to spend time with who has outgrown Polly Pockets and Duplos."

Joy laughed and left the house at last for the first time in several days. She knew that Luca and Marie were away for the day, taking the girls to see the children's museum in Norwich, and she was still a bit wary of exposing Katie to even a chance of bacteria. She drove to her aunt's house instead, without calling, figuring that even time spent in someone else's kitchen would feel like an escape from her own.

Joy had avoided alone time with Joann for the past few weeks. She'd seen her often, at worship and Bible study, of course, and they'd had fun with the entire family several times, but she hadn't sought her aunt out for any confidential conversations or initiated any one-on-one time with her. Joy had been debating about how to present her dilemma with her book to Joann, afraid that Sheila's opinions about the character Joann was modeled on would hurt her aunt somehow. She'd only told Joann that Sheila had requested some character changes she wasn't sure about, and Joann, probably sensing Joy's need for privacy in her decision-making process, hadn't pressed her. Joy was thankful for her aunt's perception, but she knew she couldn't continue to stay away without Joann becoming concerned.

Joann was climbing into her jeep when Joy drove up. She got back out to hug her niece. "You're leaving," Joy said. "Don't let me keep you from anything."

"Did Paul tell you to get out of the infirmary for some time to yourself?" Joann asked her, laughing.

"Yes, he did. It's obvious I've escaped this plague, and I've been at home for *days*. But I can go somewhere else if you're busy..."

"Just come with me if you'd like. I'm going ice skating."

"Alone?"

"That was the plan, but I'd love your company too."

"Are you going to a rink where I can rent skates?" Joy said.

"No, but I have another pair in the house. I'll get them if you're up for it."

"Sure," Joy said. "Thanks." She got into the jeep to wait while Joann disappeared into her house again. She leaned back in the passenger seat, sighed with pleasure at the opportunity not to have small fingers touching her for a few waking hours, and enjoyed a few moments of peace. Joann's vehicle, unlike Joy's van that had a colony of crumbs and used napkins and dirty preschooler socks at any given time, was tidy and smelled of some sort of essential oil instead of decomposing apples. Soft classical music was playing on the CD player, and the car diffuser was running.

Joy leaned forward, closer to the diffuser, closed her eyes, and took several deep breaths, trying to determine the identity of the oil in it. She was still uncertain when she opened her eyes and saw her aunt staring at her though the windshield, grinning.

Joann dropped into the driver's seat and tossed a pair of skates into the back floorboard. "It's bergamot," she said.

"What? Oh, the oil. How did you know what I was thinking?"

"I assumed you weren't paying homage to my gear shift," Joann teased her.

"Ha. Yes, well, it's a nice scent. I've never smelled this one before."

"It is nice. It's one of the best for respiratory issues. I re-organized the attic yesterday, and my sinuses are grumbling at me a little...so bergamot and fresh air it is!"

"That may be my next oil purchase," Joy said. "You've got me way more hooked than I care to admit."

Joann smiled but didn't answer.

"Whose skates will I be wearing?" asked Joy. "Alex's? A random relative's? Goodwill's?"

"Mine," said her aunt. "They're a bit big on me, so I know they'll fit you."

"But whose will you wear?"

"One of the benefits of re-organizing the attic yesterday was that I located my old skates from when I was first married. They're half a size smaller, but they still fit me. They look awful, so Alex bought me some new ones a few years ago, but the blades are still sharp, and they work fine."

"Oh, thanks," Joy said. "I hate for you to have to use the old, ugly ones, though."

"I'm not going skating for the fashion aspect," snickered Joann. "Have you not noticed that I'm wearing sweatpants? Sweatpants! Ugh!"

Joy hadn't noticed, and she took one look at the bulky, baggy pants and snorted. Joann was no fashionista, for sure, but she did prefer well-fitting jeans or trim slacks. "This is the first day in five days that I *haven't* worn sweats," said Joy.

"You're overdressed today!"

Joann drove to the small rink in the nearby town of Greenburg; this rink was a parking lot that was flooded and then maintained for ice skating in the wintertime. Admission was free, but there were no skate rentals available.

Joy and Joann had the place to themselves other than one teenage couple who weren't skating. They skated around for quite a while without stopping or saying much. Joy relished the cold breeze on her cheeks as she scraped along. It was the perfect day for ice skating – 25 degrees and sunny. She also allowed herself a moment of pride that she could not only keep up with Joann on ice skates but even was more skillful on them. Joy had grown up skating on big-city rinks and could still skate backward and land a simple jump, to her amazement. The first time that Paul, who'd grown up skating on bumpy pond ice, had seen her spin and jump, a bit clumsily, he'd almost fallen in surprise.

Despite her skating ability, Joy's endurance was low because she didn't exercise aerobically as often as she wanted to, so she sat down on a nearby concrete wall to rest after a few minutes. Joann joined her soon.

"Whew," Joy said. "This is wonderful. I need to come here more often without the kids so I can get my heart rate up and work up a sweat."

"I love it," Joann said. "I'll never do any fancy moves like you can, but I love gliding along fast on the ice. It's like flying without the ear pressure or the security lines!"

"Thanks for bringing me along today. It seems like a long time since our hike, and with the holidays and other craziness lately, I've been neglecting exercise again," Joy said.

"It's easy to do," Joann said mildly.

They sat in silence for a minute. "Aunt Joann," Joy said at last. "I don't know what to do about the movie situation. It's a big dilemma for me. I *don't* want her to change my characters, but I can't imagine turning down this opportunity – and this money."

"That must be a tough decision, kiddo, but I'm sure you'll make the best choice."

"But I don't know which choice is best! Here it is, practically Christmas, and I'm still fluctuating every time I consider it." She took a deep breath and continued. "The – the character Sheila is requiring that I alter is Julia, Aunt Joann. You know better than anyone else how much my storyline means to me – that these characters basically *are* me – and you – and Uncle John, and that most of the plot is true. How am I supposed to change any of that?"

"Oh, Joy. I understand now, I think. You're not only facing the idea of changing your special creation, but of changing a piece of your life story."

"Yes!" Joy's eyes were filling with tears. Dumb tears. They came at all the most infuriating times. "And I wrote about you the way I remembered you, except for the name, and of course the fact that I couldn't recall the precise wording we all used in every conversation, or the exact order of events for the entire summer. But Aunt Julia *is* you, to me, the you I perceived when I was 14. Casting you any differently seems impossible, and...and almost wrong!"

"Hmmm...did she think I was a bit too plain and boring for the big screen?" Joann said quietly.

Joy flushed and stared at her lap, tracing the seam on her jeans with her index finger. Here it was – what she'd hoped to prevent...

"Joy, dear heart, please listen to your old aunt for a second. Your book is beautiful. I love it. It is a work of art, and I'm proud to be included in it. If you want to expand your horizons, though, and to become more well-known as an author, please, please do not hesitate to let them add

231

some more interesting things to the character based on me!
The very fact that Sheila wants to change Julia for a movie
proves that you portrayed me accurately, because I would
never flatter myself that my life is movie material."

"That's what's wrong with the movie industry, then,"
said Joy, rubbing her eyes in frustration. "It's all fake."

"Maybe so, but I believe your book – abridged or
unabridged – would make a wonderful movie. Don't worry
about me."

"It doesn't hurt you that Sheila feels that way about
Julia – about someone based on you?"

"Not at all, Joy."

"And you wouldn't be offended if I decided to go
through with it?"

"No, absolutely not. I promise."

"Oh," Joy breathed.

"Is *that* why you haven't been talking to me about it
lately, kiddo? Because you were afraid to hurt my
feelings?"

"Ahhh…yeah…"

Joann leaned over and hugged her niece close.
"Put your mind at rest, dear heart. I will be just as proud of
you no matter what you choose. Now – dry your eyes
before your tears freeze…let's skate!"

Joy squeezed her back, sniffed, and scrambled to
her feet.

CHAPTER 26

Joy blinked, and it was Christmas Eve. After she and Paul coaxed the wound-up triplets to bed at last, the two of them sat on the couch for a long time, cuddling and watching the lights twinkling on their Christmas tree. Under the tree were all their presents – four for each child, one for Joy, two for Paul, and stockings too. The plan for the following day was to share a leisurely brunch at home, open all their presents from each other, and head to Katie's house in the late afternoon for Christmas dinner with her, Clark, Luca, Marie, their children, Jennifer, Alex, and Joann. There would be more presents there, no doubt, and then board games and snacks until bedtime.

"There's not much from me under the tree for you this year, sweetheart," Paul said, stroking Joy's hair.

"I would hope not, after those perfect hiking boots you bought me in October," Joy said, smiling up at him.

"I'm so glad they worked for you."

"Yes, all that hiking, cold turkey, and I didn't get a single blister!"

"I do want to give you a gift that isn't under the tree, though," Paul continued.

"A pony?"

"Shhh...don't spoil the surprise!" he chuckled. "No, what I'm going to give you is an entire day at home to yourself. No cooking or cleaning allowed. You can write or think or sleep or watch an insipid Hallmark movie or anything relaxing that you want."

"But – where will you and the kids go all day?"

"Oh, we'll manage," Paul said.

"It – it sounds so amazing," Joy said. "I don't think I've had a whole day alone at home since – since – well, since before the kids were born!"

"Exactly. And with this big decision looming over you, I thought you'd appreciate the peace and quiet, even if you choose not to use your day actively thinking about it."

"Oh, yes. It will be so helpful. When? Which day? Obviously not tomorrow…"

"How about Monday? It's the only day anytime soon that nothing has been planned yet, and still a few days before I start back to teaching…"

"I will be looking forward to it – so, so much," she said, kissing him. "Did you know that you are a genius at gift-giving?" Paul grinned and kissed her back.

It didn't take long for them to rip into all their presents the next morning. For the past two years, Paul and Joy had been buying each of the children one present in each of four categories, want, need, wear, and read. This strategy had drastically reduced the number of junky toys to enter their household each Christmas, especially since Katie and Alex and Joann were considerate about giving them experience gifts or art supplies too. All three children were enthralled with their "want" and "read" presents and played contentedly until it was time to eat brunch – another benefit of fewer presents – no toy overwhelm.

The extended family celebration time was comfortable and joyous as well, filled with meaningful conversations, fun but competitive game time, and thoughtful gifts. The hit present of the day was Paul's gift to his mother – an exquisitely refurbished baby grand piano.

"Paul!" Katie gasped when he, Luca, and Alex brought it inside from his truck. "How did you know?"

"I know that old piano we had growing up is the only piece of furniture you regret not moving out of the farmhouse when you left, and that you've really missed playing," he said. "So, I took an educated guess that you'd enjoy it…"

"Enjoy it! Paul!" Katie grabbed her oldest in a bear hug. "It's – it's just right. It's beautiful. But how could you do it? You – you don't need to be buying grand pianos for your old mama!"

"Well, this is the only one you're getting," he teased her. "Don't worry, Mom. I found it online. An old music teacher was selling it a couple of weeks ago for peanuts -

$50, if you must know. We made a trade, too – he tuned it for me, and I used the snowblower on his driveway and walkways, so he didn't have to hire someone that day. I sanded down a few spots on it and slapped some new finish on it. And I'm no super pianist, Mom, but it sounds about right to me."

"Try it out! Try it out!" shouted Jennifer, so Katie plopped right down near the front door and played "Silver Bells" from memory, hesitating on a few chords now and then, but she got through it, even after half a decade without playing. They all cheered, and then the men moved it into an empty corner of the living room, and Katie played some more. When she grew tired, each triplet plunked out the short melodies they were learning, and then Joann and even Paul took turns playing. The evening was full of music after that. Clark spent most of his time staring at Katie, and everybody noticed, but nobody minded.

The only off-key note in Joy's day was in the Christmas card she received from her mother, which had gotten shoved under the couch by mistake before she even saw it. Joy discovered the card late Christmas night as she was cleaning up the remaining bits of wrapping paper on the living room floor. She sat down on the couch and opened it.

Inside was a generic, cheap holiday card, with a simple greeting, signed with Amelia's name. A half sheet of notebook paper fell from the card into her lap. Joy read it in a flash, read it again more carefully, and then crumpled it fiercely in her hand.

Amelia had written," Dear Joy, I hope you and your family are having a safe and healthy Christmas season. I am still here in Pennsylvania, living in the Dawdi Haus, but I am no longer of much service to the Yoder family. In September, I suffered a mild heart attack, and although I am recovering, I tire easily. The Yoders have told me that I may rent their place indefinitely, so I most likely will, as I have no energy to make additional plans. Do not come racing down here to see the dying invalid. I am not well, but I detest pity, and it is best for me to assume that I will fully recover eventually. I will write to you again to let you know if anything changes, or if I feel strong enough for a visit from the grandchildren in the future. Also, I suppose you will be relieved to know that I studied the Bible with the Fischers soon after your visit and was baptized. I have not been strong enough to return to church until recently, but I am attending again now.

"Love, your mother."

Joy was still clutching the paper and attempting some calming breathing exercises when Paul came downstairs from his shower to find her.

"Oh, there you are," he said. "I thought you were coming up a long time ago – what – what's wrong, Joy?"

She passed him the crumpled paper without a word. Paul had already abandoned his glasses for the night, but with some skillful maneuvering in the air toward the overhead light, he managed to get most of the rumpled words. "Oh, sweetheart," he whispered.

"How could she be so – so cold and offhand about it – about her heart attack, and about her baptism? How could she not assume I'd want to know right away, so I could help her if possible, or rejoice with her, or something?"

"I don't know, Joy," Paul said, taking her cold fingers into his big, warm hands.

"Do you realize that if Jacob hadn't called and told us, and if she hadn't survived her heart attack, I literally might have never known she'd been baptized? I might have had to live the rest of *my* life dealing with the pain and guilt of thinking she was lost forever."

"Yes, Joy, but that's a lot of ifs, and they didn't become reality, thanks to God."

"Every time I believe I've moved past the – the hurt – the anger – the disbelief that Mother is still so – Mother, something happens that brings it up again. I'm so angry at her right now, Paul. That letter was just – just awful."

"It was. Do you want me to throw it away?"

"Yes!" Joy ground the word out. "Yes, now!"

Paul complied, and then he took her gently by the arm and led her upstairs, and once they were in bed, he rubbed her back until she fell asleep.

When it was Monday at last, Joy woke, alone and quite late, to delicious aromas coming from downstairs. She smiled, stretched luxuriously, and lay in bed listening happily to the voices in the kitchen. Soon, the bedroom door banged open, and the triplets entered one by one, each carrying something to her bedside. Annie, the most cautious child, painstakingly carried a half-filled glass of juice, while Micah and Gideon brought napkins and silverware. Paul brought up the rear of the procession with a tray of food.

They all hugged and kissed her, and the children chattered about all the cooking Daddy had been doing. Joy listened, beaming at Paul between their sentences. On her plate lay a small, fluffy omelet full of minced bell peppers, cheese, onions, and ham, a quarter of a homemade waffle drizzled with melted butter and maple syrup, and three strawberries. Paul cooked so rarely these days between his teaching job and the million other tasks that he handled that Joy had nearly forgotten how good at it he was. At Micah's prompting, she took bites of both the omelet and the waffle, closed her eyes, and smiled. "It's delicious," she said.

"Good. Now, kids, say bye to Mommy. We're headed to Grandma's house. Joy, lunch is in the freezer, and we'll be home around 5:30 to start supper. Remember – no cleaning!"

Joy gave out another round of hugs and kisses, and then they were gone. Joy finished her meal, savoring every bite as the flurry of departure noises sounded around her. And then, after they drove away, there was silence. Total silence except for the hum of the heater Paul had installed before her third winter in the farmhouse. It was almost magical.

After her meal, Joy took a long bath with steaming water full of rose-scented oil. She didn't rush or allow herself to worry about anything – she just soaked. Next, she dressed in her comfiest sweater and worn out jeans, wrapped up in an afghan, and sprawled on the couch with her Bible and her journal. She read the entire book of Philippians, more consecutive verses than she usually managed to read in several days, prayed without losing her train of thought or dozing off, and then set her mind on her dilemma.

When Joy's mind couldn't ponder her situation any longer without spinning on the same tracks again and again, she prayed once more, specifically about whether she should accept Sheila's offer. "Why is this so difficult for me?" she asked herself. Finally, she opened her journal, the same one she'd had for years, that held only a dozen or so entries from her time as a mother. She flipped to an empty page, scrawled "Pros and Cons" at the top, and began to list the benefits and negatives of signing over her book.

Joy surprised herself. She wrote slowly at first, pausing often to ruminate, but soon she was scribbling as fast as her hand could go...not only listing the pros and cons anymore, but describing her feelings in great detail about each item on her list. She ignored everything except her writing process for a long time, unburdening her mind onto the pages. "I'd forgotten," she thought. "I'd forgotten how much more easily I can work through decisions on paper!"

Four pages later, she threw her pen to the floor and let her journal fall to the couch from her lap. She lay back, thoroughly spent, with a burning wrist. She didn't move or even open her eyes for at least five minutes. When she could move her hand again, she read what she had scrawled, or at least attempted to read it...some of her handwriting looked more appropriate for a prescription than a journal!

One of Joy's list items and corresponding stream-of-consciousness observations slapped her in the face as she read it. She had written that one pro of having her book become a movie was that she would feel more accomplished – that she would feel as though she had done something other than her typical mundane tasks. But what did she need to prove? She realized that she'd allowed this decision to become another battle of her expectations of herself versus what she actually needed – or maybe wanted. Being famous, even on a small scale, and earning some much-appreciated money, would be helpful and exciting, but Joy discovered with a jolt that when it all came down to the wire, she did not want to alter her book in any significant way to meet anyone else's demands. There it was…plain and simple…the truth she had been running from for almost four weeks. She didn't want to. She'd only been considering slashing one of her characters into ribbons because she thought she should. Should should should.

Joy jumped up and went out on the front porch, throwing the afghan around her shoulders against the frigid sunlight. The porch had been one of her thinking spots years ago when she'd first moved to the farmhouse, and she flopped down on the porch swing to see if the fresh air would help clear her mind. She looked around at the cozy, old-fashioned porch and the big yard littered with children's riding toys covered in snow. This place had been her home now for over seven years, and she loved every square foot of it. She and Paul had updated the house gradually, as they'd had time and funds, and while it was still far from modern, it was much more comfortable now. She was thankful for a home with plenty of space to spread out and to be able to practice hospitality.

Joy tried to snap her mind back to the issue at hand, but then it dawned on her that she'd already made her choice. Now, she had to own it. She hurried back inside and grabbed her journal once more. "I've done it," she wrote. "I've made my choice. I choose to allow my book to remain genuine and *mine*. I choose to maintain the identity of my characters so that they reflect accurately my experiences. I choose to keep Aunt Julia as the secondary heroine – Aunt Julia in all her denim-clad, no frills, housewifely glory, because not all heroines have to be glamorous or have naughty pasts. I choose to let my book stand on its own – to be enough even though it may never be famous. I choose to let my own life – my own tasks – be enough too even though I will most certainly never be famous. And I pray that I will grow more successful in choosing contentment and peace with myself, my relationships, and my decisions." And then Joy jumped up in search of lunch, feeling a bit lighter already. She opened the freezer, as Paul had instructed, and found two of her favorite guilty pleasures inside – frozen burritos from the grocery store. She laughed in delight and heated them up.

Joy debated about whether she should go ahead and tell Sheila her decision, especially since it was still the holiday season. She had planned to tell Paul first if she made her decision today, but after lunch, she decided to go ahead and finish the process immediately, while she possessed the gumption and the solitude. If Sheila didn't answer her cell phone, she'd write her a nice, long, grateful email.

Sheila did answer right away, to Joy's relief. They exchanged pleasant holiday greetings, and then Joy blurted out, "I can't do it. I – I thought I would be able to, but I can't."

"I'm sorry to hear that, Joy. Why did you reach that decision? Was the offer too low – because I might be able to raise it by about – oh, $250…"

"No, no. The offer was high enough, and your terms were totally fair. I suppose it all came down to the character changes. I discovered that I wasn't willing to alter Aunt Julia's identity for any price, primarily because, you see, she's based almost 100% on a real person."

"Ahhh…I wondered that when I sensed your initial resistance."

"Yes." Joy took a deep breath. "Um, so, I'm actually the main character. Her story is nearly identical to mine. And Aunt Julia is based on my own aunt – who is my only close relative and now one of my best friends. She – she's more like a mom to me than an aunt. I – I couldn't change her."

"I understand now, Joy, and, as much as I would have enjoyed creating a beautiful film from your book, I believe you've made the right choice. I didn't realize your novel was such a thinly veiled memoir. You're right not to change it."

"Thank you for understanding, and for your patience in letting me have time to think it over."

"Of course! And I'll be watching for your next novel, even if it's only so I'll have a good new read."

Joy laughed ruefully. "You'll probably have to wait at least a decade. My creativity seems to have taken a major hiatus while I'm raising little ones."

Their conversation concluded not long after that, and almost the moment that Joy tapped the end button on her phone screen, she felt as though an immense burden had been lifted from her shoulders. She almost felt like twirling through the house like a little girl pretending to be a fairy princess. But what should she do next? Twirling for the next – she checked the kitchen clock – 3.5 hours wasn't feasible. Neither was running around in circles in the front yard, although it was tempting...

In the end, Joy sat down at her bedroom desk with her laptop that was older than her marriage. She blew a layer of dust from the desk, opened a new document on the computer, and sat for a moment, motionless. Over the past few months, she'd begun considering what she'd write about if she ever had the opportunity to create another novel. The idea that had continued to swirl in her mind at random intervals resurfaced again. What if she wrote a book based on her decision to relocate to Vermont, and about how she had worked through her struggles to find herself? She could begin it with her breakup with her old boyfriend, Calvin...

Joy placed her fingers on the keys and typed – slowly at first, and then faster and faster until sentences came pouring from her brain onto the screen. She'd typed three pages before she even stopped to ponder. Funny, she'd always preferred to create fiction by handwriting first, but today, she'd chosen to try the laptop since her hand was so sore from all the journal writing earlier. As it turned out, her thoughts were flowing *better* electronically! She dove back into the sea of words that she had no idea had been rippling inside her head.

The next time Joy came up for air, it was almost dark, and Paul had sent her a text message. "Do you mind if your aunt and uncle come over for supper?" he wrote. "We're at their house, and when I mentioned what I'm cooking tonight, Alex got excited…"

Even though Joy assumed they'd share a quiet dinner as a fivesome, she was suddenly desperate to see Joann and to share about her day with her. "Sure! Invite them! Invite anyone you'd like!" she texted, laughing aloud.

"Um, are you sure you don't mind?" he replied. "If you'd prefer it to just be us, I'm certain they could wait until another time."

"I'm sure," she responded. "See you soon!"

Joy saved her work and read over it – all ten single-spaced pages. When she'd read it, as objectively as possible, she sat back against her chair with a thud. It was good. Better than anything she'd written in years. It was real. It was sincere. It was natural. And she could hardly wait to start writing again! How strange – how utterly odd that her years of writer's block would dissipate on the very day she had refused a movie contract. After this revelation, Joy discovered that she was crying, but her tears were from relief instead of sadness. She felt as thought she'd jumped into that sea of words – that refreshing lake of creativity – with both feet after spending years thirsty in a desert. It was beautiful. Joy closed her eyes on the spot and thanked God.

The front door banged open downstairs as Joy concluded her prayer. Joy ran to the landing, anxious to greet her family. Alex and Joann had come over already also, and Joy dashed down the stairs two at a time to greet everyone, her enthusiasm surrounding her entire being.

Joann was the first to hear her above the din of three cold and hungry children. "Mercy, dear heart," she declared as Joy bounded over like a child, her cheeks still damp. Joy gave her a bear hug without saying a word, hugged and kissed each triplet, and then kissed Paul on the lips right in front of everyone.

"Wow!" Paul said. "I guess we should try this day of solitude thing more often."

"I wrote ten pages of fiction at one time," Joy announced to them all. "Ten pages! Ten typed pages! And I could have easily written ten more! Oh, and I turned Sheila's offer down. I couldn't do it. I couldn't change my book. And then I wrote – and wrote – and wrote! I'm so happy!"

Paul grabbed her and held her close while the triplets clamored around her in confusion. "I knew you could do it," he said. "I knew you'd be able to make a choice you'd be happy with – and I knew you could write again. I'm so glad."

Alex gave her a hug as well, and then Joy turned again to her aunt, who'd been silent since her first greeting. "I couldn't change your character," Joy whispered, smiling at her.

"I don't care about that," Joann said, her voice husky. "I care that I haven't seen you this happy in years. And I care that you've chosen to do this because it feels right to you." She wiped her eyes and then hugged her tight too. "I'm so proud of you, Joy."

Supper was a meal of both peace and celebration. Joy was too emotional and exhilarated to eat much, although she could tell that Paul's homemade lasagna was delicious. Mostly, she sat quietly and drank in her family. It was almost as though her day of introspection had given her an entirely fresh perspective on everything, including her loved ones. She basked in Paul's calm, capable strength and the way had had cared for three wild children all day but barely seemed tired. She marveled at the intelligence and wit of Micah, Gideon, and Annie, the amazing people she had helped to create. She smiled as she watched Alex serving her aunt with another portion of salad – how kind and generous he was to all of them. When her eyes rested on Joann, she almost cried again.

None of this – none of these blessings in her life – would have been possible without the love and influence of her aunt Joann for so many years now.

Joy knew that life would never stay simple, and she knew that this creative mountaintop high tonight would fade. But she wasn't the same person as she'd been yesterday. All the pieces of herself – Christian, wife, mother, niece, author – had slid into place, and she would never be the same again. She was, at long last, Joy complete.

THE END

ABOUT THE AUTHOR

Sarah Floyd lives deep in a Vermont hollow with her husband, two little boys, and Australian Shepherd dog. It took her more than fifteen years of dreaming to get to Vermont, but she finally made it. Sarah enjoys reading, writing, traveling, crafts, sports and games, learning languages, spending time with family and friends, and occasional moments alone. And hugs. Oh, how she loves (and misses) hugs. It *is* 2020, after all. She doesn't enjoy folding fitted sheets.

Sarah is also the author of *Finding Joy* (2015), *Enough Joy* (2017), and *Joy Begins* (2020), the first and second books and prequel in the Voice of Joy series. Sarah loves to hear from her readers. To contact her, send her an email at voiceofjoy123@yahoo.com.

Made in United States
Orlando, FL
14 September 2022

22409965R00141